UNSPOKEN
Promises

Book Two of the Unspoken Series

GABBIE S. DURAN

Dedication

To Yamara and Cezanne, who always reminded me to never rush this story, and to my daughter, Stephanie, thank you for always listening.

Prologue

HAVE YOU EVER wondered why everything happens? I do …
I cannot seem to understand why I woke up in that hospital without my memory, or why I haven't gotten it back yet? Although,
at this point, I'm beginning to cope with the fact that I might
never get it back. Even if I did, do I really want to go back to
being the person I once was?

I was known to the world as a stuck up, conceited bitch. I
was a person with a controlling agent, who just happened to be
my cheating fiancé. He didn't love me. He only loved my money. According to the tabloids, I was someone who had no care in
the world for anyone but myself, and although I had no memory
of who I once was, I knew it was true.

But that was my past and now I'm in the present.

The last three months have been a challenge for me, but I
wouldn't change a moment of what has happened. Three months
ago I woke up in the hospital not knowing who I was, or why I
was there; a blessing in disguise. It was the day I actually woke
up for the first time to the person I wanted to be. I no longer care
if I recover my memory of who I was. All that matters is who I
want to be.

Now that I've left it all behind, I don't regret a moment of
walking away, especially from Bill. Walking away was the best
decision of my new life.

If it weren't for Emily's memories I would have never
found Matt. He might have only been a memory the day I first

dreamt him, but my reality of him is far from a dream. I long for those memories now, as well as treasure them. They help me understand Matt, even though I don't require them for me to love him. He's everything a girl could ever wish for, and right now I feel like the luckiest girl in the world. Knowing that his promising love for me will be the answer that I was never looking for gives me hope of a better me.

The day I knocked on his door, I never expected for my life to be turned upside down and inside out. I never expected that I'd have to fight the feelings I was having towards Matt, causing me to build a barrier around my heart to protect it. But I guess love always wins in the end. He found a way to break down that barrier. He found his way into my soul with his compassion, sexy smile, and his warm, tender eyes. He is my weakness.

I knew from that moment on that I was holding onto him and never letting go. Matt was mine to keep, and there was nothing that was going to take him from me.

At least that is what I believed until I woke up this morning.

Every girl grows up believing in happily ever after, the kind of happily ever after that will last forever. Every girl wants one, she dreams of it. She lives for that one day she will finally find her prince who will give her that happy ending.

I thought that's what I had finally found when Matt said he loved me last night. I thought I had found *my prince* when he said I was the one. The one he had chosen, and the one he loves, finally giving up his past for me.

I thought when we declared our love to each other that we would be a happily ever after from that moment on. But do they always last forever? I was about to find out.

Chapter One

Matt

I STARE DOWN at Abigail as she sleeps. She's the most beautiful thing I've ever laid eyes on. Since the moment I saw her standing at my front door that day she came looking for me, I thought I was the luckiest bastard in the world just being able to lay eyes on her.

She looks so peaceful as she takes shallow breaths, in and out, in and out. I know she's exhausted. Shit, I'm just as exhausted at this point, but I just cannot resist waking up to watch her sleep. She's lying on her stomach, her face in my direction. She has a light smile on her face, as if she's in a peaceful dream. I wonder if she's dreaming about us.

I kept her up for most of the night, unable to satisfy myself with her body until the early hours of the morning, but it's because it's Abigail.

She's different.

Even with Laura, while in high school, it was always a rush just to sneak sex in. Then as we both left to college, it was rare if we got to spend more than a couple of days together. It was usually just a weekend at a time, if we did see each other. Even within those couple of days with her, I wouldn't crave having sex with her.

I just cannot get enough of Abigail.

Shit, I already wanted her again, but I know she needs her sleep. Her body needs to rest after the ordeal she was put through this weekend. Realizing that if I keep lying here next to her, my boner will not ease up, I would either have to relieve myself or go against my own word and take her again.

Nope. I'm going to be a good boy and let her sleep.

I lean down and kiss her on the shoulder, unable to resist feeling her silky skin against my lips one more time before I get up. She lightly twitches as if feeling my touch, but doesn't stir any more than that.

With a smile I get up and out of bed, already searching for my boxer briefs, not knowing where the hell they're at. Last night we were both in a hurry to get each other's clothes off. They went flying everywhere.

Giving up on clothing since I cannot find them in the dark, I quietly open the door, not wanting to wake her, and do the walk of shame to my own room. With a chuckle, I think, it's not a fucking shame what we did last night. If I could, I would announce it to the world that Abigail Adams was now my girl.

I'm almost at the guest room when I pass Trey on his way out of the bathroom and he stares at my naked body with a raised eyebrow.

"Can't say I cock blocked you last night. From the screaming and pounding coming from the room, I guess you've kissed and made up."

Wanting to pound his face for his comment, I force myself to keep it under control. He's right. Abigail had no reason to forgive me for the way I've been fucking up with her, but I promised her I wasn't going to do it again, and I intend on keeping that promise.

"Just drop it, Trey," I say, knowing if I don't shut him up, he'll continue.

"Whatever, dude. Just don't fuck this one up. I like her, and by the way Kelly was about ready to attack you last night, I'm thinking she already has a cheering squad behind her. Myself included."

I nod my head knowing he's right as I walk into the room.

After getting dressed in my go to basketball shorts and t-shirt, I throw on my shoes and head to the kitchen to cook Abigail some breakfast. I decide to make pancakes for her, knowing she cannot get enough of them. She earned them after getting her qualifying time in San Francisco and it killed me knowing I wouldn't be able to cook them for her when she was done to celebrate.

Better late than never.

As I'm reaching into the fridge for the eggs, I hear a knock at the front door. I immediately rush to open it, praying whoever it is doesn't ring the doorbell. I don't want them to wake my beautiful girl up. Swinging the door open, I see Lisa, the girl that Abigail caught me fucking on the table, standing there with her eyes bloodshot red, and crying. I tense, knowing this is not going to be good.

"What are you doing here, Lisa?"

She sniffles and says, "I need to talk to you, Matt."

I look over in the direction of Abigail's room, making sure it's still closed before I pull the door back to give Lisa access to come in. As I shut the door, I do a recheck down the hall one more time before I follow Lisa into the living room.

She's already taken a seat on the sofa, forcing me to my reclining chair so I can keep as much distance between us. The last thing I want her thinking is that I want to be next to her.

"So what's up?" I ask, hoping I can get her out of here within the next couple of minutes.

Lisa continues to sniffle as she cries, twisting her hands in her lap and it's annoying the fuck out of me that she's not saying something.

"I'm late," she lets out, barely above a whisper.

"What are you late for?" I ask with a confused look on my face, thinking she's lost her mind. Shaking my head, not knowing what she's talking about, she repeats, "I'm late, Matt. I haven't gotten my period," she clarifies.

My heart sinks and I stop breathing as I take in her words. Unbelieving what I've heard, I stand up and start pacing in front of the fireplace, wanting farther distance from her.

"What the fuck do you mean you haven't gotten your period?" I ask, still shocked. "Are you sure?" I add, still not believing her.

"I took a pregnancy test and it was positive," she says, nodding her head, sniffling again.

"That's not possible. I used protection. There's no fucking way you can be pregnant," I practically shout at her.

Thinking back to that night, I know I used protection; I always make sure I use protection. Since the first time I dipped my dick into a pussy I made sure I was gloved up.

Then it dawns on me and the blood drains from my body. I didn't use a condom with Abigail last night. Not once in the five or six times I made love to her. It didn't occur to me because I was so desperate to be inside her. I loved the feeling of her warmth wrapped around my cock. Even if she would have asked me to glove up after that first time, I would have begged her to reconsider. There was no way I was not feeling her like that again.

Hearing a gasp come from the hallway, my head whips in that direction, my eyes finding Abigail's. I should have known she was there. I had almost sensed her before I heard her. Normally I can since my body is always craving her look or touch. But this time I'm feeling the dread of knowing that she might have heard what we've said.

She's still standing in it, as if she's attempting to stay hidden, but failing because I can see her hand holding onto the corner of the wall revealing her presence. I see her pull her head back and her hand disappears. I rush to the hallway wanting to hold her, wanting to reassure her that this is all a mistake, but as I turn the corner I see Trey blocking the entrance and she's already disappeared behind the door.

Trey shoves me back into the living room. "Leave her the fuck alone. She doesn't need this shit from you!" he says, shouting as he points in Lisa's direction.

Heated from not being able to get to Abigail, I shove Trey back, but he's already expecting it. He blocks me, shoving me again with his shoulder, making me fall on my ass on the ground behind me.

This is why he's my center, he protects me with force, letting no one through, and it's exactly what he was doing with Abigail, protecting her.

"Abigail, please!" I shout, not knowing what else to say as I scramble to get myself up off the floor.

I feel someone grab at my shoulder. Confused, I turn to see Lisa's pleading eyes. "Leave her, Matt."

Pissed that she would even say that, I snarl back at her. "Go home, Lisa. I'll call you later."

I don't want her here when I'm begging on my knees to Abigail.

"I'm not leaving until we figure out what to do."

My blood is boiling from the shit that's happening. I hate that I cannot talk to Abigail and I want to kick Trey's ass, but I don't want to deal with Lisa right now. Knowing my only choice is to leave, I walk over to the island where I keep my keys and grab them and my wallet as I walk straight out of the door.

Digging my phone out of my pocket, I start dialing Abigail's number, but it goes to voicemail. That doesn't surprise me; she probably hasn't turned it on since yesterday.

I jump into my car and turn it on, listening to the roar of the engine. I throw it into reverse, peeling out of the driveway and up the street. Hitting the steering wheel, hoping it will compensate for the pain that is tearing me up right now, I picture a broken Abigail back at home. But I already know, no matter how hard I try, she isn't going to talk to me right now, especially so soon after fucking up.

I cannot believe this is fucking happening right now, but in reality there's no one to blame for my stupid mistake but myself. I had stopped screwing girls the day Abigail moved into the house. I didn't want to give her a reason to confirm my lifestyle. Why, I don't know. But knowing she was there was all I needed to make the shit stop.

Then I go and fuck it up because I had come home with a case of blue balls one night. Remembering her face when I had looked up to see her and Kelly standing near the doorway nearly kills me. What the fuck was I thinking? That was the first time I had fucked up with her and I could not stop doing it ever since, no matter how hard I tried not to. Not even twenty-four hours after promising her I wouldn't ever fuck up again, I was already breaking that promise.

I keep driving, knowing I need to see the one and only person who will make me feel better.

Chapter Two

Abigail

MY BODY IS numb, unable to move. The firmness of the wooden door behind me is the only thing keeping me standing as I lean against it. My arms are wrapped around myself as I keep my eyes tightly shut, wishing I was dreaming, and at any moment I will just wake up. I keep praying what I heard is another memory, one that doesn't really belong to me, but belongs to Matt's sister instead.

But I know I'm awake, which makes it hurt more.

I had woken up to the other side of the bed being empty, my mind wondering if *last night* was instead a dream when I had opened my eyes, but the warmth of Matt's body was still present. It left me with hope that I wasn't dreaming. His smell was still on the sheets, teasing me with need to still have him next to me, which is why I got up to go look for him.

At first I thought that he had snuck out again before I woke up, like he's done in the past. His absence made me think he might regret what happened last night, but I just as quickly forced myself to push the thought from my mind as I remembered Matt's words yesterday; the promises he had made. That was the reason why I got out of bed.

Now I regret getting up.

Had I stayed in bed like my body was begging me to do because I was still exhausted, I would have never heard their conversation, or even known she was here. But as I stare into the space of air ahead of me, I question whether Matt would have even told me she had come. Would he have told me the truth?

"Supermodel, you okay in there?" a concerned Trey says as he knocks at my door, the vibration hitting my back from the force he adds into it. Suddenly, I feel the door being pushed behind me, making me step forward as it opens. Trey steps into the room, the light from the hallway illuminating the room a little.

He takes one look at me and his grim appearance speaks for itself. It's telling me just how pissed he is and he isn't attempting to conceal it at all.

Staring at me, he says, "They're both gone now, so you don't have to keep hiding in here." He folds his arms in front of his chest before he continues. "You want me to call Kelly?"

Unable to speak, I shake my head at him. He nods, still standing there, as if refusing to leave. It's as if he's waiting for me to give him some sort of reaction. What the fuck does he expect me to do? Begin sobbing like a lunatic or go psycho with rage? I don't have the strength or will to do either. The only thing I want is to be left alone.

I slowly begin walking over to my bed, staring down at the disheveled sheets that Matt and I had managed to toss in every single direction. It's a reminder of the hope that I had for us, the hope that is no longer there.

The reminder only pisses me off, making me start yanking at the covers. Grabbing them with the force of anger that I have inside of me, I pull with all my might; I want them off the bed. I toss them across the room, not caring where they land, as long as they are not anywhere near me right now. They smell too much like Matt and I don't want a reminder of what I don't have.

I throw myself on the bare mattress, curling myself into a ball, forcing myself to shut out the world. After a minute I hear the door shut, the darkness engulfing the room again as I hear

Trey's footsteps retreat down the hallway.

My body starts trembling, the shock of the morning catching up to me as I hold myself tight. With my eyes closed, the exhaustion takes over as it pulls me into the darkness of my dreams.

I'm excited. The blissful feeling that is inside me is uncontainable as I'm beaming from ear to ear. It's hard not to smile, even with the doubt that is coursing through me, but deep down inside my heart, I know it's worth the doubt to know I'll make him happy.

I take one last glance at the piece of metal sitting in front of me before I turn to go back into the house. Matt is expected home soon. Since he didn't have practice today, I informed him to come straight home after school, but hadn't told him I would be here when he arrived. I wanted that to be part of the surprise.

I shut the door leading to the garage and I can already hear him walk into the house through the front door, a rowdy crowd following him in. I shake my head as I chuckle at myself. Of course he would bring the crowd here, as usual. It shouldn't surprise me. I am a little disappointed, though. I had wanted it to simply be the two of us when I gave him his present, but what can I do now?

I make my way into the living room, the crowd already taking up refuge on the couches, Laura sitting in Matt's lap since there isn't enough room, making me shake my head. They've been getting a little too close lately, worrying me and making me wonder just how close they have become. I know I've had the talk with him, so I'm hoping my words stayed with him, something I had dreaded doing, but was necessary, regardless.

From where I'm standing, still hidden from their view, I watch when he starts kissing her. Simple at first, but it quickly grows heated, even with the crowd. When I see his hand start to creep into her shirt my eyes grow wide. "Matthew!" I shriek at him, freighting both of them as Laura jumps off him, allowing Matt to stand up.

I give him the fiercest glare I can give as he turns to look at me, making sure he can see the shock in my eyes. "Em, I didn't know you were home," he tells me, looking ashamed as his head whips back and forth between Laura and me. He should feel ashamed. I know I raised him to respect women.

He walks over in my direction, placing a kiss on my cheek. "Do you really think you kissing up to me is going to make things better?" I ask him, trying to sound as if I'm still disappointed, even though I no longer am.

He leans back, looking at me with his lips turned up to the side as he smiles, a twinkle of laughter in his eyes as he answers, "Of course."

I can only roll my eyes as I turn to walk away from him, leaving him to follow me. "I have a surprise for you," I tell him, still walking into the kitchen.

"Oh really?" he says, his curious tone making me smile.

"But, now I'm beginning to wonder if you really deserve it," I tease him.

When I reach the kitchen, I go to pour myself a glass of water, waiting for his curiosity to kick in and start questioning me. It doesn't take long before it does. "So, what's this surprise you've got for me? You're finally going to let me get a tattoo?"

"No," I respond while glaring back at him, making him laugh. "You know how I feel about tattoos. You can get one when I'm six feet under and I don't have to see it on your body," I tell him.

He shrugs his shoulders. "I thought I'd try again," he says with a teasing smile.

Tilting my head, I ask, "How badly do you want a car, Matt?"

"Badly."

I act as if I'm considering his answer, the desperation clear in his eyes as he waits for a response. "Okay."

"So when can we go car shopping?"

"I already bought you a car."

His eyes light up, but his smile turns into a frown. *"You didn't buy a damn hybrid like yours, did you?"* The scowl in his expression is tempting me to laugh.

"And if I did?" I question him.

I watch as his face grows disappointed and I force myself to contain the laughter threatening to escape. *"It's sitting in the garage,"* I tell him.

He sighs to himself, dragging his body over to the door leading to the garage. As he gives me his back, my lips gradually form into the smile I've been containing. When he turns on the light, I watch as his body freezes up as he takes in the car. His body spins around, eyes wide in shock as he looks at me then back at the car.

"Are you serious?"

I nod my head as I'm smiling at him.

He turns to look at the car again, rushing to touch it. *"It's obvious it needs a lot of work done to it, but it's your responsibility to come up with the funds to do so. I want you to get a job to pay for the repairs. Don't expect me to give you a penny out of my pocket for the car. I'm only paying for the insurance. Even the gas money is your responsibility. Do we have an understanding?"* I ask him.

He turns around, the exhilaration still in his eyes as he rushes back to me, picking me up to spin me around. *"Of course, I'll do anything you want me to do,"* he replies as he places me back down on the ground.

I reach up to place my hand on his cheek as I look him in the eyes. *"As much as I hate this car, you deserve it, Matt. You deserve a little bit of happiness."*

Disoriented, he draws his eyebrows down. *"You really think I need this car to make me happy, Emily?"* he asks, shaking his head. *"I was happy without the car and I'm pretty sure I would have continued being happy without it."*

"I know, Matthew, but you wanted this car and after much consideration, I decided you deserved it."

"Thank you, Emily. I won't disappoint you. Ever."

I smile, pulling him towards me to hug him, making sure I convey just how much I love him in return.

My dream slowly begins to fade as I wake up, the despair taking over my thoughts as I open my eyes. With every new memory I discover something important about Matt, and with this memory I've fallen deeper in love with him. My love for him came so easily, even when I knew it wasn't the right thing to do. I'd known it wasn't safe and now I'm paying the price. As badly as I want to hold onto my love for Matt, I was going to have to learn to live without it and let him go.

My body is completely weak, feeling lifeless, and my head is pounding. My eyes are burning, even with the darkness that is surrounding me. My head feels like a heavy weight on my shoulders and I don't have the strength in me to move.

The outside world means nothing to me at this moment. I don't care. The only thing I want to do is sleep. So I do. Letting the darkness drag me back with it.

I AWAKEN, THIS time my body is demanding I get up. Willing myself out of bed, I slowly tread my way off to the bathroom, not bothering to turn on the light when I enter. The darkness is a reminder of what I've lost and I welcome it.

Still weakened, I stretch my arms down on the counter, allowing my mind to escape to the memory I hold from being in here. The agony of those last words cause the tears to return, my heart surrendering to the pain all over again. I relinquish to the pain slamming against my shattered heart, allowing it to remind me that I have nothing left of his promises.

Gripping the counter, I scream; the anger replaces the pain with every bellow I let out. I want the agony to end, but it won't. It's only gets worse.

I'm still screaming when Trey comes bursting into the

room, the door slamming against the wall as he rushes into the bathroom. "What's wrong?" he asks, his panicked voice booming in the small space. I keep screaming, collapsing to the floor, my body now convulsing from crying as I give up the fight to hold it in. I feel his large arms wrap around me, engulfing me against his warm body as I sob, refusing to fight against the pain anymore.

"Let it out, supermodel, let it out," he whispers against my ear, his arms tightening around me as he rocks me back and forth, allowing me to cry into his chest. I don't know how long Trey holds me, but he never once complained or said anything more. He simply sat there on the floor with me, holding me, letting me know he wasn't leaving.

My body is soon weak again, unable to move, my tears now dry, and my throat feels raw. With my eyes still shut tight, I cannot get the image of Matt's desperate face begging for forgiveness out of my mind. No matter how hard I try to push it away, it doesn't leave, so I do the only thing I can do to make it go away. I sleep.

I awaken once again on the bed, but I'm not alone in the room, which makes me panic thinking it's Matt. As my eyes adjust to the darkness, I take in Kelly's form across the room. Squinting my eyes against the illumination of the bathroom light, I watch her take clothes from the hangers in my closet, stuffing the items into my large travel bag.

"What are you doing?" I ask, the words gnawing at my throat.

She spins around at the sound of my voice, her face at first startled, but soon relaxes. "What does it look I'm doing? I'm packing your shit," she grimly replies, going back to her task.

"Why?"

With her back still facing me, she says, "Because I'm pretty sure you no longer want to be here. Unless you do?" She turns to me with a curiously raised eyebrow.

Still miserable as I lie in bed, I take in her question before shaking my head to respond. "How did you find out?"

Dropping the bag, she slowly makes her way over to me, taking a seat on the bed. "I kept trying to call your phone to see how you were doing today. When you didn't answer I called Trey. He told me about Lisa," she explains with a bitter tone.

Pushing the same bitterness aside, I ask, "Can you get me some water?"

"Of course," she answers before she heads out of the room, soon returning with a glass of water. I didn't realize how thirsty I was until I completely drank it all. She takes the empty glass from me, placing it on the bedside table. "Why don't we finish packing up your clothes so we can get you out of here?" she asks, the animosity clear in her voice.

I don't have to answer, even if I tried to deny her request I know she wouldn't let me stay here. I can tell by her determination of how she continues packing. I sit there unable to do anything else at this moment but watch her at the task.

"I didn't know what you wanted to do with this," she says as she hands me something.

Kelly's body is blocking the light preventing me from seeing what it is she's handing me, but the moment my hand wraps around it I already know it's my bracelet: the only token I have as a reminder of him. I sit there, pondering what to do with it. It doesn't take me long to make the decision as I clutch it in my hand, refusing to surrender it. Besides the memories, it might be the only reminder of Matt that I will ever have.

Looking up at Kelly, my vision is blurry again; I fight the tears and force myself to stand up. After going to the bathroom, I walk back into the room and take one last look at it. I remember the night I had found a sanctuary from the pain I was running from, but now I was leaving it with the same type of pain, if not worse.

Grabbing for my purse, I head out the door with Kelly's arm wrapped around my shoulder to guide me into the living room. My eyes are already searching for Matt, feeling disappointed that he isn't here.

"He hasn't come back," Trey's deep voice startles me. "So you're just leaving?" he asks, taking a look at the bag in Kelly's hand, then back to me with his eyebrow curiously raised.

"Trey, I can't stay here," I reply. The words pierce at my heart as I say them, wishing I didn't have to.

"Why not?"

"Trey, don't," Kelly asserts back at him.

He ignores her. "I don't see why you have to leave, super-model. I thought you were done running?" he mocks, making me glare at him. "You've both had your problems before and still managed to live under the same roof, what difference is it now?"

The reminder of his words takes me back to the night that I found Matt with Lisa on the table. "Not this time, Trey," I clip out.

Trey frowns, but comprehending my words he gives me the briefest of nods. He walks over and hugs me. "Don't become a stranger. Give me a call if you need me to kick his ass," he says into my ear.

His words make me smile, but not enough to evaporate the ache deep within my shattered heart.

"Thank you, but this is my battle to fight," I muffle into his chest. I pull myself away from him and start walking towards the front door without looking back. It would hurt too much to do so. I make my way to Kelly's car, climbing into the passenger seat, but I cannot help myself as I steal one last glance at the house while Kelly pulls away.

My thoughts return to the night I showed up to it needing somewhere to escape. I had run to Matt in hopes that he would be the answer that I was looking for, praying that he wouldn't turn me away. Ironically, I was doing just the opposite this time. The only difference now was I wasn't escaping because of fear. I was leaving because I was brave.

Chapter Three

Matt

HAVING DRIVEN ALL night, my mind is now feeling exhausted. I didn't even stop to rest. I hadn't wanted to at the time. With the endless open road ahead of me, it left too much time to think. My mind was in a constant battle against itself as I kept remembering all the mistakes I made.

It had gotten to a point of pure torture trying to fight my thoughts. I keep remembering all the times I had with Abigail, kicking myself in the ass for not taking my chance sooner than I had. That alone was the biggest mistake of them all. There was no one to blame but myself. Maybe if I had given in to my heart long ago I wouldn't have fucked up the first time.

The idling roar of the engine is the only thing keeping me relaxed as I sit in my car. The whole drive here I could not wait to get here. I needed to see her, but now that I'm parked on the street, I don't have the courage anymore to get out. Regardless of the mistakes I have made, she will never judge me. It is the reason I need to talk to her. Tell her how I've fucked things up … yet again.

I kill the engine, but stay in the car looking over in the direction of where she is at, pondering what I plan to tell her. No matter how much I go over my words, there is no simple way to say I've fucked up and I need her forgiveness.

Taking one last deep breath to prepare myself for what I'm about to do, I open my door and get out of my car. The day is cloudy, an overcast gloom from the clouds in the sky, as if it's replicating the depression deep within me. The chilly air adds to the bitterness of my mood.

Staring out at the hills ahead of me, I take the first step needed to get me to her. I know exactly where she's at; it feels like years since I've seen her, although it hasn't been that long. The realization of knowing that I'm going to see her again is starting to sink in and I have to force myself to keep walking. Each footstep forward feels heavier than the next.

When I reach her, I look down at her below me. The guilt of not coming sooner cuts deep inside of me as I hang my head in shame. It's been nine months, to be exact, since the day I buried her. When I walked away I'd made the decision to never return. The reality of knowing I was never physically going to see her again had torn my heart apart. Regardless whether I can see her or not right now, I need to be here with her; to know this is as close as I'm physically going to be with her.

Emily always had a way of making me see the answer to my problems. While growing up, she was always there to lend an ear. Listening without judgment to every single word. I don't know how many times I depended on her for an answer, and no matter how many times I asked, she always responded.

The day she died, it felt as if she took a part of my soul with her, and I had let her. She deserved it more than I did. It wasn't until the day Abigail walked into my life that I knew that part of my soul had returned. It's as if Emily was giving it back to me, knowing I desperately needed it.

Abigail was the light at the end of a darkened tunnel that I was trapped inside of. I had refused to keep walking forward when Emily died, but Abigail finally forced me to take the steps to awaken *her*. She helped me find the light within myself.

Dropping down to the ground, my knees hit the earth, sending a jolting pain up my legs. I stare down at the grave marker, realizing it's the first time I've laid eyes on it. The elegance of the black marble represents the extravagant taste of her husband's family. I had blown off their countless phone calls when they had contacted me to help choose the marker. I didn't care. It would have made me face the reality that she was never coming back. The agonizing disbelief of seeing it brings tears to my eyes.

I sit there with the silence surrounding me as I allow the tears to fall and the agony takes over me. I miss her so fucking much. I keep wishing that she were still here with me. Just a phone call away like she was before. I'm selfish, I know, but I hate the fact that she's no longer by my side when I want her to be.

After what seems like hours of sitting there crying alongside her, I somehow find the courage to speak. "I fucked up, Em," I say crying at her grave. "And I don't think she's ever going to forgive me. You always told me that me fucking around was going to come back and bite me in the ass and you were right." The words come out as a whisper as I continue to speak. "I can't stand the thought of losing her, as I did you," I cry down to her, expecting an answer, but all I receive is silence.

Eventually my eyes grow heavy, forcing me to lay my head down on my knee. My body comes to a point of relaxation and it's then that I see her. She looks no different than the last time I laid eyes on her. Her smile is breathtaking, as is her beauty. Her eyes are sparkling against the sunlight, telling me that she's just as happy to see me as I am her.

I run to her, lifting her up off the ground to spin her around. I'm unable to control my excitement as her laughter beams into my ear. It's what I've missed the most. It's music to my ears. When I stop spinning us and place her back on the ground, she's still smiling at me; the blissfulness on her face is contagious.

"I've missed you so much, Emily," I tell her as I hug her once again, unable to resist holding her.

"I've missed you, too," she whispers back to me.

When I pull away, the joyfulness inside of me is now replaced with apprehension and fear. Her palm comes up to my cheek and I cannot resist leaning into it as I stare down at her. "Why are you crying?" she asks with a worried frown, making my eyes go glassy and full of tears.

I'm scared to tell her the truth. "Matt, I know what has happened," she murmurs, taking me by surprise. "I know because I've been watching over both of you. As I always will. No matter where you're at."

My eyes go wide in dismay, wondering just how much she's been watching, earning me a chuckle from her lips. "Trust me, there are times I don't watch," she tells me with a twinkle in her eyes.

"Matt, I don't understand why you're so hard on yourself. You're both young, and bound to make mistakes," she explains.

"I chose Abigail because I felt you deserved her in your life. I know everything will work out in the end because you both truly love each other and will learn from these mistakes."

I want to believe her, I desperately want to, but deep down inside I feel as if I no longer can. "I swear I never meant for any of this to happen and I have no excuse, but I swear I will fix it somehow," I promise as I drop my head in shame.

"I know you will, mijo, and until then you can count on me to be watching over both or you."

When I look back at her she is smiling again. The wind starts to pick up and the scattered leaves on the ground begin to blow around us in a vortex. She slowly begins to fade as I stand there reaching out for her to stay, but my begging is nothing but muted words.

My head snaps up as I awaken with a shock, gasping for air as I desperately search for her, but she's nowhere in sight. The cemetery is just as empty as it was when I arrived. The gloominess of the grey skies is still high above my head and the bitter cold is beginning to seep into my body. I welcome it, hoping it will take over the pain still deep down inside of me. The agony of knowing she is once again gone is allowing my sorrow to continue to take over my thoughts.

The hours slowly creep by until eventually my eyes grow heavy and I know I have to leave. I stare down at Emily's name. "I'll be back, Em, but next time it will be with Abigail so you can meet her," I promise, staring down at her name before I turn to walk away.

I'm going to get Abigail back, even if it kills me doing so.

I get into the car and drive to my next destination before I make the long journey back to Portland. I need to see Emily's house again. I could not find it in my heart to sell it. She was already renting to a family when she died, so it made it easier to keep it that way. I had inherited it when she died, along with all the insurance money from both her and her husband, but no amount of money was going to make me as happy as she did.

I pull up near the house and park across the street where I have a clear view of the house. It's already dark out, but the street lamp gives the house a softened glow. From the street I can see the family inside and it makes me think back to the reason why I never could bring myself to sell the house. I had hoped one day I would move back with my future wife and raise my family in this house. Back then I had thought in my stubborn head it was going to be Laura, but now I know it could never be her. She wasn't the one I wanted a future with.

Closing my eyes I allow the exhaustion of the last couple of days to take over, and I fall asleep. My mind wanders into dreams of Abigail. A dream of a future I want with her.

Abigail

I SPENT THE entire car ride to Kelly's with the world existing in a blur. My thoughts were too consumed with the memory of

Matt having sex with Lisa. I should have known from that night there would be consequences to falling in love with Matt, but somehow I had ignored them.

Kelly parks the car and I climb out, my body still numb as I follow her to the door. I'm still in shock, feeling as if I'm a puppet being commanded to walk. David is waiting for us as we reach the door. His smile is a mix of pity and reassurance, but I accept it as he moves aside to allow us entrance, my legs automatically leading me to the couch. Within minutes Kelly is standing in front of me, shoving a bottle of tequila in my hands. It's déjà vu of the last time I had come over to her apartment. The only difference is now I'm here because of the result of that night.

Her face grows confused. "Are you sure?" The tequila may continue to numb my feelings, but it's not going to make them disappear, which is why I'm still shaking my head.

David comes over to take the bottle from Kelly. "Alcohol is not her answer," he says, as if reading my mind.

Kelly sighs before sticking her tongue out at him. He chuckles at her response as he places the bottle on the coffee table. I've always envied what Kelly has with David. By the way they act with each other, it's obvious how much they're truly in love. It's the kind of love I'd craved with Matt.

"Are you hungry?" I hear Kelly ask from the kitchen.

I shake my head to answer. I don't have an appetite for food right now. I'm so depressed it would only made me sick if I tried to eat.

David stands and walks over to the kitchen, offering to help cook. "Get out of here. The last time you helped me cook you almost burned down the kitchen."

With a shrug of his shoulder, he walks away with a mischievous smile on his lips. "I purposely burned the food last time I cooked so she wouldn't ask me to help anymore," he says with a wink.

Kelly must have heard his response. "In that case I'll make

sure my renter's insurance is up to date as soon as I'm done and *you're* cooking tonight," she yells from the kitchen.

His face turns pale and his eyes go wide. I cannot resist laughing at his expression. It's just what I need to push my sorrow aside, but my thoughts soon return to Matt.

My life in the last three months had always included Matt, one way or another, since I'd woken up in the hospital and received my first memory of him. But now I was going to have to learn to live without him. I already knew it wasn't going to be easy.

Matt

I DRIVE UP to my block and it's full of cars, already making my stomach turn from dread. My driveway is full, forcing me to keep driving and park my car up the street. Taking my anger out on the car, I slam the door shut wondering what the fuck is going on in my house as I walk towards it. It's obvious there is a party going on, which make me grow furious. The fact that Abigail is in the house adds to the anger. The need to protect her and the thought of knowing she may be in fear from having this many people surrounding her boils my blood. I better not find out she's been touched either, I may just murder someone.

The music gets louder as I get closer to the door. It's wide open, allowing people to come and go.

"Hey, Matt," a drunken classmate cheers from my doorway, blocking my entrance. I shove my way past him. "Go home, party's over!" I shout over the music.

The lyrics of *I Know You Want Me* are blaring from the speakers, a throng of people dance around as I continue to maneuver my way through the partygoers, my eyes automatically searching for Abigail. I don't see her amongst the crowd in the room full of people.

"Take her back to your room to fuck her, Trevor," I shout to the couple in the corner practically fucking, making my blue balls grow tight. They remind me of having Abigail in that same position not too long ago.

They both turn to look at me, but I tilt my head towards the door, demanding they leave. Glaring at me as they stand and leave, I continue to scan the room, still unable to think clearly. I soon find the other person I'm looking for... Trey. The sight of him doesn't do anything but peak the rage inside of me when I take him in.

He's standing on the table. The table I bought for Abigail. He's dancing on top of it in his boxers as he swings his white t-shirt above his head in circles. His hips are thrusting back and forth to the music as if he's a male stripper.

If I wasn't pissed before, I am now. I cannot believe he's on *her* table like that.

I say hers because she's the reason why I bought it. It was to make up for the fucked up mistake that I made on the other table. A mistake I'm now paying for.

When I see him reach down for the girl looking up at him to invite her up, I lose it. There is no fucking way some tramp is going to get up on *my girls* table. The girl that should be on that table is Abigail. Regardless of why she's on it.

"Get the fuck off," I furiously growl at Trey as I stalk my way over to the table, already yanking at the girls arm to pull her back.

Trey sees me, his face lighting up with a drunken smile. "Hey fucker!" he shouts above the music, making me scowl at him. "What the fuck is that face for? It's about time you showed up," he adds in a drunken slur.

The girl's whose arm I'm holding is now giggling, her hands starting to glide down my body, aiming south for my dick. I push her hand out of the way, watching her face grow annoyed. Ignoring her, I turn to glare back at Trey.

"Get. The. Fuck. Off. The. Table!" I shout up at him again.

He jumps off the table, landing in front of me.

"What the fuck got up your ass?" he asks, looking perplexed from my reaction.

"Do I really need to answer that?"

He shrugs his shoulders without a care. "You're the one who got yourself in this position," he says, thrusting his hips forward to mimic fucking someone.

I ignore him, not needing a reminder of my mistakes. "I told you, no more parties while Abigail lives here," I bellow as I walk away from him, but I only make it a couple of steps before I hear him shout behind me. "She doesn't live here anymore."

My feet are rooted to the spot as I turn to face him. "She left with Kelly," he states with a humorless expression.

My hearts drops into the pit of my stomach hoping it's a lie. I feel as the world has stop moving. I don't want her to be gone. This is her home, it will always be hers, whether she realizes it or not… It's her future. I silently say the words in my mind, I'm already rushing towards her room. Pushing the door open with force, it slams against the wall and instead of finding her, I see a couple on the bed about ready to fuck.

"You have two seconds to get the fuck out of this room before I drag your sorry asses out!" I shout at them.

Angry, they both start scrambling off the bed as they dress before they leave the room. I slam the door behind them and take in the empty room. Every single one of her possessions is gone. It's as if she was never here. Seeing the empty room confirms Trey's words. She's gone.

I walk over to the bed, sitting on it as I place my head in my hands. My eyes close as the pain of knowing she is no longer here rips at my heart. I just keep repeating in my head: I don't know what the fuck I'm going to do, but I know I'm going to get her back.

Chapter Four

Abigail

IT'S BEEN ALMOST a week since I left Matt's house. I've chosen to do nothing but sulk in my misery in bed. I haven't had much of an appetite. Although I tried eating, the food is tasteless, so I gave up.

It doesn't help knowing this is the week of Thanksgiving. It would have been our first Thanksgiving together. Instead, we are spending it apart. Kelly had insisted I go with her to spend it with David and her family, but I refused, not wanting to bring my misery to her family. Instead, she left me to wallow alone for the two days she was gone. I needed this time to myself. I had to figure out what the hell I was going to do now. I had become so dependent on having Matt with me all the time that I now felt empty without him.

Being the friend that Kelly is, when she returned, it was back to our normal routine. She would come in the morning before she left for work, returning after to bring me something simple to eat, but the attempts were turning into failed endeavors. I keep reassuring her I am fine, although she knows I am lying through my teeth.

Having to pee again, I get up and make my way over to the bathroom. As soon as I wipe myself the aspect of my concern from this previous week is evident on the toilet paper. The worry of possibly being pregnant with Matt's child has consumed my thoughts. The longing of getting my period is now granted, but the pang of disappointment just as quickly takes over. It hadn't occurred to me until Lisa's announcement of her pregnancy that I too can be pregnant, but the agony of waiting to find out was now over.

Digging under Kelly's sink, I find what I need and quickly clean up. After washing my hands I head back to the bed and take up my previous position. The warmth of where my body was once laying is still there between the covers. Staring up at the white ceiling, I keep telling myself that I'm lucky. It would have been worse if I had been pregnant as well. Now I can move on with my life.

After an hour of lying there and thinking to myself, I come to one conclusion: I cannot risk taking the chance again. Knowing that I will need Kelly's help, I search for my phone and turn it on. I've been dreading having to do it, knowing that the minute it comes alive there will be countless messages from Matt, but it's the only way I can get a hold of her right now without having to wait until she shows up tonight.

Within seconds of being on, the phone starts pinging, confirming my thoughts. It takes close to a minute before they stop and when I take them in, I notice most of them are voicemails from Matt. My heart is telling me to ignore them because I just cannot bring myself to listen to them right now. I know if I risk listening to his voice I will break down again and I'm not strong enough yet to face that demon.

I do open up the text messages from Trey, noticing his consistency of asking if I'm doing okay. What am I supposed to tell him? He already knows I feel like shit, but I know it's not fair to ignore him.

Me: I'm alive, but that's as much as I can give you.

It doesn't surprise me when I don't receive an answer since he's in class, so I get up to go take a shower knowing I need to wash off the funk that I'm in. When I'm done and dressed, I receive my answer back from Trey.

Trey: Hey supermodel, I know you're alive.

As well as a message from Matt.

Matt: Beautiful, please, I need to talk to you.

I choose to ignore Matt's request. He should have already gotten the point I don't want to speak to him. I send off a quick "*fine*" to Trey with no further explanation and call Kelly.

She answers. "Hey girl, how you feeling?" she asks, sounding concerned.

"Better. What time do you get off work today?"

"In about an hour. Why, what's up?" she asks sounding excited I'm actually asking the question.

Sighing to myself, I say, "I need a ride to a doctor's office. Or clinic."

I get an unbearable silence on her end, worrying me. "Why?" she curiously asks. "You're not pregnant, too, are you?" she says, now sounding shocked.

"No, I'm not pregnant!" I screech back at her. "I just got my period, but that's why I need to go to the doctor. I need to make sure it *won't* happen."

"It's pretty slow right now so I don't think they'd mind me leaving. I'll be home in twenty minutes," she tells me.

Feeling relieved, I reply, "Okay, see you in a bit."

Less than twenty minutes later she's walking in the front door. "First of all congratulations on not being pregnant," she states as if I've just won a huge prize. "Don't get me wrong, I'm pretty sure both of you would have made a beautiful baby, but I'm happier you're not knocked up."

"Gee, thanks for the support if I would've been," I sarcastically respond with a chuckle.

She rolls her eyes. "What you need is Planned Parenthood and I know exactly where it's at since it's where I go."

"I don't care where we go as long as they take credit cards as payment since all I have is Matt's debit card connected to my account," I say, already grabbing for my purse that is on the counter.

She nods her head in agreement and we're soon walking out the door.

Three hours later we're back and I'm good to go. Matt tried calling me again, but I simply ignored his call. I was tempted to turn my phone off again, but I couldn't bring myself to do it. As soon as I make myself comfortable on the couch the door-bell rings. The simple sound of the bell is enough to make me tense up, the dreadful memory of what comes with that sound still haunts me to this day. But I have every reason to add to the dread when I see Matt walk through the door, followed by Trey close behind him. This is what I was attempting to avoid when I was ignoring their phone calls. If I had wanted to see or speak to them I would have let them know.

He spots me the minute he walks in the door as he ignores Kelly's angry protest to get out.

"I don't need your shit right now," I bark at him, already marching my way towards the bedroom. I'm halted to a stop when Matt blocks my way. Trey is already at his side grabbing for Matt's arm, trying to drag him away from me.

I look over at Kelly who has already made her way to my side. She looks livid and ready to attack Matt as she glares at him.

Matt continues to ignore both of them as he takes my hand and leads me to the bedroom. I try yanking it back, but he keeps a gentle grip on it as he tugs me along. The warmth of his hand is too familiar, leaving me to cave to his request.

As we near the room, Kelly rushes to stand in front of Matt. "She already told you she doesn't want you here, so leave," Kelly snaps at Matt, the irritation clear in her voice. "Stay out of it Kelly, this is between Abigail and me."

Still not budging, she tells him, "You should have thought about that the day we walked in on you fucking Lisa on that table. You're lucky I didn't kick your ass then," she threatens as she shoves her finger into Matt's chest.

Looking back to me, his eyes are full of regret. "Please, beautiful, hear me out," he pleads. The remorsefulness in his words breaks me down. "I'll be fine, Kelly," I say, eagerly giving in to Matt's plea.

Still furious, her eyes lock onto Matt, "You better be nice."

Without answering he leads us around her and into the room. The reality of knowing I'm alone with Matt hits me, but the trance is quickly broken when I hear, "You make her cry again, Garcia, and I'll fuck you up!"

I cannot help but chuckle before Matt's eyes find mine. The misery beaming from them is matching my own. We both continue standing there as the anguished silence surrounds us like a darkened cloud.

"Abigail, what do I have to do to get you to speak to me again?" he desperately asks, his eyes pleading for my forgiveness. I don't answer because I'm scared I'll forgive him.

My heart has descended into the pit of my stomach and the pain in my chest is increasing with every second that passes. My heart is begging me to reach out to him, to forgive him, but I keep telling myself it would be a mistake.

I watch his eyes gradually rake my body. His eyebrows draw forward as if narrowing down on something specific. Puzzled, I look down at the object of his attention, grasping my wrist up to my chest.

"You're wearing your bracelet," he happily says as I hold onto my wrist. Looking back up to him, I see his lips curve up in a satisfied smile. "I'm not giving it back," I sternly tell him.

Without hesitation, he reaches for me as he engulfs me in his arms. "I would never ask for it back. It's yours to keep no matter what happens between us."

The realization of his words hit me like a wall slamming against my emotions. I wasn't prepared for him to say them. Uncontrollably, I start to cry as if I haven't cried for days.

"Please don't cry, beautiful," he whispers against my ear,

making me sob even harder. "I swear I never meant for this to happen," he says as he holds me tighter.

"I know, Matt, but it did," I tell him, unable to keep the hurt inside any longer.

"This doesn't have to change anything between us. It shouldn't. I still love you."

As I sob against his chest, taking in the meaning of his words, I know what he wants, but I'm still not ready to forgive. Forcing myself to speak around the lump lodged in my throat, I say to him, "I can't be the other person in your life. It wouldn't be fair to her."

"How can you be the other person when there wouldn't be anyone else for me?" He muffles the words against my hair. "I love you, Abigail. Nothing will ever change that."

I take in his words, but regardless of the meaning behind them, they don't change my decision. "I love you, too, Matt, but I can't be with you knowing that you're going to have a baby with someone else. You need to put that little life before anyone else right now. Especially me."

The exasperated sigh he releases tells me that he's given up. It pains me, but deep down inside I know it's for the best. I don't know how much time has passed, but we eventually hear a knock at the door before it opens and Trey enters, making me pull away from Matt.

When I lift my head from Matt's chest and look over at him his eyes go straight to Trey. "I warned you not to make her cry, fucker. You're really looking for me to kick your ass, aren't you?" he threatens him, making me laugh. Trey looks back down at me, giving me a satisfied smile.

"Shut the fuck up, Trey." Matt snarls back at him, the humor in the situation not fazing him.

"I'm fine," I say to Trey, realizing how weakened my body feels as I said those two simple words. With a curt nod, he turns to leave the room, leaving Matt and I alone once more.

"I'm not giving up on you, beautiful," Matt declares against my ear.

His warm breath glides against my skin, sending a shiver down my spine as it reminds me of what I dearly miss of Matt: his arms and words. It's when he places a kiss below my ear that I nearly succumb to my weakness and ask him not to leave. He doesn't give me the chance as he pulls away from me to follow Trey, leaving me to watch him walk away. At the same time I ask myself, am I going to regret letting him leave?

Matt

MY EMOTIONS ARE a mess as I drive away from Kelly's house. I expected Abigail to be angry with me, but I never expected her to try to break us up. She may not have said the words, but I know deep down inside she was telling me it was over. I wasn't accepting it.

Seeing her again shattered me from the inside out. The spark that I've grown to love about Abigail was completely diminished, as if it never existed. It reminded me of the night she came to live with me. I'd vowed to never let her feel that way again, yet this time I was the one provoking it, which is the reason I walked away tonight. I need time to figure out how to make her glow again.

"Dude, you can't blame her for not wanting to live in the same house with your baby momma," Trey states with bitterness.

"Lisa is *not* moving in," I throw at him without a sideways glance. I refuse to let anyone else other than Abigail move into my house.

I hear him utter under his breath, but I ignore him. I don't give a shit what he says. The only thing I can think of is Abigail. It's a torture in itself knowing I'm the reason she moved out. The reminder of her sorrow filled eyes as she stared back at me today will stay with me forever. It will be a constant reminder that will twist at my heart until I earn her forgiveness.

Deep down in my gut I knew the night she came to me it would only be a matter of time before I fell in love with her. It's why I promised myself, regardless of what happened between us, that she would never have to leave. But now I was the one she was running from.

With Abigail gone, it feels as if my world has collapsed around me. I feel like a failure to myself, as if I no longer have a reason to move on or exist.

"I'm surprised you didn't bring her back with us," Trey sarcastically claims at my side, breaking my thought.

His words make me smile. He's right. Had it not been for him or Kelly holding me back I probably would have brought her back against her will, but I knew it wasn't right. She would have resented me even more for doing it and it wasn't the way to earn her heart back.

My main concern now is to figure out how I am going to get her to move back in again. It's going to happen, one way or another, because I wasn't giving up on the notion. I meant my words. She's mine and I'm not letting her go.

Coming to a red light, I grow frustrated with the wait, my thumb irritably tapping on the steering wheel as I wait for the light to turn green. At that precise moment I'm reminded of how Emily would always tell me to be patient when I was driving.

Patience. That's the answer I need.

The thought makes me close my eyes and I silently pray. "*Emily, I really need an answer,*" I plead to her.

"Fucker, the light is green," I hear Trey shout at my side.

I open my eyes with a smile as I lift my head to mouth a silent *thank you* before I drive away. Focusing on the road ahead of me, I contemplate what I have to do. And then it hits me, but I already know it's only possible if I play my cards right.

Abigail

I STARE AT the door as if expecting Matt to walk back through it again. It isn't Matt who reappears through it, but Kelly. Her hands are on her hips, and she's glaring at me.

"Now that you're out of this funk, we're going out."

I roll my eyes at her demand. "I don't feel like it, Kelly," I answer, earning me a scornful expression. It doesn't faze me in the least.

"I'm not asking."

"Fine," I give in, knowing she will drag me out of here even if I continue to protest.

There was one demand she was willing to grant me: not going to the Brewhouse. Going there meant I was running the chance of seeing Matt. Kelly's suggestion was that we hit up a local dive bar a couple of blocks away so we can easily walk there and grab a cab on the way back if needed. Somehow in my gut I already know what it means, and I wasn't looking forward to it.

Quickly texting Julio to inform him of my plans so he can meet us there, we're soon walking out the door. I am hesitant to go, but I do. As soon as we walk into a bar called Pop's, I can already tell it's run by an old man named Pop. The floors look like they haven't been cleaned in weeks. The chairs and tables could be on their last leg, and the wooden bar has duct tape on it. At least the pool tables look decent enough from what I could see.

Tugging me along, Kelly heads straight to the bar, already shouting our order to the bartender. Two double Patrons, which reminds me this night isn't going to end well. When he hands them to us, I throw my shot back and regret it the moment it runs down my throat as I cringe. I'm barely taking a breath before Kelly is ordering our next drink.

I don't make the same mistake twice as I grab the drink

from her hand. Instead, this time I make my way over to a corner table, giving Kelly no choice but to follow me.

You Give Love a Bad Name is blaring through the speakers of the bar and it makes me want to down the drink I have in my hand to flush out the words. It's exactly how I feel as the main chorus bellows out, but the only thing keeping me from doing so is remembering the last time Kelly got my ass drunk.

It was because of Matt…

Kelly starts swaying to the music as I'm left watching her with amusement. I can already feel the alcohol taking its effect on me as well. I start looking around the bar when I suddenly hear, "Hey pretty ladies, haven't seen you in here before," says a guy standing next to me. I hadn't noticed him until now.

Taking him in, my eyes go wide in shock. If there were an ad for "my thug life," he would be the poster child with his bald head that he rakes his hands across before placing his red hat on backwards to cover it. The t-shirt he's sporting with the letters "Tapout" across it looks two sizes two small on his body.

His tongue rakes across his top teeth, but finishes by licking his lips while his eyes narrow down in a hooded slit. I'm pretty sure the nauseating feeling coursing through my body is not from the alcohol.

"Hey yourselves," Kelly flirts back to him.

I start to firmly shake my head, my body tensing up as my eyes shoot daggers at her to shut up. I know she's already buzzing and the liquid courage coursing through her body is going to get us in trouble. Encouraging Mr. Thug Nasty standing next to me is the last thing I want to do right now, especially with the look on his face. I'm pretty sure he thinks he's going to get lucky tonight.

He starts raking his hand under his shirt as he lifts it to allow us to see what's underneath. His roaming hands on his body and the smile accompanying it is threatening the alcohol to come up.

"I've got smiley face tattoos on my chest. I'd be happy to

show them to you," he says with a widening smile.

"Um, no," I reply, trying to stop myself from completely throwing up from the mental picture.

"You sure, sexy baby? I've got nipple rings to match. Trust me, once you get a taste of those in your mouth, there's no going back," he says near my ear.

I crane my head back to avoid him coming any closer.

"I want to see," I hear Kelly eagerly say from across the table.

Gasping in disgust as he starts to lift his shirt, I notice his eyes go wide in shock as his body is jerked away from us. He's now face to face with a very angry Julio. "I wouldn't try it unless you want me to kick your ass," he snarls in his face.

From the look on Mr. Thug Nasty's face, I wouldn't be surprised if he pissed his pants. When Julio is pissed he looks ready to kill. Normally I would try to stop him, but this time I'm not going to.

It doesn't take much for the guy to run away in fear. "I don't know why he had to scare him away. He could have been the only fun we might have tonight," Kelly says before tossing her drink back and waving down the waitress for another.

I'm the one now rolling my eyes as I look back at Julio. His eyebrow goes up at Kelly's remark. "I'm surprised you picked this place. Mateo wouldn't be too happy if he found out you're here," he acknowledges. I'm now the one scowling at him as he awaits my response.

"Since when do I need Matt's permission to live my own life?" I crudely throw back at him. With a sorrowful expression now on his face, he sighs. "I didn't say that. I'm just saying you should take in mind how he would react if something were to happen to you, Abigail," he replies.

His words pathetically affect me. I know Julio isn't happy with Matt's mistakes, but for some odd reason I feel like he's still siding with him.

Kelly is already handing me another shot. "Drink up, bitch.

You have some catching up to do," she shouts. I take the drink from her, tossing it back, hoping it will numb the uncertainly overtaking my mind.

Slamming the glass on the table, my eyes find Julio's again. I have no further words for him, but from the sympathetic looks he's giving me, I'm pretty sure he understands.

Chapter Five

THE SKIES ARE black; Mother Nature's mood is drastically matching my own. The skies above me are a perfect representation of the pain deep inside my heart. The pouring rain is beating down upon my body, but I welcome the beating of the raindrops to help mask my pain. My legs are protesting and begging me to stop their throbbing, but I refuse to give in. It would only mean defeat. The constriction of my lungs as they strive to give me my next breath is making me gasp for air. The will to keep pushing harder, to go faster, is overpowering all the protest thrown at me. After every run, the strain of finishing is worth knowing I've completed my goal.

This is my runner's high.

Alcohol is not my answer. Nor will drugs ever be. Those won't do it for me. At one time it was Matt who had all the solutions, but now I'm running to help myself find my own answers. He may have helped me discover my newfound love, but our running together will now be memories. Memories I will cherish forever.

I'M LYING ON the couch, confused as I stare at the TV. I cannot help but scrunch my face in confusion as I watch the girl pace back and forth in the small span of the living room, nervously biting her thumbnail. As far as I can understand, she's waiting for someone, but I'm still trying to figure out why she's wasting her time. Suspenseful music is playing in the background, already telling me this is going to be good, which is why I'm still watching. It's adding a dramatic effect that is holding my intrigued attention.

The music comes to a dramatic pause as a guy walks in the door. The girl begins attacking him with words. "Pinche Disgracido, ya se que me has enganado, pero ver me en la cara y otro ves mentir me? Que piensas que estoy pendija? Que vas a poder enganar me otra ves. No, esta ves, te puedes ir a la chingada."

My eyes go wide as I continue to hang onto every word said. I cannot help but think of Matt. The similarities of the drama appearing on the screen are too similar to my real life, which makes me chuckle. The woman grows angrier from the silence she receives; I'm pretty sure from the expression on the guy's face he's been busted. This darn show has been my guilty pleasure for the past week. My only excuse is I need a distraction from my thoughts. Since Kelly has no cable, this is what I was stuck with. I can't complain, it's better than constantly watching the sports channel.

"What are you watching?" Kelly's voice startles me, making me scramble to find the remote to turn the TV off, but it's too late. I'm busted. The couple on the screen continue to argue, the man desperately pleading she forgive him.

"Story of my life," I grimly tell Kelly as I sneak another peek to continue watching the debate on the TV for a couple more seconds.

Finding the remote, I turn off the TV realizing that I don't need to know the outcome of the performance. Regardless of what happens, it's obvious he's going to do it again since he *did* technically just leave the bed of another woman before it came back from the commercial. *Cheating douchebag.*

I sit up on the couch to face Kelly and I see her eyeing me

with her eyebrows curiously raised.

"What?" I ask, masking my embarrassment from being caught.

"Why are you watching a Mexican soap opera?" she questions with a snarky smile. "Are you trying to learn Spanish for a certain someone?" she adds.

"No. If that were the case I'd buy that stupid program to teach me Spanish."

She rolls her eyes at me. "You don't need to waste your money. It's how I learned Spanish," she informs me and I'm surprised by her words.

"I would have assumed you grew up speaking it."

She shakes her head. "Nope. One summer with my grandma and those soap operas was all I needed. It didn't take me long before I was fluent in the shit," she says with a snap of her fingers. "You'll pick it up in no time."

"Yes, Miss voice of reason," I tease.

"What time is big man getting here?" she asks, looking down at her phone.

I stand up from the couch already heading to the counter where my purse is. "Julio's mom has a doctor's appointment today, so he won't be coming with us."

Her eyes go wide in complete surprise. "You sure this is a good idea? You know Julio doesn't like you going out without him. And Matt will blow a gasket if he finds out," she states.

Hesitantly looking back down at her phone, she opens up the screen and goes straight to the call log.

"What are you doing?"

She sighs. "Abigail, you know it isn't a good idea to go anywhere without any of the guys," she replies.

From the anguished look in her eyes, I know she wants to call someone.

"You don't have to remind me *how* Matt feels about me going out without Julio, but I promised him the day off and this is *your* only day off this week," I remind her. "I'm tired of depending on everyone else to be my chauffeur. Besides, I have my glasses," I say holding my big oval shades up to show her.

Kelly knows she's been defeated. "Fine, then, let's go. But I'm still texting David and telling him where we're going just in case we have a repeat of the mall," she mumbles while texting away on her phone.

With a guilty sigh, I do the same to Julio. She's right. He should at least know where I'm at just in case. My excitement is increasing with the thought of my plans today, but the excitement is soon replaced with nervousness the closer we get to our destination.

Two hours later, the knots that I got in my stomach as we arrived have been replaced with frustration. Who knew buying a damn car would be such a confusing decision? Kelly brought me to what they called 'the mile of cars' hoping it would help make the decision easier, but for some reason it made it harder. There was too many to choose from and no particular one was catching my attention.

"How about this one?" Kelly asks, walking over to a white Mercedes Benz. I look as I rub at my forehead to try to ward off the headache I have. Taking in the car, I crinkle my nose, making her roll her eyes. "What's wrong with this one? The color?" she asks, making me sigh again.

"It's not the color, it's more the car," I tell her, staring at the price tag on the window. "I just can't justify spending this much money on a car."

She grows confused. "What do you mean? You can easily afford it, Abigail. Why wouldn't you want it?" she asks, looking back at the car. Unfortunately, I don't hold the same excitement she does.

"I'm not always going to be loaded," I claim as I walk away.

I try my best to ignore the disappointed sigh she gives me as she sadly looks back at the car. I think she wants the car more than I do. At this point I've pretty much given up on the decision. This day was beginning to feel like a failure. I visited over five dealerships and still could not decide on a car. But in my defense, Kelly kept escorting me to the high-end models.

Giving up, I begin to walk back to Kelly's car. It's when I'm about to climb in that I take one quick glance across the street and see it. My car. I head straight in its direction, leaving Kelly confused as she rushes to catch up to me.

I reach her taking her completely in.

"Hello ladies, are you interested in test driving the car?" the old salesman asks as I picture myself behind the wheel. "I don't need to test drive it. I'm taking it home," I inform him.

"This is the one?" Kelly doubtfully asks as she takes in the Dodge Challenger sitting in front of us.

"Yes, without a doubt."

With a humoring smile on her face, she shakes her head. "Why doesn't it surprise me?" she says chuckling.

I glide my fingers across her candy apple red gloss of paint that is shining under the sunlight, a beacon that was calling for me to come get her. To me she's the most beautiful thing I've ever seen, making me smile because I know she's going to be mine.

The salesman is already excited. He knows he's made an easy sale without having to put any effort into trying to convince me. Even if anyone tried to talk me out of buying the car, I wouldn't allow them. I was going home with *this* car.

Two hours later I'm walking out the door with the keys to my new car. All I had to do was authorize the transfer with the bank and I was signing the paperwork needed to register the car. They have already brought her up to the front of the dealership, primed and ready for me to drive her home. I climb into her for the very first time, taking in the new car smell that is effusing into air. The brand new leather beneath my skin feels like silk against my body and when I start her up the purr she gives me sends a prickle through my body as I close my eyes and take in the sound. It sounds like music to my ears as I listen to her sing to me. Before putting her into drive I turn on the radio, the lyrics of *Wide Awake* sing through the speakers, making me smile. This could not have been a more perfect song for me at this very moment. Throwing her into drive, I step on the pedal and drive out of the parking lot feeling on top of the world.

I make it back to Kelly's place faster that she does because I was pushing the speed limits on the open freeway that was clear of traffic. Matt never let me pass the speed limit when I drove his car, which caused the need for me to do it in my car.

It doesn't surprise me when I see Julio standing next to his car as I pull up into the spot next to him, his eyebrow going straight up as I climb out of the car. "I leave you alone for one day and this is what you go buy?" he answers with a smirk on his lips.

I'm shocked by his words. "I needed a car," I answer.

"When you said you were buying a car, I thought you would've chosen better," he replies.

"How can you say such a thing? Lola's an awesome car," I sternly tell him, defending her.

He grunts. "Really, you named your car Lola?" The look on his face telling me he hates the name, but I don't care.

"It's my car."

He takes in the car again. "I guess it shouldn't surprise me you chose this car," he casually states.

My smile widens. "Nobody is going to tell me I can't drive Lola. We're going to ride off into the sunset every day with no one to tell us we can't," I say, holding my arm extended out towards the already glistening horizon where the sun has started to set.

Julio looks off into the distance with me while he laughs. His laughter is contagious as I too take in my own words. When our laughter dies down I see Kelly walking up to us with a smug look on her face. "I take it you're still happy with your decision?"

"Of course I am. Why wouldn't I be?"

"I just feel like you chose the car because you can't get

Matt out of your mind," she replies.

Shocked, my jaw drops. "I didn't buy the car because of Matt," I defensively answer.

She takes in the car one more time. "Okay, if this is the car that is going to get you out of your funk, then so be it," she conveys with a smile.

All three of us stand there staring at the car. I'm feeling happier than I have in days.

Matt

MY BODY IS aching and sore from my game just moments ago. I'd pushed myself harder than I normally would, needing to rid myself of all my pent up tension I had inside of me. Our win is bittersweet. It's the win we needed to help push us into Nationals, but the entire time my heart was aching from the absence of the two people I wanted in the stands cheering me on.

My heart was desperately wishing Abigail would have been in them, but I knew she wouldn't be. Alone in an empty locker room with my thoughts to keep me company, I relinquish to my misery surrounding my heart. I could not resist glancing up to the stands before I exited the field, wishing Abigail were there, but I knew she wouldn't be because she's still mad at me. Pushing the disappointment aside, my thoughts wander to my last homecoming game, a smile tugging at my lips from the memory.

Gradually making my way to her, she's already beaming with pride as her smile illuminates her face. Reaching her, I lean down to engulf her in my arms, my lips firmly press against her cheek. I hold her longer than expected, listening as she giggles against my ear. She's already shoving at my chest to let her go, but I swing her around in a circle so I can continue hearing her sweet giggle.

"Matthew, you're going to make me smell," she playfully

chastises as I bring us to a stop. "Most girls would kill to be in my arms at this moment, Em," I tease as she slides down my body.

She snickers. "Of course they would. I don't know whether it's a privilege or a curse that you seek me out first," she implies with her nose scrunched up.

"How was your flight?"

"Well, as always. I'm sorry I couldn't get here sooner than this afternoon," she expresses, the guilt now replacing her smile.

Grasping her tight against my chest again, I ignore her pro-test to release her. "You're here, and that's all that matters," I express against her hair.

Emily has been to every single one of my games, regardless of where it was. Most of the time she barely makes it on time because of her schedule, but to me it didn't matter. All I cared about was that she made it.

She gently pushes away so she can look up at me. "Speaking of girls, where's Laura? I haven't seen her," she states, al-ready searching for her amongst the crowd.

"She's not here," I answer as I pull away from Emily. "She's sort of mad at me right now for forgetting her birthday," I shamefully admit.

Tsking. "I don't understand that girl sometimes," she re-plies.

Her response doesn't take me by surprise. Although she's tolerated Laura, recently she's been expressing how we both need to move on. It was I who was stubbornly holding onto the hope that things would get better. "Homecoming is the most im-portant game of the season. She should have been here," she says.

Pushing the bitterness I'm now feeling from the realization of her words, I force a smile. "It's okay, Em. You were here, which is all I need," I somberly say.

"As I always will be. I wouldn't miss your games for the world," she states.

I'm now genuinely smiling from her words. She's right. Girls may come and go, but knowing that I'll always have my sister at my games is all I need. She's the most important person in my life and no matter what happens, I know she will always be there for me, as I will her.

My memory is broken with the bang of the locker room door slamming shut. Hanging my head, I rake my hands through the strands of my hair, miserably sighing to myself. The sound of footsteps nearing makes me start removing my gear. The action is more to disguise my emotions to whoever is approaching and is now at my side. Glancing up to see who it is, I see Trey already taking a seat on the bench next to me. As I continue to remove the pads from my shoulders, I roughly toss them onto the floor; an exasperated sigh leaving my lips.

"I miss her, too," I hear Trey mummer.

From the corner of my eye, I see him bleakly staring at the lockers ahead of us. Those four words tear at my soul, reminding me she's gone. I cave to the tears that were threatening to release and allow them to fall. Slowly they trickle down my cheeks as I sit there and somberly remember Emily.

Trey remains silent and dazed at my side, but from the sigh that soon escapes from his lips, I know he's grieving alongside me. Had it been anyone else besides him, I would have never submitted to my pain, but knowing he understands, is the reason why I had. Emily might not have his blood, but she treated him just the same, and her death hurt him just as much.

It isn't long before the rest of the team gradually makes their way in, forcing my tears to dry up and disappear, but the thoughts and memories that were in my mind are still there. They forever will be.

Composing myself the best I can, I shower and dress. Since Trey's family flew in for his game, he had invited me to join them for dinner after. Exiting the building with Trey, we make our way back onto the field to find his family. When we near the small crowd, I see Abigail standing with them, lighting up the darkened skies that had loomed above me. Julio is discreetly standing behind her as he stands at Kelly's side to converse with Trey's mother. I cannot help but quicken my steps to reach her faster. Her eyes find mine and the smile she gives me radiates from ear to ear.

"There they are. It's about time. I'm starving," Trey's dad declares when he eyes us walking in their direction.

Trey's mother nudges him. "We all know you're hungry, but do you have to keep complaining about it?" she scorns, extending her arms out when I reach them.

Happily, I give in to her request. "You disappeared without a word after the game," she says, pulling away to look at me with saddened eyes.

"I'm sorry," I quietly reply, knowing from the expression on her face she understands why I disappeared so quickly. The sincerity in her eyes as she continues looking at me while she pats me on the cheek makes my eyes go glassy.

She gives me a reassuring smile. "It's okay. You're here now," she states before stepping away. My eyes automatically find Abigail's. I cannot resist pulling her into my arms. "You played a really good game today," she expresses.

"I didn't think you'd be here," I admit.

Yanking her head back, she's wide-eyed as she asks, "Why would I miss your game?"

Testing her, I say, "Because you're mad at me."

"I am, but I wasn't going to miss homecoming. You always told me it's the most important game you play," she replies.

Her response takes me back to my earlier memory and the words Emily gave me. Without hesitation, I kiss her. She is taken aback at first, her body going rigid in surprise. But within seconds, she's returning my kiss and I forget we're surrounded by a crowd of people as I hungrily kiss her. I've missed her lips... I've missed the taste of her.

"Dude, you don't have to eat her face off to prove she's yours!" Trey exclaims.

His words cause Abigail to pull away, her head already whipping in his direction. "Shut up, Trey!" she scornfully shouts at him with her signature, *I'm going to kick your ass* look. The sight of her angry at him makes me laugh, until she turns to give me the same look, but it doesn't faze me a bit. Leaning down I happily kiss her again, earning me a softened mumble against my lips.

When I'm done I turn to face everyone. "You've all met Abigail, right?"

Clearing her throat before speaking, "Yes, she told us you were *friends*, but I'm a bit confused by the definition at this point," Trey's mom states, still looking confused.

I feel Abigail pull herself from my arms. "Yes, Mrs. Johnson, we're just friends," she clarifies.

"Abigail."

"Nothing else," she throws back at me as she fixes me with another glare. As much as I want to argue her point, this is not the place to do it. "Fine, friends it is," I reply with a fabricated smile.

"You better not be kissing me like that, dude. I don't do tongue with guys," Trey sarcastically jokes, making everyone laugh and lightening the mood.

"What *do* you use then?"

"How about I take you under the bleachers and show you," he responds, thrusting his hips in my direction. His mom immediately smacks him upside his head. "Trey Johnson, I did not raise you to be speaking that way in front of the ladies," she reprimands. "You apologize."

Glowering, he looks over to Abigail. "I'm sorry," he mumbles as he rubs the back of his head. Mrs. Johnson nods her head in a silent approval before turning to me. "And you, young man," she says, pointing her finger at me. "If I find out you break this young girl's heart, you'll be answering to me," she sternly lectures. By the tone of her voice, I *know* she will kick my ass for sure if she knew I've already broken both our hearts.

"Yes, ma'am," I answer, looking once again at Abigail. "I'm sorry," I apologize down at her. She looks baffled. I keep my eyes locked on hers hoping she understands. By the way her lips go flat, I know she's finally understood.

"Good, now let's go eat. You boys must be hungry," Mrs. Johnson announces.

Taking advantage of the fact that Abigail is here and willingly speaking to me again, I ask, "Do you all mind if Abigail and I take a rain check on dinner?"

"Matt," Abigail apprehensively replies.

Deeply looking into her eyes, I implore, "Please, just you and me?" I tuck her hair behind her ear before saying, "We have a lot of time to make up for." Her shoulders drop and a smile creeps into her lips.

"Of course," Mrs. Johnson cheerfully replies, and in the corner of my eye I can see everyone retreating away.

"Okay, but we're eating food, nothing else," she warns, but with a hint of laughter which is evident in her eyes.

Understanding her meaning, I lean down to whisper into her ear, "If you change your mind, I wouldn't mind giving you something else for dessert." Feeling the goose bumps rising against my lips as they touch her skin, she shoves me away and I hear a protesting mumble, "Never mind," before she turns to try to walk away. Quickly catching up to her, I wrap my arm around her waist and continue walking with her as I say, "You win then. Food it is," I express, unable to resist laughing as I continue holding her all the way to the parking lot, leading her to my car.

Looking behind my shoulder, I convey to Julio he's got the rest of the night off before helping Abigail into the car. Climbing into the driver's side, I see Abigail curiously eyeing me from the corner of my eye. "What's your weakness tonight?" I cannot help but notice how her eyes roam by body. It takes every ounce of resistance to not smile from her reaction. "Pizza. My favorite," she says, biting down on her bottom lip when done.

"Do you want sausage on that pizza?" I tease, now smiling from her earlier reaction as my eyes are matching the same hunger staring back at me. A blush creeps up her cheeks and a glimpse of a smile spreads across her lips. "However you prefer," I hear her shyly reply.

Holding in my laughter, I start up the car and drive off to my destination. To help speed up time I called ahead for her pizza. "Give me a minute. I'll be right back," I notify Abigail when we arrive. "We're not eating here?" she asks, looking confused. "No, I thought we'd picnic somewhere today," I relay before I rush out of my car to pick up our dinner. Back in the car within minutes, she's already asking, "Where are we going?"

"It's somewhere special. I promise."

I'm driving up a winding road with the time quickly going as I try to remember how to get to my destination. Right as I think I will never find it again, it comes into view. When I put the car in park, I look over at Abigail to find her eyes wide in amazement as she stares over at the skyline of Portland in front of us from the top of the mountain. "Come on, the view is better from the outside," I tell her, grabbing for the box of pizza. Popping my trunk, I reach inside for a blanket I always keep for emergencies and nod for Abigail to follow me so we're sitting in front of the car.

Handing Abigail the pizza once again, I lay out the blanket and pull her to sit next to me on it. Opening up the box, I hand her a slice of pizza as she says, "How do you know about this place?" she warily asks. I can hear the cautiousness in her words, as if testing me. "I accidently found this place a couple days after Emily died. I sort of got lost while I was driving around attempting to forget what happened. I stopped to figure out where I was. I hadn't noticed the view until I was forced to take in my surroundings. I haven't been here since then," I reveal, remembering the sorrow I felt on that day. My words strike me as I take them in myself. In my heart, the moment seems like only yesterday, instead of the months that have gone by.

"It's beautiful," Abigail says, looking back down at the city.

"Just as beautiful as you," I add, earning me a smile. Within minutes we're eating our pizza as the sun is gradually setting. Taking a chance, I move to wrap myself behind Abigail, and she willingly leans back against my chest, allowing me to wrap her in my arms. We sit in silence together as we watch the sunset on the horizon. When all that's left is the glow of the setting sun in the skyline surrounding us, I place a kiss below Abigail's ear. "Thank you for bringing me here," I hear her whisper. I tilt her chin up with my hand so she is facing me, greedy with the need to kiss her.

Our kiss is gentle and sweet. "I love you," I say against her lips. I feel her smile before she returns the kiss, but doesn't return the words. I'm feeling dejected from her lack of response, but she surprises me when she responds. "I love you, too," she whispers. It's enough to tell me I have hope, which is all I can wish for at this point.

Chapter Six

MY PHONE STARTS vibrating in my back pocket as I'm leaving class and walking back to my car. Digging it out of my pocket, I grow disappointed when I see the screen. I had hoped it would be Abigail. She hasn't called me since the day I took her atop of the mountain, but I've managed to get her to respond to my text messages.

The name on the screen doesn't help suppress my disappointment, either. "What's up, Lisa?" I clip into the phone, not bothering to disguise my agitation. I called her over a week ago to inquire how she was doing, which I'm already regretting. "Why haven't you called me?" she whines into the phone.

"I've been busy," I lie back to her, already wanting to end the call. She hasn't stopped calling or texting me since I first contacted her. It was beginning to get annoying.

"Too busy to ask how the mother of your child is doing?" she asks. "I haven't been feeling well, by the way," she irritably adds.

"I'm sorry," I reply, not knowing what else to say. "Lisa, unless it's something important, I really have to go," I tell her, already dreading what she might say.

"I was calling to tell you that I made a doctor's appointment for next week and you're going with me," she demands.

Sighing to myself, I keep walking towards the sports building, slowing my pace as I near it. "Fine, text me the date and time and I'll pick you up," I say.

"You can't avoid me forever, Matt. It's not fair," she whines. "I'm not avoiding you, I just got other things on my mind right now," I tell her, which is true. "I'm sorry, but I really have to go, Lisa. I'll call you later," I add for good measure, but from the snicker on the other end of the line before I end the call, I know she doesn't believe me.

The call only makes me think of Abigail again and the promise I made to her. It's only been a couple of days since the homecoming game, but the days are beginning to feel endless since Abigail left. Every night I fall asleep I'm wishing she were next to me.

A minute later my phone is already ringing again. "What now?" I angrily answer, thinking it's Lisa calling me back.

"I'm sorry, is this Mr. Garcia? Abigail Adams' assistant?" the voice on the other end of the line asks.

Immediately I resent answering the way I did. "I'm sorry. Yes it is."

The voice pipes up. "My name is Thomas Pierce. I'm calling on behalf of Rebecca McDonald from *Running World Magazine*. Mrs. McDonald had briefly spoken with Ms. Adams in San Francisco in regards to doing an interview for our magazine," he reminds me. "I was calling to set up a time and date for said interview."

I cannot help but ask, "Will she be paid for this interview?"

"Of course," he replies.

I can't help the smile that comes across my lips. This is the perfect excuse I need for me to speak to Abigail again. "What time is best for you?" I ask, hoping he will say something soon.

"The earliest we can do is Saturday," he states. At the same time I hear the ping on my phone telling me I have a text message. Ignoring it, I continue my conversation. "Saturday would be perfect. Where and what time would you like to meet?" I enthusiastically ask him.

I spend the next few minutes wrapping up the details with

the gentleman on the phone. Ending the call, my earlier excitement is now replaced with doubt. They insisted on an early shoot due to the predicted weather. It meant it required Abigail to wake up at the crack of dawn. Abigail is not going to be happy about having to wake before ten A.M., but I'll deal with her on that matter. I was *not* going to let her miss this opportunity. She earned this interview and it's exactly what she needs to get her publically back into the modeling world.

Opening up my text app, I take in Lisa's message, noticing the appointment is next Friday. I guess I'm going to have to skip class for the appointment. As I'm putting my phone back into my pocket, I'm already thinking of ways that I can convince Abigail to get up that early, but just as quickly it occurs to me and I already know she isn't going to resist my offer. With a confident smile on my face, I enter the building, excited about my plans.

Abigail

MY PHONE STARTS singing the words to *Red.* I know it's Matt because it's the ringtone I've designated for him. I hesitate to answer, but when the musical tone comes to an end I grow disappointed.

Ever since the night we watched the sunset together, I've been more than confused. My heart is aching from wanting to forgive him, but the will to keep him at a distance is what keeps me from doing so. I hate how he can easily make me feel as if his mistake had never happened. Nor that it doesn't exist. That night I let myself get whisked away by Matt as if we were still dating and our love was stronger than ever. For that hour as I sat tightly wrapped in his arms, I had completely forgotten about our troubled relationship. It wasn't until he was driving me back to Kelly's that I was reminded we were no longer living in a fantasy of a happily ever after.

My thoughts are broken when I hear my phone announcing I have a text message. Curiosity is my weakness and I'm already opening it up to read it.

I have a job for you. – Matt.

He conveys, simple, and to the point.

The urge for more details is the reason why I'm quickly calling him. "Hey, beautiful," he answers within the first ring. He sounds amused, as if he knew I wouldn't resist the bait. "I love you," he adds, knowing the vulnerability I have to those words.

"Matt, please get to the point," I irritably snap at him, trying to mask my vulnerability.

I hear him disappointingly sigh on the other end. "I got a phone call from that running magazine. They want you to do an interview and a photo shoot."

"Really?" I ask, unable to contain my excitement.

"Yes, I already told them you would do it," he informs me.

"Shouldn't you have asked me first if I wanted to do it?"

"No," he answers. "You need to start working again. I'm not letting you turn down any opportunities that will get you back into modeling," he states, the tone in his voice refusing to allow me to challenge him. It adds to the fueling flames coursing through my body that began only seconds ago. "I already told them you would do it. You're scheduled for tomorrow."

"Fine," I clip out to him. I'm about to inform him to send me the detailed information when I hear a hard knock on the door, along with a simple, "Good," from the other end of the phone.

The knock startles me. Immediately, I'm frightful of who's on the other side.

"Matt, there's someone at my door," I fearfully whisper into the phone.

"It's me beautiful." My once frightened mind is replaced with confusion. "What the hell are you doing here?" I irritably ask, already climbing out of bed to make my way over to the front door, peeking through the peephole to verify it's really him. I see him standing there with the phone against his ear and waving back to me.

"I know you're behind the door, Abigail. I heard you walking up to it," he states, laughing into the phone, further irritating me.

I yank open the door, already scowling at him, as we both end our phone calls. Without an invitation, he steps into the apartment carrying grocery bags with him. "You haven't answered my question," I inform him as my eyes follow him into the kitchen after shutting the door. My arms are tightly crossed at my chest as my eyes glower at him, still waiting for an answer.

"I'm staying the night," he casually replies, already removing the items from the grocery bags. "You have to be at the shoot by seven A.M." he adds, surprising me to a gasp. I'm undecided over which has shocked me more, the fact that he thinks he's spending the night or that I have to get up so darn early. His chuckle isn't helping to defuse my mood.

"I knew you'd take some convincing to get up early, so I brought stuff to make you pancakes in the morning."

Dammit, the promise of his pancakes is enough for me to cave to any of his request. He clearly knows I've missed his pancakes, since he's declaring to make them. Gradually, I take the leaded steps needed to get me to the kitchen, but stop at the entrance of the doorway. Leaning my body against the frame, I keep my arms defensively crossed across my chest to prevent me from unwillingly reaching out to Matt.

Yes. Distance is my weapon.

"You're not staying the night, Matt," I grimly tell him.

Ignoring my reply, he continues removing the items from the grocery bags, placing them on the counter. "I don't see what the big deal is. You're going to have the place to yourself tonight," he states.

My mouth falls open. "How did you know that Kelly wasn't

going to be here?"

He chuckles before answering, "I made sure of it," adding a wink after his reply.

No wonder why David had come over and insisted Kelly pack an overnight bag. At first I had felt a pang of jealousy knowing why he wanted her to stay the night at his place. Now I'm pissed he would let Matt manipulate him to get me home alone.

Placing the eggs into the fridge, he leaves everything else on the counter and slowly walks his away over to where I'm standing. His lips are mischievously curved up to the side and his eyes look dark as he keeps them locked onto mine. My breath hitches and my heart flutters with excitement. I know that look. It's the look he gives me when he's hungry for something, and I'm pretty sure that something is *me*.

Still striving to catch my breath, I say, "I'll see you in the morning," my voice raspy as he reaches out to me. His hands find my hips, pulling me towards him, forcing me to lean against him. Taking in his unique smell, I'm reminded of how much I miss being in his arms. My body is already igniting as I remember how easily he can satisfy my every need, the twinge of sparks exploding from the simplest of touch.

"I'm not going anywhere," he answers, his husky voice breaking my carnal thoughts.

I can feel the warmth of his breath as his lips brush against my ear, mocking my desire. "Do you want a kiss, beautiful?" he asks in a husky tone. The sound of his voice sends a chill down to my toes as his nose nuzzles my neck. My body is already drained of its blood from the realization of knowing how close I am to caving to his request.

I remove his hand from my hip to try to pull away. "I don't think it's a good idea, Matt," I reply, still trying to dislodge myself from his arms.

Pulling me tighter against his chest, he whispers in my ear, "Abigail, I'm not giving up on us."

"You have to stop doing—" are the only words I get out before I'm rendered speechless from his lips crashing down upon mine.

The kiss is simple, but I'm still left breathless. "I knew that would shut you up," his warm breath utters against my lips and he's kissing me again. My eyes find the darkness behind my closed lids and I savor the taste of his mouth as I greedily return his kiss. My hands are gripping at his shirt, pulling him closer to me. The feeling of his tongue moving against my own awakens my need to have him. I'm cursed when it comes to the willpower to deny him.

How am I supposed to keep the walls of my heart guarded against him when my body is defying what is needed to keeping him afar? All my thoughts of refusing him are forgotten when I feel him reach down and lift me up against his body, my legs automatically wrapping around his waist to hold on tight.

Within seconds we're in Kelly's room, my back against the mattress of her bed. "Kelly is not going to appreciate us doing this on her bed," I say against his lips, but holding him firmly on top of me, resisting letting him go.

"I'm pretty sure they've fucked on my bed. Payback is a bitch," he says, smiling against my lips.

I'm already yanking his shirt off, my lips returning to kiss him every so often between managing to rip each other's clothes off. Within seconds our bodies are naked against each other. My legs again wrapped around his waist, eagerly pulling him to me.

Abruptly, he yanks his head back, breaking our kiss, pulling his body away. "I've got to get a condom," he quietly says, surprising me he even has one. I'm left perplexed by his words as I look up to him. "I don't want to risk getting you pregnant," he explains, looking apologetic for stopping. The words are like a bucket of cold water awakening me. His declaration is a reminder of why I've been erecting the walls around my heart.

I scramble away from him. "What's wrong?" he asks, his eyes searching mine for an explanation. Sitting at the head of the bed, I bring my knees up to my chest trying to cover my naked body.

"We shouldn't be doing this," I rasp around the lump which is now lodged in my throat. He looks shocked, but just as quickly his expression turns remorseful as he briefly drops his head to sigh. Lifting it again, it's now full of regret. "Abigail, I don't know how many times I have to apologize. I know you don't want to hear it anymore, but I truly do mean it. I will always regret my mistakes, but I don't understand why they have to tear us apart?"

I grow angry at his words. "You got her pregnant, Matt. *She* is the one that is going to be having *your* baby," I argue back at him. Already having the courage, I continue. "That should have been me!" I throw back at him before I can stop myself from saying the words. I cannot hide the yearning of my words for it to be true.

He looks taken aback, as if I've physically slapped him. "Abigail," he softly says my name. "You don't think I wish it were you having my baby instead of her?" he asks, his words breaking as he asks them.

I cannot help the tear that escapes my eye, but I let it fall as I gravely sit across from him, mourning the loss at the chance. The ache from my shattered heart has resurfaced and is a painful reminder of why I have to keep myself guarded against Matt. "How do you think I feel knowing that from now on she will always come first?" I know the words may sound selfish, but they are how I feel.

With sincerity in his eyes, he says, "I will never put her before you, Abigail."

"You have to, Matt. At least for the baby," I answer.

My words suddenly strike him, the realization clear in his eyes when he takes them in. "You're right," he answers, my heart dropping into the pit of my stomach as he agrees. "I will always put my child first, but she will never take your place. I will always choose you," he declares.

I take in his words, my heart skipping a beat. They're the words I desperately want to hear, but are they the words that I should be allowing him to say?

As if my silence is what he was hoping for, he leans forward grabbing my hand to tug me to sit on his lap. Relinquishing my need to continue fighting him, I grant him his request and return to his body as he wraps his arms around me, allowing him to hold me. My face finds the crook of his neck as we silently sit there in the dark.

It isn't long before he gently places a kiss below my ear. I know it was to comfort me, but the warmth of his skin against my face provokes my desire again. My inner demons push my earlier words away with the need to taste him. Bravely, I place an open mouth kiss against his skin, taking in the taste of him. I keep kissing my way up his chin and I can feel his body go stiff against mine.

His hands provocatively begin gliding against my body, engraving a trail of electricity from his touch. The heat from his palms is igniting a flame inside of me, awakening my desire, eagerly succumbing to his touch.

I can feel his erection nudging against my thigh. Knowing he's ready for me makes me want him inside of me right now. Lifting my body up, Matt helps me straddle his waist and slowly sink down onto him, taking him completely inside my body. The feeling of being filled by him prompts me to moan. I'm about to move, when his hands grip my waist, preventing me from moving. "Beautiful, I really should put a condom on," he forcefully says against my mouth, the words sounding strained as he says them.

Still gripping his head, I confess, "I'm on birth control."

Without hesitation, his hands that are gripping at my waist lift me up, practically pulling himself from me. I'm about to protest when I feel the tip of him at my entrance, just as quickly slamming me back down against his hips, filling me completely as I moan into his mouth from the pleasure.

My need for him is overtaking me completely. It's as if I've lost all control as I aggressively rock my hips against his body, needing him deeper inside of me. His strong hands are gripping at my hips and I can already feel I may be bearing the imprint of his hands tomorrow. The intensity of his touch is driving me wild.

Fiercely gripping his hair to give myself something to hold onto, our mouths are tightly connected as our tongues continue to duel in a battle to outdo the other, demanding to taste more.

Every time my clit brushes up against his body, the pleasure inside of me builds as it demands its own release. My moans are becoming feral with the increased speed to reach our peak. I'm desperately trying to prolong my orgasm, but his words are making it inevitable.

"I've... Missed... You... So... Fucking... Much..." he moans against my mouth with each thrust, ultimately throwing me over the edge. My orgasm feels like dynamite exploding inside of my body, shattering me from the inside out. Slamming me one last time against his body, Matt throws his head back, letting out an animalistic growl.

My body slumps against his as it slowly continues to spasm. I'm exhausted and weak from my orgasm, my breathing labored, feeling as if I've just finished the most intense run I've ever had with Matt. Opening my eyes to look at him, I see he has the same reaction. His labored breath pushes his chest back and forth against my body.

We're both drenched in our sweat, my arms still wrapped around him, my face once again in the crook of his neck. I don't want to let him go just yet, but as if hearing my silent plea, he lies back onto the bed, bringing my body down with him. Our bodies are still tightly flushed against each other as he rolls us to the side. Wrapping my leg around his waist, I pull him tighter against my body, still refusing to let him go.

My eyes are already growing heavy when I hear him say, "I'm staying the night, beautiful."

Weakly attempting a chuckle, I tighten my arm around his waist as I surrender to my thoughts. My mind may be telling me to fight him, but my heart already knows who it belongs to, and he's lying right next to me.

Chapter Seven

Matt

I HOLD ABIGAIL in my arms, remembering the last morning I woke up with her at my side. It was the day I believed she would always wake up at my side from that day forward. It isn't until today that I realize how much I wish she truly were waking up with me every morning. It entices me to fight harder to have her at my side again.

The feeling of her silky skin against my body feels amazing, even more so when she's naked. The way her body molds into mine proves she's made for me. My dilemma is figuring out a way to make her realize it as well.

Inhaling the scent from her hair awakens my craving for her. I didn't sleep much last night, having stayed up most of the night savoring the feeling of having her in my arms. Although I didn't make love to her again, I desperately wanted to. My already awakened cock is proof of how badly I want to make love to her.

The screeching of my phone's alarm starts blaring, breaking the silence in the room as it announces it's time to get up. I had set it last night before I called her. I'd already known we were going to need it. Dislodging my body from hers, I go in search of my phone, finding it within the pile of clothes on the floor. After disengaging the alarm, I climb back into bed with Abigail, the coldness of her absent body already giving me the chills. She immediately wraps her body back into mine, her face finding her favorite spot in the hollow of my neck. I don't protest, but wrap her tighter against my body. I already know I'm going to have a hard time waking her. Abigail has never liked waking up early, unless it was for a run.

The day I agreed to the interview, I knew I was going to have this problem, which is why I asked David to keep Kelly at his place. It allowed me to be here with Abigail to wake her up myself. But now I was regretting agreeing to the early time. I would rather stay in bed with her all morning.

Her slow breathing informs me she's still sound asleep. Nudging my nose against her earlobe, I glide my tongue against her skin, making her stir. "Beautiful, you have to get up now," I whisper into her ear, wishing the words weren't true and we could stay in bed all day.

I feel her mumble into my neck in a silent protest. Using the leg she has hooked around my hip to pull me closer to her body, I cannot refuse her request, but instead push my hips deeper between her legs, letting her know how hard I am for her. When I hear a satisfied moan, I know I'm playing with fire, but I'm willing to take the risk to feel her heat. I start to trail my hand down her body. The warmth of her skin against my palm is driving me wild, especially when I reach her ass... my favorite spot.

I know it was only last night, but it's felt like an eternity since I've made love to her. The distance she's placed between us has been torturing me. My need to be inside of her again is keeping me from following through.

She pushes herself against me; her lips are already kissing against my neck, igniting the flames that are inside of me. I dip my finger in her wetness, testing to see if she's ready for me, because I'm about to fuck her, and I'm not holding back.

My need to be inside her has completely overpowered me. Grabbing her by the waist, I turn her body to face the mattress as I thrust my hips forward to enter her in one rapid movement.

This is my way of proving how much I need her.

The sound of her gasp weakens my ability to keep myself under control as the walls of her warm pussy surround my cock. I stop to gain control, but Abigail wants otherwise as she pushes herself back against my hips, demanding I give her more. With the glow of the outside light coming in through the window I can see her naked body below me and she looks like a naked goddess from this position; it drives me to start pumping faster. Her moans grow stronger, louder, encouraging me to push her over the edge. My speed increases as I watch her grab the sheets in her bare hands, begging me for more.

"Harder, Matt. Fuck me harder," she moans, driving me wild.

I've lost all control at this point as I give in to her command. I tighten my grip on her waist as I feel her body inching forward on the bed to keep her connected against my body. I can already feel I'm not going to last long, but I keep pushing. The strain makes my body tense, but I want to satisfy her first. When I see her throw her head back, letting out an elongated moan and her walls tightening around my cock, I feel every nerve inside of my body explode as I let myself go and spill myself inside of her, filling her completely.

Slowly, I bring my body to a stop. Abigail's breathing is labored and her bottom half is collapsed onto the bed from exhaustion. Leaning forward to place a kiss on her back, I taste the saltiness of her sweat. Although I'm just as exhausted, I cannot bring myself to dislodge from her warm body.

"I prefer you waking me up like this than you slapping my ass," she breathlessly says, making me laugh.

"Me, too," I say against her skin, feeling her shiver.

I pull myself up from her body and my eyes go straight to the rounded globes of her ass. Unable to resist myself, I give her a light slap, earning me a small yelp. She turns to pierce me with her fiercest glare, which only makes me laugh again. Pulling her body up to lean against my chest, I place an open mouth kiss against her shoulder. "We really should get up already," I whisper against her skin, nipping it this time.

I feel her mumble against my body as she stays slumped against my chest.

"Why don't you take a shower while I make you some pancakes," I tell her as I keep my arms wrapped around her body, unable to let her go just yet, although I know I should.

"Mmm, pancakes," she seductively says, rubbing her ass against my cock, making it twitch.

I'm now groaning as she tantalizes with my ability to contain my desire. I know if I don't force her to get up now, I'm going to cave and keep us in bed all day. Giving her a light shove to get up, I climb off the bed to look for my clothes. When I glance back down at her, I already see her getting comfortable again within the covers, pulling the sheets up to her chin ready to fall back to sleep.

"Abigail, if you don't get up you're going to be late," I sternly tell her. She still doesn't move. With one hand I yank the cover from the bed and bring my other hand down, aiming straight for her ass, knowing that it's the only thing that will wake her up. She lets out an angered howl, her face glaring daggers at me as she throws the pillow at me. "You fucking asshole!" she shouts as I catch the pillow.

I can't help but laugh. "I might be an asshole, but I'm *your* asshole," I state as I let the pillow drop onto the bed, still looking down at her. "You made me do it. I tried getting you up another way," I tell her, pulling her arm to help her up.

She's about to take a step when she stops, turning on the spot as if searching for something. I know it's probably her phone, so I start to dial her number to help her out. I hear it ringing on the floor and pick it up, the words shocking me.

"What happened to the ring tone I put on there?" I bitterly ask.

She attempts to grab for the phone, but I hold it high in the air out of her reach. "The other one was no longer appropriate.

I like this one better," she answers, pulling at my arm to get to her phone.

"No," I throw back at her, turning my body so I can change the ringtone. "Matt, give me my phone!" she whines, trying to reach around me.

"Go get in the shower. I'll give you your phone back when you get out."

Glaring at me, she stomps her way to the bathroom. From the corner of my eye I watch as she irritably takes one last glance at me while walking naked to the bathroom. I'm left staring at her, mentally telling my dick to calm itself. When I hear the shower turn on, I go back to my task. When done, I make my way to the kitchen and start making her pancakes. Thirty minutes later she's joining me, showered and ready.

"Give me my phone," she demands, holding her hand out for it. Handing it to her, I'm already calling it so she can hear her new ringtone. The lyrics to *Faraway* begin singing from her phone and she stands there taking in the words. When it's done, she snaps her head up, taken aback by what she hears. "You forgive me?" she asks, looking baffled.

"It's the rest of the words I was aiming for you to take in."

Watching her lips go flat as she contemplates my answer, I turn to continue making breakfast. "I don't know why you scheduled the shoot so damn early," she utters, pulling herself up to sit on the counter.

"It wasn't me that chose the time. I know better," I respond with a smile as I watch for her reaction from the corner of my eye. The glare I'm given tells me she doesn't believe me, but I ignore her and continue making breakfast. Transferring the pancakes to a plate to hand to her, her lips go wide into a smile when she eyes it, lighting me up. I turn off the stove and stand in front of her watching as she eats. After the second bite she curiously looks at me. "You're not going to eat?" she asks around a mouth full, looking for my own plate.

I open my mouth, requesting a bite, as my eyes find hers.

She feeds me the piece that is on her fork and I slowly close my lips over the fork, keeping my eyes locked onto hers. Her eyes go wide and when I pull back I see her squirming on the counter. She struggles to cross her legs, as if trying to hide her appetite for something other than my pancakes. Grabbing onto her knees, I spread her legs, pushing my body in between them to bring our bodies flush against each other. I'm about to satisfy both our hungers when a knock on the door startles us both.

"It's Julio. I called him last night," I notify her, knowing she's probably terrified from not knowing who it is.

Pulling myself away from her, I go over to make sure it's truly Julio before I open it. Verifying that it is, I open the door. With an acknowledging nod he enters. "I made pancakes," I tell him as he walks past me.

His eyes light up when I tell him, watching him head straight to the kitchen to serve himself. With Julio now here, there is no way I'll get Abigail to feed me anymore, so I serve myself and we all eat in silence in Kelly's tiny kitchen. The entire time my eyes avert every now and then to Abigail wishing we were alone, but my carnal mind knows better.

"I guess we should start heading out," I say to Abigail and Julio while placing my plate in the sink. I hope Kelly doesn't chew my head off about the mess I'm leaving, but we're already running late because of our delay this morning.

I'm grabbing for my keys when I see Abigail grab a pair of keys of her own off a hook on the wall. "We're taking my car," she says with a smirk on her lips.

"When did you get a car?" I ask her. "You haven't asked me for any money lately," I state.

Throwing the strap of her purse over her shoulder, she says, "I don't need to ask you for money anymore. You're the one who insisted I be added to the account," already walking to the front door without a backwards glance. She's right. I did insist for her to be added to the account because, in all technicalities, it's her money and I have no control over it. I'm just surprised she made the decision to buy the car without me. I would have liked to be there with her.

I push the resentment aside. "Let's go see your new car," I say to her, holding the door open as she follows Julio out.

I follow her down to the parking lot, leading us towards a red shiny new car. Not just any damn car, but a brand new Dodge Challenger, making my lips go up to one side as I desperately try to hide my smile.

"It's a nice car."

"Yes, it is, and *you* don't get to drive it," she distinctly states as she disengages the alarm with her key fob. "Is that so?" I sarcastically ask.

She pauses at the driver's side door, her eyes narrowing at me. "Payback is a bitch, isn't it Matthew? Now get your ass in the car before I leave you behind," she demands, making Julio laugh. "Oh, and you get the backseat since Julio is too big to fit in the back." Normally with a demand like that I would have already been walking to my own car, but being that it's Abigail and I love her, I miserably climb into the backseat. This might be the same model car as mine, but it's far from the same size. At least there's more space in my backseat compared to the cramped space I'm currently sitting in. I wouldn't be able to fuck Abigail comfortably in this car.

The thought stays with me the entire car ride to the photo shoot, including what I plan to do to her in *her* car as I watch her drive. I can tell how nervous she is by the way she's nibbling on her thumbnail every now and then. It leaves me wondering if this is routine for her before a photo shoot.

Soon we're arriving at the photo shoot and I'm grateful the weather has decided to be cooperative today. I would have hated if they had to reschedule the shoot. The surrounding trees and greenery add a majestic backdrop for the location. It's exactly what she needs to feel comfortable. The first thing I learned about Abigail is how much she loves nature. The moment I get her to a trail, she instantly calms and a smile spreads across her face, which is why I'm always pushing her to go for a run.

With all of us out of the car, I see Abigail's face go pale the minute she sees the camera crew and equipment. Making my way over to her side, I ask, "What's wrong, beautiful?"

She doesn't bother glancing at me, but keeps her eyes locked onto the set. "Is it strange that I feel really nervous?" she asks, looking to me for an answer.

I push a strand of hair away from her face so I can better look into her eyes. "Did you feel this way at the last one?" I curiously ask, since I wasn't with her. Biting her lip she nods her head, her eyes taking a quick glance at the set again before they nervously lock back onto mine. "You have nothing to worry about, Abigail. The running company said you did a great job at that one, and you said yourself that you had fun," I remind her, recalling how excited she sounded when she had told me all about the previous shoot.

"I know," she answers, her shoulders slumping forward. "But what if these people don't like me?" she nervously responds.

I wrap my arms around her, engulfing her against my body, hoping to help calm her discomfort. Within a couple of seconds I can already feel her relax, which is what I was aiming for. "You're Abigail Adams... the famous supermodel," I tease.

I feel her chuckle against my chest before she looks up at me. "That's not who I am anymore."

"The last time I checked your name was still Abigail Adams, right?"

She rolls her eyes up at me. "That's not what I meant. I really doubt they look at me anymore as a famous supermodel." I reach down to give her a kiss on her nose. "Regardless of how you're labeled in the modeling world, it's still you. So go show them who you are," I tell her, earning me a shy smile.

I feel her deeply sigh against my chest before she pulls away to walk in the direction of the crew. I proudly follow her, knowing she's going to be all right. Before long they have her changed, prepped, and ready to start the shoot. The photographer gives her a few quick ideas of what he expects from her and within minutes I see him lift his camera to his eyes and the clicking of the camera is heard.

Watching Abigail in her element is mesmerizing. I say her element because it's obvious this is what she was born to do. The poses come naturally to her. The photographer doesn't need to give her much instruction. He tells her what he's expecting in the next shot and she delivers, flawlessly. I knew since the day I met her she was beautiful, but watching her work is amazing. The entire time she's focused and doesn't disappoint. No wonder she was beginning to rise in her career. At least that was until the fucker Bill took it from her.

The photographer takes a moment to quickly glance at the screens in front me which are rapidly displaying the photos he's taken, and I cannot help but glance at them as well. I know he's taken some good shots and he must have thought the same, as he calls it a wrap. With a satisfied smile on her face, Abigail makes her way over towards all of us, taking a peek at the scene. She stands there, staring at it and I take the moment to move up behind her. "Beautiful," I whisper down into her ear. She turns, her face now displaying a worried frown. "You think so?" With certainty, I nod to her.

She turns to look at the screen again as image after image continues to appear on the screen, captivated, as if she cannot believe with her own eyes that she's the girl on the screen.

The photographer hands his camera over to his assistant and is now looking over to Abigail. "Thank you, Ms. Adams," he says, his eyes looking seductively over at her. "I hope to be able to work with you again in the future." The flirtatious tone telling me he means more than just work. I cannot resist wrapping my arm around her waist, pulling her closer to my side. She attempts to pull away, but I keep my hand firmly gripped on her waist, refusing to let her go as I stare the photographer down.

"If you're done, she'll be moving on now," I sharply say

to him. He gives Abigail a curt nod and is soon walking away without another attempt. She turns to face me with fury in her eyes. "Why did you do that?" she snaps out.

"I didn't like the way he was looking at you."

She narrows her eyes at me and is about to argue, but is interrupted when we're approached by a lady who is now staring at us both with a curiously raised eyebrow. "Hello, Ms. Adams. My name is Samantha Clark and I'll be conducting your interview," she states, holding her hand out to shake Abigail's. Abigail obliges with a friendly smile. "It's nice to meet you," she answers.

"It's nice to meet you, as well. If you don't mind, I'd like to start now," she tells Abigail, nodding her head to where there are two directors' chairs.

"Great," Abigail responds, already pulling away from my hold. She takes two steps before whipping around to face me again. "The next time you try to stake a claim on me, remember I'm not the one who put us in the situation we're in," she utters before turning again to stomp away. I'm left watching her as I agonize over her words.

She catches up to Samantha who is now sitting in one of the chairs a couple of feet away from us. I stay behind with Julio. "It's going to be a while before she forgives you," Julio mocks behind me.

"Yeah, I know, but I have to keep trying," I solemnly state, watching from a distance as Abigail begins to answer her questions. "It'll pay off in the long run," I add, hoping he understands.

Abigail

"SO, MS. ADAMS, why running?" the interviewer asks, her

eyebrow going up to one side as she taps her pen against her notepad, which is beginning to annoy me.

At first my earlier nervousness began to resurface the minute I sat in the chair, but it's easily replaced with irritation as she taps her pen. She started the interview with basic instructions to answer as truthfully as possible. It had sounded easy then, but I'd grown nervous as soon as I nodded my head to answer.

The annoying thump, thump, thump is increasing as she waits for an answer. Her obnoxious stare is a reminder that I need to answer. "It's relaxing," I nervously say. "It also helps with the stress," I add for further explanation. She lowers her head to takes notes, but just as quickly snaps it back up. "What would you say your stress is from?" she inquires.

"Life," I say abruptly and without further explanation, but she seems unsatisfied. "Would you say your amnesia plays a major factor with your stress?" she asks, sounding as if she's trying to convey a statement rather than ask a question.

"No," I respond directly. I can already tell from her unsatisfied expression that she's going to push the subject. "Have you recovered any memories from *before* your accident?" she asks, continuing her annoying interrogation, still tapping her pen. I shake my head at her, making her pen pause; her disoriented expression is now worrying me. "And that hasn't worried you?" she asks, looking puzzled.

"No," I clip out.

Dropping her head, she resumes her scribbling, but is already asking her next question. "How do you feel now that your amnesia has impacted your career and life?" adding before I can reply, "Since obviously your career is no longer the same."

I look over in the direction of where Matt and Julio are standing as I consider her question. "No, it isn't, but I'm satisfied with it how it's turned out," I utter, still staring at Matt. When I had turned to face him, he was briefly focused on Julio as they carried on a conversation, but the moment his eyes found mine, he gave me a smile that lit me up from the inside out.

Any doubt Samantha was attempting to put upon me is quickly pushed away.

"Do you plan on returning to modeling?" she asks, bringing my attention back to her. "It would be a waste if you didn't," she adds.

"Regardless of what my future plans are, they're going to be decisions *I* make for myself," I affirm, already starting to feel irritated by the interview.

"You recently broke your engagement from your manager. Would that be a major factor as to why you haven't returned to modeling? Or has the amnesia affected your memory that contributes to your career?"

"My amnesia had nothing to do with my career. I did well during the photo shoot, didn't I?" I clip out, earning me a simple nod. "Obviously my lack of knowing who I was before my accident has nothing to do with my modeling. I needed a break from it. The breakup with my manager was due to personal reasons that I'd prefer not to discuss in this interview," I mutter. My blood is beginning to boil at this point. My leg is beginning to slowly twitch from the irritation. Feeling as if I need to further explain my answer, I add, "And like I stated earlier, it's my future I should be focusing on, not my past," I growl out.

"You resurfaced with a recent running company. Was that because of the loss of contract with your manager as well?" she continues to prod.

At this point I'm ready to jump and strangle this bitch. "I didn't lose my contract, I *fulfilled* it to term. If you don't mind, I'd prefer to no longer answer any more questions in regards to my previous manager or my amnesia since it's irrelevant to your magazine. I thought you were a running company," I announce, feeling agitated. "Shouldn't you be asking me something in regards to running?" I ask as calmly as my enraged state will allow me to without sounding like I'm ready to bite her head off. "If you'd prefer," she retorts.

She turns, her face finding Matt, and I do the same to find

him already giving us his signature smile, his lips up to one side before he gives us a quick wave. I already know the gesture is aimed at me, but from the blushed color on Samantha's face when our eyes meet again, she must have believed it was aimed at her.

"Is your new boyfriend the reason for your new fond love of running?" she inquires. My eyes go wide in shock. "He's not my boyfriend," I snap out.

Her lips go up in a smirk. "What would you say he is then? From the way he was protectively guarding you from our notorious photographer, I would have thought otherwise."

"He's my assistant, but most of all, a loyal friend," I state, watching her eyes turn doubtful.

"He's in most of the pictures provided from your races," she claims.

"To answer your earlier question, yes, he's the reason why I took up running. He's the reason why I've run most of them. He did sign me up for them," I explain.

"Are you implying that you didn't want to run them?" she pushes with a raised eyebrow.

"No," I answer as nicely as I can without allowing my anger to surface.

"I was just frightful to sign up for them myself," I tell her. Of course only a select few know that Matt sort of threw me under the bus to run them, but I still ran them. I was the one with my feet at the starting line and they were the same feet that were crossing the finish line. Whether I signed up for them myself or not, I earned the recognition to say that I *ran* them.

By the way her lips go flat, it isn't the answer she was hoping for. "Given the opportunity to run Boston, do you plan to?" she asks. It's about time she ask me a question I *want* to answer. "Of course I'd want to run Boston. It's the Super Bowl of all races. What runner wouldn't want to run Boston?"

"Of course," she adds with a smile, taking her usual notes. "Well, I believe that's all I need," she informs me before standing up, leaving me dumbfounded.

"That's it?" I feel cheated as I ask the question. I feel as if she's pissed that she didn't get the gossip she wanted, so this is her way of punishing me. I suppose I should feel ecstatic she's no longer grilling me, but I feel disappointed nevertheless.

Out of the corner of my eye I see Matt and Julio making their way over to my side. It's when Matt reaches us that Samantha lightens up. "All done?" he asks, looking satisfied himself.

"Yup, all done," Samantha quickly answers, beating me to the reply.

"Ms. Adams, if you'd kindly come with us, you'll be allowed to change over here," a member of the camera crew tell me, her arm extended towards a tent they have constructed. I'd forgotten I still was still wearing the running apparel they had provided for their shoot.

"I'll wait for you here," Matt informs me with a blank expression, but Samantha's excited expression worries me.

I follow the girl with Julio closely behind me. When I reach the tent, I take one quick glance back in their direction. As suspected, Samantha is already talking Matt's ear off as he listens with interest. His face is still expressionless, giving me the reassurance needed to step into the tent.

Five minutes later, I'm stepping back out, but the sight I left is not what I find now. Matt is smiling at something that Samantha is saying. His once bland expression has been replaced with his carefree smile as he gives her his full attention. I watch as she reaches up to flirtatiously caress his arms as if she's feeling his bulging muscles. Both throw their heads back laughing. The sight of her touching him ignites the anger I had managed to tamper down before I left them. I'm practically stomping my way over to them now. Matt sees me as he continues to smile, somehow making me angrier. "You ready to go?" I snap at him.

"You're leaving already?" Samantha whines up at Matt.

"I did arrive with her, so yes," he replies with a small chuckle.

"I can give you a ride home," Samantha says, her hand once again coming to rest on his arm as she bats her eyelashes up at Matt. "I'm sure Abigail would be nice enough to give you the rest of the day off," she states.

I look straight at Matt, my eyes narrowing at him. "Of course. He has a nice *new* table that needs to be broken in," I slowly clip out through clenched teeth, already regretting the words as I turn to walk away without a backwards glance.

I reach Lola and I'm about to open my door when I feel Matt grab onto my wrist, preventing me from opening it. When I turn to face him, he's inches from me, our bodies practically touching. I step back to get away from him, but my back crashes against the cold metal of my car. I'm trapped with Matt closely leaning into me. My body starts prickling with excitement, knowing how close he's standing in front of me. My body might be awaking with excitement, but Matt's reaction is far from it as a frown is casted across his face. I know he understood the meaning behind my message. "Why would you say something like that? What's wrong?"

Narrowing my eyes at him, I attempt to control the rage building up inside of me, which is keeping me from answering. A frown spreads across his lips. "Did she say something during the interview to upset you?" he grimly asks.

"It wasn't the interview," I snarl out. "I don't like her."

He still looks perplexed, but slowly his lips creep up into a grin. "You're jealous of her, aren't you?" he mocks, the question making me resent my earlier reaction.

"It's stupid... I know. I don't know why I'm acting like this," I admit with a sigh. His lips come near my ear. "No one can ever compare to you, beautiful," he huskily whispers into my ear. If I weren't leaning against my car for support, I'm pretty sure I would collapse to the ground from those words. The sound of Julio clearing his throat makes both Matt and I look in his direction. I see Samantha walking her way over, looking astounded. Unintentionally, I shove Matt away from me.

"I thought you said there was nothing going on between both of you?" Samantha asks upon reaching us, looking between the two of us with a puzzled expression. Matt gives me an angry scowl, but I frantically shake my head when I remember my interview.

"There isn't," I state, my eyes pleading for him to understand. He looks torn whether to feel angry or disappointment by my words, but when he looks over at Samantha, the calmness in his face conveys he understood. "No, there isn't," he indicates with a forced smile.

To most people his answer would sound true to his word, but I can hear the pain of declaring those words in his voice. It isn't until I heard them from his own lips that I regret asking him to state them. I might have fought tooth and nail to make those words sound true, but I'm beginning to wonder if I could accept the meaning behind them.

"Have a good day, Samantha," Matt announces before stalking his way over to the passenger side of the car. Yanking the car door open, he climbs in. I look at Samantha, shrugging my shoulders at her before climbing into my car, allowing Julio to shut it for me. My eyes find Matt's in the rearview mirror staring back at me, looking torn all over again. It's when Julio climbs into the passenger seat that I break our eye contact. From the resentment taking over my soul, I already know the car ride is going to feel like the longest one home.

Chapter Eight

Matt

I STARE OUT the car window. I'm raging inside, but slowly try to calm myself before we make it to Kelly's. I don't want to be angry when I get out of the car. I don't want to risk taking it out on Abigail; it's the last thing I want to do. When I speak with her, I want to be as calm as possible so to not push her away further.

Abigail has only seen me out of control once, and even then I saw the fear in her eyes. I know deep down in my heart it was from both my actions and what the fucker had done to her that had caused my reaction, but I'd promised myself she would never have to see that side of me again, unless needed. I take another deep breath as my thoughts wander to when Emily had so passionately clarified how woman think.

"Women are sensitive creatures, Matt. You have to be careful with their emotions. If not, they'll come to resent you for your actions."

It's exactly what Abigail is doing. She's resenting me for breaking her heart. She's pushing me away. Her denying our relationship to everyone is her way of hurting me in return. She may not be doing it intentionally, but nevertheless, it was happening. She pulls into the parking lot, my eyes closing as I picture Abigail's smile to help calm me. Her smile has a way of soothing my anguished heart.

Climbing out of the car, I'm already walking to her side, determined to find an answer to her reaction at the park. I reach her and she's already squaring her shoulders, as if ready to argue. She opens her mouth to begin speaking, but I grab her face and take her mouth passionately with my own. The need for her to understand she's mine clouded my thoughts the moment I saw her ready for battle. I no longer wanted to fight with her. I never had.

I continue to possess her mouth, knowing I'm robbing her of the only breath she had as she was going to speak, but that was my intention. Her nails dig into the skin of my back as she grips my shirt, as if she's afraid I'll pull away. It's the last thing I intend on doing for the next few minutes. I hadn't planned on kissing her, but seeing the vulnerability in her body language, telling me she was ready to argue, fueled me to kiss her to make it disappear.

She whimpers into my mouth, awakening my greed to take her back to the apartment and make love to her. I already feel my cock stirring to life and I have to mentally tell my dick this isn't the reason I'm kissing her. Minutes later, our kiss is coming to an end as I drag it out, not wanting it to stop. Still holding her face in my palm, I gently pull away to watch her eyes flutter open. Her mouth is still slightly open, and her chest is rising and falling. I can feel the strong pulse of her vein in her throat rapidly beating against my fingers. It's matching my reaction of how she's made me feel. With her eyes now open, I can see her beautiful eyes staring back at me at a loss for words. Exactly how I want her.

"Now can we talk about what happened back at the park?" I quietly ask her. For a moment she looks confused, but just as quickly her eyes are scowling back at me. As much as I want to kiss that expression from her face again, I *do* want to discuss what happened earlier.

"There's nothing to talk about, Matt. It's obvious you're never going to change," she utters. "What the hell is that supposed to mean?" I clip out.

She tries to push me away, but I trap her against the car with my arms at her side, not allowing her to escape. "I want to know why you keep telling people we're not together."

"Because we're not!"

What the fuck?

"You can keep saying that to everyone else, but I'm not taking that as an answer. We might not be living together anymore, but we *are* still together," I clarify to her, but by the look on her face I believe she thinks otherwise. "Is it truly what you want, Abigail?" I force myself to ask.

Her eyes are glassing up as her lips tremble, resisting the urge to cry. "Give me a reason why?" I dreadfully ask.

"Lisa," she quietly answers, the pain evident in the single name.

"Abigail, I already told you I refuse to let her come between us," I plead to her.

"How can you say she isn't going to come between us? She already has Matt," she snarls out, angry and irritated. "You *fucked* her and got her *pregnant*, Matt. How would you react if the tables were turned in our situation? Did you honestly think I was going to stick around and pretend you getting her pregnant was okay?" she retorts.

Both shocked and confused by her declaration, I whisper, "You're right. I wouldn't like it, but that shouldn't change us, beautiful," compassion clear in my voice, hoping she will change her mind.

She shakes her head. "All we can ever be now, Matt, is friends. Nothing more," she whispers back. I cannot resist wrapping her back up into my arms and I'm relieved when she doesn't pull away. "I'm so sorry, beautiful. I promise I'm going to fix us," I say around the large lump in my throat.

"Just promise we'll always be friends," she says, her voice sounding broken and raspy. I place a kiss upon her temple as I say, "If that's what it takes to keep you in my life, then friends we'll be," I state, hating having to say the words, but meaning them just the same.

I continue to hold her for a couple more minutes before she speaks again. "I really want to thank you for scheduling the interview. You're right, I really needed this interview and I enjoyed the photo shoot."

Her words make me smile. "You're welcome."

"I should go inside and take a shower," she voices.

"You want me to help you scrub your back?" I tease.

Her eyes playfully narrow back at me. "Friends," she reminds me of her earlier words, making me sigh in disappointment. She pulls away from me and this time I let her go. I watch her walk away and when I see she's safely inside the apartment, I make my way over to my car, leaving the broken pieces of my heart behind.

From the corner of my eye, I see Julio standing near his car that is parked on the other side of mine, solemnly looking at me, letting me know he had been watching the entire time. It doesn't surprise me he would still be here since we were out in public. He gives me a quick nod before he climbs into his car. I don't care what Abigail says. I already promised to never give up on her and I don't intend to start breaking any more promises.

I'M LYING IN bed, staring up at the ceiling, dreading what the day will bring. I have mixed feeling over what to expect today. Aren't fathers supposed to be excited about going to their kid's appointment? Unfortunately, I'm not.

Forcing myself to get up and dressed, I exit my room, taking a quick glance at the end of the hallway where Abigail's room is. The room is still unoccupied because I could not bring myself to move back in. I'd contemplated it the night I got back, but soon changed my mind when I realized how lonely it feel without her. I'd rather keep the pleasant memories from the room in my heart until she returns. Until that day, I'll keep my residence in the spare bedroom.

I make my way over to the living room, surprised to see Trey already awake and watching television. Taking a take a seat across from him in the recliner, he looks to me with a raised eyebrow. "What's up with you?"

Sitting back, I rake my hand down my face before I answer. "Today's Lisa doctor's appointment."

"Fuck." The single word comes out sounding like an apology.

I love you – Matt. I text Abigail, hoping it will help soothe my mood.

I'm not expecting an answer since she's most likely still asleep, but knowing that she will see it when she wakes up is enough to make me smile.

"Something's been bothering me for a while," Trey says, bringing my attention back to him. His face looks both confused and worried at the same time.

"What's been bothering you?" I amusedly ask.

It looks as if he's contemplating his words, which is astonishing for Trey. "I remember you telling me Abigail walked in while you were fucking Lisa." The smile on my face now replaced with a furious frown. He ignores my expression and continues. "How is it that you were able to finish? I know that shit would have made my dick go limp in a heartbeat," he declares.

My blood is now boiling from remembering the night. I told myself I wasn't going to bring it up again, yet I'm forced to when Trey asked the question. He silently sits staring at me, giving me a moment to reflect back to that night. I had thought my world was beginning to look towards a brighter light, but it came crashing into darkness because of my weakness to keep my dick in my pants. Reluctantly, my thoughts escape back to that night when I'd come home sexually frustrated. I'd starting drinking the minute I walked in the door and since I hadn't eaten anything all day, the buzz hit me fast and hard. Lisa had knocked on the door by the time I'd been on my fourth beer. Her face was blurred into a vision of what looked like Abigail. Without thinking, I grabbed her and starting kissing her. By the time my mind had comprehended it wasn't Abigail, Lisa had her hands down my pants enticing me. I'd lost all will power to push her away. Within seconds, I had her on the table and rolling on a condom. I remember in detail, making sure I got that thing on. My drunken fazed mind was picturing Abigail as I fucked Lisa, but the minute Kelly shouted my name and I saw Abigail, I knew then I had fucked up.

Bringing my mind back to the present, I answer Trey. "Abigail walked in as I was finishing," I answer through clenched teeth, the image of her shocked face still appearing in my mind.

"Did you check the condom to make sure it *actually* broke?"

I'm stunned he would consider something like that, being it's Trey. "That night I wasn't too concerned about checking the condom at that point. The only thing I was worried about was getting Lisa out of the damn house fast enough so I could start kissing Abigail's ass to get her back here."

"I guess you're screwed," he says before his eyes go back to watching TV. I don't know whether to feel pissed or confused by his reaction, but since it's Trey, I'm not surprised.

Grateful he's at least dropped the subject, I stand up to grab my keys off the counter when my phone rings. The name on the screen doesn't lighten my mood. "What's up?" I casually say into the phone, not wanting Trey to know who's calling.

"I was calling to tell you my doctor's appointment got rescheduled to Monday," Lisa states, sounding disappointed. In a way, I feel both relieved and frustrated at the same time. As much as I wasn't looking forward to this appointment, I wanted to get it done and over with. "What time?" I gravely ask.

"They gave me three P.M.," she replies. "Fine, I'll pick you up at two-thirty then," I tell her, hanging up the phone without saying goodbye.

Looking at the clock on the wall, it tells me I can still make it to my class. Rushing back to my room to grab my backpack, I'm soon heading out the door. With as many days as I've missed during the week when I disappeared to go visit Emily, I'm risking failing the class if I continue missing much more. The professors have already threatened to fail me, which is something I cannot afford being on the team, so this rescheduled appointment is a blessing in disguise. Another thing I'm grateful for: I don't have to see or put up with Lisa for now.

Chapter Nine

Abigail

YOU SHOULD NEVER browse the Internet when you're bored. It will lead you to bravely do things you never thought possible. It began with an email from a running company announcing an upcoming race. Of course I could not resist looking at it, but the more I read about the cause, the more determined I was to run it. Even without Matt.

Without hesitating, I was soon entering my information on the registration page. As I'm pushing confirm on the webpage, I see Kelly walk into the living room, sleepy eyed as she begins to yawn. I know we're both late sleepers and she doesn't usually wake until it's nearly time for her to leave. Most of the time she's rushing to get ready and out of the door.

"God, why the hell are you awake so early?" she asks, her eyes squinting against the sun shining into the living room.

Her yawn is contagious and now I'm yawning. "I went for a run this morning. Why are *you* up? You don't have to start work for another couple of hours?"

She considers the question. "I figured I'd get up and spend some time with you."

As much as I appreciate her thoughtfulness, it also makes me feel guilty. I know she's only doing it so I won't go back into the usual slump I've been in lately. I'd managed to revert back to it after my photo shoot. Matt's daily text messages weren't helping either. They only made me miss him more. She yawns again, making me lecture her. "Quit yawning, you're making me yawn," I tease her as I yawn behind my hand.

"Watcha doing?" she inquires, craning her neck to look into the screen of my phone when she's finished yawning.

"Signing me and Julio up for a race this Saturday morning."

I watch as her perfectly arched eyebrow goes up, an amused smile spreading across her lips. "You're actually signing up for a race on your own?" she skeptically asks now, looking enthralled by the notion.

"Yes, I'm signing up for a race on my own," I sarcastically tell her. "The proceeds go to a shelter that houses abused women and their children."

Her eyes light up. "That's good," but just as quickly she apprehensively looks at me. "But wouldn't you rather run it with Matt?" she asks.

"I don't need him to run a race. I didn't run San Francisco with him," I state.

Still sleepy eyed, her lips go flat as she takes in my reply. "I just thought it was your thing with him. Running."

"It used to be my thing with him, but by the way things are going between us, it isn't anymore," I admit.

She nods her head in understanding. "Abigail, what's going on with the whole situation involving Bill?"

My heart stops. The dread mixed with a hint of fear is laced together when I hear her question. "I don't know. I got a phone call from the arresting officer giving me an update. He was let out on bail, but they're still trying to serve him his restraining order," I rasp out as I remember that I'm still not safe from him.

"So what does that mean?"

"I have no clue."

Kelly looks sympathetic at this point. "What does Matt say about all this?"

Now I feel guilty. "I haven't talked to him about it," I admit. Her eyebrows go up telling me her next words may just come out as a lecture. "As much as I don't like the douchebag right now, he deserves to know," she shares her opinion, just as I expected.

"I have to be talking to him in order to tell him," I remind her.

A curt nod verifies she agrees with me. She stands up, already heading to the kitchen to start making her coffee. I stare at the confirmation page on my screen, already feeling proud of myself. This is the first race I'll be running without someone convincing me to run it. I no longer need Matt to make decisions for me.

I PICKED JULIO up bright and early on the day of the race. I'd informed him of my signing him up for the race on one of our daily runs, but was more surprised when he learned it was only the two of us running it. He had expected I would have included Matt, earning him a lecture from his assumption. He took it kindly, but had also managed to throw in his own opinion; I should quit denying myself the pleasure of running with Matt instead. The rest of our run was spent in silence from my bitterness over the subject.

Sadly, Matt's absence on my runs was starting to affect me. With each run, my mind would ponder whether I had made the right decision by demanding we just be friends. Every time the thought came to my mind, it felt like a stab in the chest from not having him at my side. On several occasions, I almost caved to my longing to run with him again, I'd nearly given in and called him, but I stopped myself and phoned Julio instead.

Now at the race, with our bib numbers in hand, Julio and I walk over to the start line. I'm standing in place fumbling with my bib trying to pin it to my shirt, cursing to myself, wishing Matt was with me to do it for me, like all the times he's done before.

As if some magical genie heard my request, I hear Matt's deep voice in front of me, making my heart skip a beat. "Here, let me help you with that." His hands engulf mine to take the safety pins from me, and my longing to touch him this past week returns tenfold as he stands directly in front of me. His absence has been excruciating. As he fumbles with my bib, my body shivers from the giddiness of seeing him again.

"What are you doing here, Matt?" I breathlessly rasp out.

Tilting his head to look at me, he gives an alluring smile and I nearly melt to the ground in a puddle. "I'm going to run this race. What are *you* doing here?" he jokingly asks, looking around. "I'm surprised you even signed up," he says with a smile, teasing me.

I narrow my eyes at his sarcasm. "I no longer need you to sign me up for my races," I proudly say to him. The smile he once had is replaced with a frown, and a hint of sadness.

He surprises me when he says, "I'm proud of you," with a sorrowful tone before he drops is head to finish his task.

"How did you know I was here?"

As he applies the last safety pin to my shirt, his hands find my hips. With a slight tilt of his head in the direction behind me where Julio is standing, I have my answer. Looking over at Julio, I glare daggers at him before I bring my attention back to Matt. He pulls me closer to place a kiss below my ear. "You ready to get your butt left in the dusk this morning?" he playfully teases.

"It isn't going to happen, because I'm not running any-more," I stubbornly reply, attempting to pull myself away from his grip.

Of course it's not possible with Matt as he tightens the grip of his hands. "Why?" he asks, looking dejected. The sadness in his eyes staring back at me makes my heart drop down to the pit of my stomach. The sorrow they're conveying is matching what I've been feeling this past week without him. He brings his hand up to my face as his thumb grazes my chin, reminding me of what I miss.

"I want to hold onto the happier memories of you. Running with you was one of them. All the others are of you with some other girl," I grimly say.

His frown deepens, his face now pale and filled with despair as I yank my face from his hand. My words have shocked him to weakness, allowing me to escape, but I don't make it further than a couple of steps before I feel his hand on my arm, yanking me to a stop. "Then let me give you one more to add. Please, beautiful, just one more time?" he pleads.

The desperation in his voice keeps me rooted, unable to walk away. My mind is repeatedly telling me to keep walking, my heart is telling me to go back to him. It's what it desperately wants.

Slowly I turn to face him. "Fine," I muster out around the lump lodged in my throat. He releases my arm as I watch his shoulders slump forward in relief. "What are the stakes this time?" I tease him, trying to break the tension between us.

His lips go up into a smile as he considers the question. "Fastest winner has to cook dinner," he jests, making me scowl, earning me a chuckle from him. "Okay, fine, no cooking. How about... If I win you move back into the house."

I don't bother to answer, but turn my body and start to walk off again. My body is once more halted when he wraps his arm around my waist, pulling me against his hard body, molding myself against him. My body is igniting with the recognition of Matt's body. "Please, beautiful, don't run from me anymore. I promise I'll do anything you want," he whispers into my ear, his plea piercing my heart.

I don't move. I wouldn't be able to even if I wanted. My heart would refuse to let me walk away at this point. "I can't move back in, Matt."

"Okay, you don't have to move back, *yet*. But please think about it," he says, making me think of his request. Taking a deep breath, I nod my head to answer his request. "I'll tell you what, if I win I'll cook you dinner. It's all I want," he adds.

The announcer is already announcing the race is about to begin as the crowd gradually starts huddling its way to the start line. Turning to face him, I ask, "And if I win?"

"What do you want?"

"I want to drive your car again," I reply with a smile.

I watch as his eyes go wide, his body going rigid. "No," he clips out.

Without another word, I turn my body away. "Fine, you can run by yourself," I inform him, knowing he will cave at my request.

"Fine," I hear him answer, leaving me satisfied. "But, moving back in is back on the table," he adds, making me freeze in my spot.

My smile has disappeared as I consider his demand. I want to drive his car again, but I cannot risk the chance of him beating me and making me move back in. Feeling confident, I turn to answer him. "Deal."

Instead of him looking satisfied with my response, he looks agitated. Pushing it aside, I focus on the prize ahead. I stand at Matt's side as we follow the huddling crowd nearing the starting line. My heart is already racing with anticipation of crossing the finish line; the adrenaline is building within me. The anticipation to run increases when I take one final glance in Matt's direction to completely take him in. He's looking at me, his lips are up to one side with a smile that melts every nerve deep down to my toes. I'm too distracted by his smile when the gun goes off, giving Matt a head start as he shoots off ahead of me.

My mind snaps back to reality and I sprint off after him, pissed he's already pulled ahead of me by a couple of seconds. Fumbling with my earphones since I forgot to insert them, adds to my fury. My playlist begins and I hear the first song come on. All bets are off as my body takes over and I run.

Matt is still ahead of me by a couple of feet as he begins to weave around people. Normally I would want to run next to

Matt, but my determination to finish first takes over. He will reach the finish line eventually. What I need to focus on is getting there first.

I'm one mile in and I'm already growing frustrated from the crowd of people choosing to stay in a large huddle as I attempt to weave my away around them. I'm now appreciative of the promotional crew for advancing me in the line for the San Francisco race. I would have never been able to make my qualifying time if it wasn't for them.

Distracting myself by focusing on the music blasting in my ears, I glance around me to look for Matt. When I see him, merely four people away from me to my left, I smile wide. The fork to separate the 5K runners from the 10k runners is within viewing distance and I'm confident I'm going to leave his ass behind. Picking up my pace, I don't bother to see where Matt is at this time, all I care about is reaching my destination. It's not long before I know that it's about to end when I see the five mile marker on the side of the road.

Ironically, *Clarity* is already blasting through my ear buds and my mind escapes with the lyrics. I absorb the words, realizing the song reminds me of my feelings for Matt and our love for one another.

I see the finish line ahead and the crowd is already cheering for everybody coming in. It's at this stretch of every race that my mind takes over. It pushes me to run faster; ignoring all protest of exhaustion. I'm focused on one thing at this point: finishing.

Out of the corner of my eye, I see Matt creep up to my side and my eyes go wide. The tempo of the lyrics quickens, and so do my legs, as I force my body to go faster. But when I see him keep his pace with me, I mentally begin to panic. I can barely breathe at this point from exhaustion, but I refuse to give up; I need to cross that finish line before him.

I feel the electronic padding of the timer below my feet telling me I've crossed the finish line, but I know Matt was next to me at the same time. Bringing my body to a stop, Matt is already next to me, a wide smile spread across his lips. His smile is worrying me. It's as if he's confident he's won. I try not to let the panic show in my eyes, but it's impossible not to worry. Begrudgingly turning to go get my water, I hear Matt say behind me, "What's wrong, beautiful? Still a sore loser?" As he catches up to my side, I shoot him with a glare, shocked at his words. "You were the one who lost. My foot hit the padding first," I declare, my inner child wanting to stomp the same foot in contempt.

"If that's what you want to believe," he responds with a chuckle, leaving me gaping at him. "I know I won," I whine back, already growing agitated. He's right, I *am* a sore loser, but I'm not going to admit it.

Grabbing the bottle of water from the volunteer, I open it and take a sip from the bottle while still managing to stare daggers at Matt. I'm distracted when I see Julio's large body come up to my side, also grabbing a bottle from the volunteer. He guzzles it completely without taking a breath. When he's done he looks over at me, still gasping for air. His chest is rising and falling, clearly exhausted. "You okay?" I ask him with a chuckle, wondering if I'm going to need to rush him to the hospital.

Holding a finger up as if asking me to wait, I raise my eyebrow and look over at Matt. "From now on I'll wait for you at the finish line," he says, sucking in another breath. "You're too damn fast for me to keep up with without the bike. I tried," he states, still gasping. "I tried to keep up with both of you. Biggest regret ever," he finishes saying, making me laugh when I comprehend why he looks so spent.

Matt comes over giving him a slap on the back. "Leave the chasing up to me or else you're going to have a heart attack." Julio nods his head in agreement.

Matt's eyes meet mine and his face is full of amusement, making me wonder just how much longer I'm going to allow him to chase me around.

Chapter Ten

Matt

THE DECEITFULNESS IN Abigail's eyes makes me laugh inside. On the outside she's portraying this hardened shell of anger, but from the way her eyes keep averting in my direction, I know it's far from it. I know my teasing has a lot to do with her being angry in the first place. I've come to learn how competitive she is, which is another trait I love about her. She's willing to fight for what she wants, not backing down until she gets it.

I'm glad I came this morning. At first I thought she had changed her mind when I arrived and she wasn't here yet. I had to push my doubt aside and be patient, hoping she would show up. With every minute I waited though, I had started to grow impatient, and fearful, thinking she'd decided to sleep in instead. The moment I spotted her, all doubt was pushed aside. Keeping in the shadows of the crowd so she wouldn't see me, I watched from afar until just the right moment to approach her.

Now I'm standing at her side as we wait for them to post the finishing times. I look over at her again with a smile on my face, which only agitates her. I know it's from nervousness. She won't be satisfied until she knows the results, but even so, she may not like the result in the end. The entire time I was running at her side, I had a gut-wrenching feeling she would finish first, which is why I've come to accept she will be driving my car home. It didn't matter to me anymore. All that mattered was seeing her smile and making her happy. If it took her driving Eleanor, then so be it.

I see her grow excited telling me they have started to post the results. When I turn to see for myself, I'm right. The flat screen we are all so closely huddled around has already begun to display the names. Abigail politely pushes her way through the crowd. I protectively follow her and use my body to lock her in place when we've reached the front. Holding onto her waist, I expect her to pull away, but when she doesn't it leaves me satisfied. I do it more because I love having her near me, feeling her body close to mine.

My eyes search for the closest time to where we came in and Abigail must have seen the result before I did. I hear a groan come from her and I feel her body slump forward. I find our names, and right there on the screen in clear view, I see my name above hers, which means my foot hit the finish line first. Her time is only a tenth of a second slower than mine, but it's all I need to prove I've won.

Bending my head down, I stop right next to her ear. "Looks like you'll be moving back in, beautiful," I softly say into her ear, adding a kiss against her skin. She shivers in my arms, rewarding me with the reaction I wanted.

She turns to face me looking perturbed, but just as quickly her lips go up into a smile. "You never stated *when* I had to move back in," she smugly replies. I'm about to argue when she adds, "I'll keep my end of the deal, when I'm ready." Her eyes are challenging me.

Knowing this isn't the time or place to argue the subject, I guide her away from the crowd surrounding us. I feel her body tense as she walks with me. "Where are we going?" she's asks, sounding confused.

"I plan on feeding you like I always do after a run," I answer, instantly thinking of my next plan.

Finding Julio, I tilt my head in the direction of the parking lot. I remember we've both brought our cars, causing me to stop and face Abigail. "I'll meet you at the house."

"Why?" she demands with piercing eyes.

I was expecting it. "Abigail, I've always cooked for you after we both run. I don't want to start breaking the tradition just because we aren't living together," I explain. Needing to feel her at this moment, I cup the back of her neck and gently massage it, already feeling her relax against my touch. Her chest rises and falls with a sigh before she replies. "Okay," she whispers with a smile that matches my own.

I'm left watching her walk away with Julio, and once she's safely inside her car, I jog my way over to mine, excited to get home. I follow Abigail and start to grow worried that she's changed her mind when she detours from the direction of the house. I keep following her, already preparing my speech of disappointment from her not keeping her word. When we pull up to a house and I see Julio climb out of her car, I understand; she's dropping him off. I see her wave me over and I pull my car up next to hers and she looks quite embarrassed. "I don't know how to get to your house from here!" she shouts. Telling her to follow me, I start to drive away.

The remainder of the drive, I have a smile on my face. Once we've both pulled into the driveway, I climb out of my car and make my way over to hers. When I approach her, I can see the apprehension in her eyes as she looks directly at the house. "What's wrong?" I ask her.

She looks as if she's ready to bolt. I wrap my arms around her to keep her from escaping, but she still looks petrified. "I don't know if I want to go back in there, Matt," she says, the crackling in her voice matching the apprehension radiating from her entire body. I look back at the house confused, until it occurs to me the last time she was in it was the morning Lisa was here. I hadn't expected for Abigail to feel uneasy about coming back to the house, but I don't want the unpleasantness of the memories to push her away. Pulling her against my chest, I kiss her on the temple, reassuring her that I'm with her. "I don't want to make you do something you don't want to do, beautiful, but remember I told you that this is your home, too." I say, hoping she remembers the night I made that promise to her. When she nods her head, I continue, "I meant it. This will always be your home, no matter what happens."

She remains silent in my arms, but returns my embrace. "Just breakfast?" she hesitantly asks, reminding me of her earlier demand.

"I will promise breakfast, but what happens after that is up to you," I convey, still hoping she will change her mind. "I wouldn't mind if you stayed longer," I sneak in, still wishful.

"Breakfast for now," she mummers into my chest.

Agreeing, knowing it's better than nothing, I guide her to the front door. Stepping inside with her feels like a small triumph. As I lead her over to the kitchen, she asks, "You going to make pancakes?" her eyes wide with excitement.

I turn to face her, pulling out the carton of eggs. "No," I reply, watching her smile turn into a frown. As much as I love keeping that smile on her face, the entire drive here I had laid out a game plan. I wanted to do something that involved Abigail. I wanted to be next to her the entire time. "We're making omelets, and you're going to help me make them."

Her forehead furrows, clearly not happy with my answer. "I thought the point of you winning was you cooking," she reminds me, folding her arms across her chest. "You're right, I did say that, but technically you lost, so *you* should be cooking, which is why I'm helping you," I clarify. "Come on, it'll be fun," I enthusiastically add.

Holding her hand out asking for the carton of eggs, I hand it over to continue taking the rest of the ingredients out of the fridge. With everything on the counter, we both wash our hands and I'm soon grabbing a knife and cutting board. Standing behind her as we both face the counter, I instruct her on which vegetables to chop. It's clear at first by how large she's chopping them she is new to the simple task.

Standing behind her so she's directly in front of me, I can help instruct her. I take her hand within mine as I assist her, showing her how to chop smaller pieces. The simple act has reminded me of how much I've missed spending time with her. Purposely, I prolong the time it takes to chop the vegetables. I'm using the excuse that I'm willing to show her how it's done, but in all reality it's so I can keep her near.

When we move onto the onions, I hear her sniffling. I turn her chin to face me and her eyes are red with tears. I know it's from the vapors of the onion, but I can't resist teasing her. "Beautiful, are you crying, for me?" I'm unable to resist the smile spreading across my face.

She shoots me with a scowl, making me laugh as she elbows me in the stomach. Leaning down, I kiss her on her lips. "It's okay, beautiful. You don't have to admit anything, but I know those tears are because you love me," I say against her lips.

She's about to say something, but is interrupted when we hear, "Supermodel, you're back?" Trey sarcastically bellows from the hallway. "I see you've kissed and made up, too," he adds.

She looks over in his direction, already pulling herself away. "I'm only here for breakfast," she corrects him. He's eyeing us both suspiciously, but in usual Trey fashion, shrugs off the words. "Abigail's making omelets," I proudly add.

His eyes go wide in surprise. "She's not going to give us food poisoning, is she?" I hear Abigail snicker in front of me. "Whatever, as long as I don't have to cook it," he adds.

"Why don't we finish up?" I say without waiting for a response so I won't scare her off.

She resumes her chopping without my assistance, but I keep my body wrapped behind her as I start heating up the pan. Another minute later I'm showing her how to make her first omelet. The delight on her face from accomplishing the task is just as satisfying to me as well.

Half hour later, we're all done eating and Trey calls dibs on the shower first, leaving Abigail and I to clean up. With the dishes in the dishwasher, I take the chance to finish the conversation that never started at the race. I pull her into my arms, wanting to hold her a little bit longer.

My hand starts stroking up and down her back as her words echo in my mind. I feel as if my heart is being torn from my chest. I want nothing more than to demand she moves back in, to remind her we made a bet. I won fair and square, but I know better; I'd be making a mistake if I push Abigail too fast.

I stand there with her in my arms, but it's when I glance at the clock in the living room that Abigail speaks again. "You have a game today?" she asks, noticing me staring at the clock. "This afternoon actually. But we have to get to the airport by this afternoon," I tell her.

"Where are you guys going this time?" she curiously asks.

I'm dreading having to answer and I know she isn't going to be happy with my response. "San Francisco." The words drop like a heavy brick into the pit of my stomach.

Her tilted head snaps up. She's silent, too silent for my taste, as she stares back at me with doe eyes. I step forward, so our bodies are closer together and I trap her body against the counter.

"Do you want me to come with you?" she rasps out. I shake my head and the reaction she gives me is the answer I needed to know she was testing me. She was expecting me to say *yes*. She attempts to step away, but I don't allow her as I continue to keep her trapped. "Then why don't you want me there?" she challenges. "Is that why you didn't tell me about the game?"

Raking my hand through my hair, I carefully choose my words. "You haven't been around for me to tell you," I explain to her. "It's not what you think, beautiful," I say, keeping her wrapped in my arms. I can tell by the way she's narrowing her eyes at me that she doesn't believe my explanation. "Things have been so hectic between us lately, it sort of slipped my mind."

She's stays silent. "Abigail, I don't want to fight with you, please," I say, bringing my mouth back down to her brow to kiss her. "I swear, beautiful, it's the only reason," I add for good measure.

"I should go," she scornfully delivers as she attempts to pull her body away from mine. I tighten my hold on her knowing I cannot let her leave angry. "No," I curtly reply. "We're not done talking about you moving back in," I say, attempting to change the subject. I feel her sigh against my chest. "I'm not ready yet, Matt," she softly replies. I can hear the agony in her words. "How can you expect me to just come running back to you after everything that has happened?" she throws at me.

I'm lost for words.

"I think it's too soon."

"I'll give you time, beautiful, but don't expect too much of it. I miss you and I *need* you back here with me." I could only pray I'm making the right decision.

With a sigh she leans into my body again. "What about Lisa?" she faintly whispers. Pulling away to look into her eyes, I'm about to speak, but the unshed tears in her eyes are keeping me from responding. Nothing pains me more than to see her this way.

"You're right, I should be focusing on Lisa," I tell her, watching her lip start to tremble from my admission, but I quickly add, "Only because of the baby, nothing more. You know I love you, and I know you love me just as much. Why can't we make this work?"

"I don't know, Matt," she whispers, her head dropping against my chest. "Every time I tell myself I can't live without you, she clouds my mind, making me mad all over again," she admits.

I embrace her head in my hand, keeping her against me. "Beautiful, isn't our love worth fighting for?"

She stays silent and the fear of telling me it isn't builds as the seconds go by. Her fingers grip my shirt as he stays silent in my arms. I can do nothing more than rub her back, trying to comfort her. "I don't want to give up on us," she declares, her words allowing me to breathe again.

When she pulls away, I worry. "Friends, we're staying friends," she indicates.

"Wasn't it in this same kitchen that you declared you'd never be one of my *friends with benefits*?" I remind her. She drops her head to my chest in defeat and I cannot resist kissing her on her head as I laugh.

"I don't want the friends with benefits thing anymore, you're staying my *girlfriend*," I profess.

I hear her muffle something against my chest, but I cannot make it out. "What did you say?" She lifts her head, her eyes narrowed at me. "Fine."

Palming her face in my hands, I kiss her again. I don't know what she meant by that response, but I'll take it regardless. Our kiss turns heated, and though I told myself I wasn't going to rush her, I've been yearning to make love to her again. By the way she's returning my kiss, I know she feels the same way. I pick her up and take her straight to the one place I've been longing for her to return to.

Abigail

KISSING HIM IS my weakness. When my lips meet his, I lose myself. His kiss will forever be my downfall. I may live to regret giving in to my weakness, but as our tongues glide together, I forget why I'm mad at him. I completely forget I'm supposed to be holding up the barriers of my heart. Nothing matters at all but to keep kissing him.

With my eyes closed, I can feel him walking us in the direction of his room. The route of his steps is so familiar to me since I've taken them many times. I should be fighting his request, but instead I willingly accept it, knowing what is to come. My passion for him is increasing with every step closer to the room. The thought of being with Matt is making me light up inside.

Reaching the bedroom, he shuts the door behind us, enclosing us in the room, not stopping until we reach the bed. When my back is pressed against the softness of the mattress, my mind awakens to the realization of what is about to happen. My thoughts return to the repercussions of what will happen if I give in to his request.

I yank my lips away from his. "Matt, I really should leave," I breathlessly say to him while attempting to push him away. His eyes are locked onto mine, making my stomach feel as if I have a thousand different butterflies in it, as if it was the first time he's ever laid eyes on me. His eyes have an effect on me. They make me weak in the knees and my heart turn into a puddle of mush.

Losing control, my hands grab at his waist, pulling him against my body, wanting the feel of his chest against mine. His lips slam back down to mine. I feel as if I might burst into flames.

His mouth skillfully kisses its way down the side of my neck and the need to have him inside of me intensifies with every second he makes me wait. When his mouth locks onto my breast, I let out a loud and desperate moan, wanting more. It doesn't take long for him to get the message and he yanks my sports bra up and over my head. I've lost all coherent thoughts that I really should leave, but when it comes to Matt, I'm easily convinced to do otherwise.

Driving his hips against my opened thighs, he rubs his hardened erection against my already dampened core, his basketball shorts and my running shorts not leaving much of a barrier between us. I cannot take the torture of needing him anymore and I start to yank his shorts down, using my hands and feet as much as I can without breaking contact. I feel his hands to do the same to my shorts and I lift my hips to allow him to pull them down and off.

His hands tightly grip my waist as he lifts my body up, tossing me to the center of the bed. He crawls up to meet my body, stopping right above me as he looks down into my eyes. He doesn't say anything, but his gaze alone is conveying the promise that I've always known Matt to give me—the promise that he will always love me and be there for me.

My legs drop open, inviting him to take possession of me. He doesn't hesitate as he plunges deep inside me in one thrust. I gasp as he spreads the walls of my core, completely filling me. His hand comes to the side of my thigh, gripping it with force, as he pulls out and thrusts deeper inside of me. Needing to feel him closer than he already is, I wrap my legs around his waist, lifting my hips so he can thrust harder and faster. My nails are digging into his shoulders trying to hold onto him as he drives into me. He's making the bed rock back and forth from the force of his thrusts, the headboard is pounding loudly against the wall. Our breathing is becoming labored and our moans are getting louder by the minute. Our sweat is building, giving us friction to move faster with each thrust against each other. I'm starting to feel my body tense up as it's getting closer to finishing and when Matt starts to thrust faster against my core, I know he's just as close.

I squeeze my inner walls wanting to feel more of him as he slides in and out of me. By body tightens before I'm thrown over the edge. My eyes are filled with fireworks exploding behind my closed lids as I yell out Matt's name. Within seconds, Matt is following me as he moans out my name, but keeps pumping his hips, emptying the last of himself inside me, rocking us to a slow stop, leaving us both breathless, but fully satisfied.

My heart is racing a million miles per hour and I can feel Matt's heartbeat matching my own against my chest. I dig my face into the side of his neck and breathe in the scent of sex and sweat that I love so much, wanting to preserve the memory. He turns his face to do the same against my neck and I can feel the warmth of his rapid breath against my skin. He gently suckles at my neck, sending another shiver through my body. Keeping us connected, he rolls us on our sides with my thighs still wrapped around him. "God, beautiful, I've missed you so much," he states as his hand grazes my ass.

Still breathless, I manage a laugh. "It's just my ass you missed," I say before I try grabbing for his hand to remove it from its location.

He doesn't let it go, but squeezes it hard before saying, "It's more than just your ass that I miss, although I'm not going to lie, it's a very fine ass." His mouth meets mine to give me a kiss. I close my eyes to savor the feeling of his lips against mine as his warm hand glides up and down my back, soothing me against his warm body before I drift off into a dream.

It's a sunny day, the heat of the sun shines down on our bodies, heating our skin. Matt and I are at the beach, the sounds of the rolling waves to the side of us as we walk along the shore, the feeling of the grainy sand relaxing me with each footstep I take. The feeling of love for the beach is coursing in my mind with every breath I take, savoring the salty scent of the sea.

"Emily, how do you know when you're in love?" Matt curiously asks at my side. I look over at him, and even though he's not looking directly at me, I notice his eyebrows are drawn tight in deep concentration as he keeps walking.

He's only fifteen, so I'm confused why he would ask such a question. "Why do you ask? Are you interested in a girl, Matthew?" I say, curiosity getting the better of me.

He looks at me in shock and I can't help but laugh at his expression. "No! I'm just curious. I wonder because you've never really dated since mom and dad died. I wonder if love is such a big deal. You sure don't seem to want it." The happiness from just moments ago has turned sour from his words, but I mask showing it.

"I haven't dated much because I haven't had time. I'm trying to start my business and I know love will come eventually."

"But don't you ever want to fall in love?" His teasing tone

makes me smile.

"Of course I want to fall in love. Back to the original question," I say trying to steer this part of the conversation from my loveless life. "When you fall in love, you'll know. You'll feel like you can't live without that person," I say with a sigh. "You'll feel butterflies in your stomach, and you'll start to want to spend every minute of the day with them. You'll find ways just to be with them," I explain, remembering how I felt the first time I thought I'd fallen in love. Of course it was a very long time ago.

Matt's nose is scrunched up in disgust, making me laugh. "Don't look so surprised."

"If it's as pathetic as you make it sound, then it's not worth falling in love," he says with a furrowed brow. "I don't know why you girls make everything sound like a love story. I was expecting you to just say I'd want to fuck the girl," he announces.

I gawk at his response, not believing that my little brother is thinking more with his penis than with his head. I'm definitely going to have to have the talk with him soon; hopefully it hasn't been too late. "Matt, it isn't always about sex."

"Whatever," he says, shrugging his shoulders at the subject. "I doubt I'm ever going to be stupid enough to fall in love. Why tie yourself down to one girl when there's a sea of them out there?" he mocks, spreading his arm at the ocean to the left of him.

Stopping, I place my hands on my hips. "Matthew Garcia, I can't wait until the day a girl makes you fall in love with her. You won't know what bit you in the butt and I look forward to the day when I get to see you grovel at her feet."

"Don't hold your breath, Emily, or you might just die of suffocation. I'm pretty sure I'm not going to be that *stupid to let a girl strap me by the balls."*

My eyes go wide, I cannot believe the words that are coming out of his mouth. "Matthew," I screech at him, "Where in the world did you learn language like that? I know I've raised you better than that," I lecture him.

He laughs. "It's called high school, Emily. Didn't you go there, too?" The mocking smile he's giving isn't helping to dissolve my anger. I do the only thing I can do, which is slap him on the shoulder. I can't help but laugh at his shocked expression.

I think back to how I liked it better when he was younger and still thought innocently, but no matter how much he's grown up, he will always be the little boy I love.

Matt's arm tightens around my body and awakens me from the dream. He's spooning me from behind and the warmth of his chest is radiating against my naked back. Knowing it's best to not be here when he awakens, I carefully unwrap his arm from my waist and climb out of bed. Before I leave, I take one last look at the bed where Matt is still asleep. He's taken the pillow in his arms, wrapping his strong arms around it as if replacing my once warm body.

After dressing, I open the door trying to avoid it from creaking and shut it just as quietly. I'm walking into the living room, making my way to the front door, when I hear Trey's chuckle behind me, forcing me to cringe and face him.

He's lying on the couch with his phone in one hand and a beer in the other. As he brings the beer to his mouth, a smirk forms on his lips. "Doing the walk of shame, supermodel?" Not hiding his chuckle as he takes another swig.

I turn three shades of crimson from being caught. "It's not shame," I grimly reply, not admitting his point. "I want to get home so I can shower."

"This is your home, beautiful, so you don't have to go anywhere," Matt's sleep laced voice says from behind me, causing me to cringe because he's caught me sneaking out.

Today is not my day.

Turning to face Matt, I see his saddened expression. "Matt," I reluctantly say, but he cuts me off by pleading. "I'll go back to staying in the extra room if that's what it'll take," he promises. I see the sparkle of hope in his eyes and his plea is breaking down my walls. "Please, beautiful," he continues to beg.

The blissfulness of his arms and spending time with him earlier is a reminder of what I desperately miss. I can feel the loss with the thought of walking away.

"Okay," I reply, hoping I won't regret my decision. "But you're staying in the other room. We still have a lot to work out, Matt. This doesn't mean I've forgiven you."

"I don't care. As long as you're under the same roof, " he joyfully replies.

"I'll go pack my clothes at Kelly's. I'll see you when you get back."

He walks me out and gives me one final kiss before I climb into my car and drive away, happier than I've been in days. Mentally, I know I'm rushing to move back in with Matt, but deep in my heart I can't take being apart from him any longer. My heart is still warning me Matt is keeping something from me, which is why I make another rash decision... One he will not expect me to make.

Chapter Eleven

Matt

I WATCH ABIGAIL drive away, my heart still beaming inside from knowing she will be here when I return. Entering the house, Abigail's earlier words come back to me and I know I have to start doing what's right. Abigail opened up my eyes, making me realize I have a responsibility to someone other than myself, a life that is growing inside of someone else. The last thing I want is for my child to feel like he or she is second best. I need to put it first. My selfishness of focusing on getting Abigail back made me forget that I needed to make sure Lisa was taking care of herself. Going straight to the extra bedroom, I do the one thing I never thought I'd do if it weren't for Abigail. I call Lisa so I can check up on the baby. Looking through my contacts, I find her name and push send, hearing her answer after two rings. "Hey, Matt, how you doing?" she cheerfully asks.

"Good. How are you feeling?" I ask in return.

"I've been better," she answers with a sigh I can hear through the phone. I grow worried. "What do you mean?" I quickly ask.

"I've been having a lot of morning sickness, but I hear that's normal when you're pregnant, but other than that everything's fine," she states, making me let out the breath I was holding waiting for her to explain. I had thought something was wrong with the baby, bringing me to a point of worry. It occurs to me this is only the beginning.

"I'm glad you called. Do you want to get together and maybe go out for dinner?"

Grumbling to myself, I realize she's taking this phone the wrong way. "I can't. I have a game to go to soon," I answer without taking her offer.

"You're still coming with me to the appointment right?"

"Yeah, I wouldn't miss it for the world," I say, trying to sound enthusiastic, but I can't. Lisa, on the other hand, is able to do it for both of us. "Okay, I can't wait."

Ending the phone call before she can bring up any further invitations, I toss myself back on the bed, letting out another sigh. I think about all that is yet to come, hoping it will all work out in the end.

I wasn't looking forward to going to San Francisco without Abigail. As I step off the plane, her absence was already eating away at my guilt. I keep telling my guilt ridden mind why I'd chosen to not to bring her along. The city held an experience I didn't want Abigail to remember. The only good I had from it was the fact it was the city in which I realized I could not live without Abigail, but it's also the city that holds my past. I kept forcing myself to push the thought away and instead focus on what I would have waiting for me when I return. It's what kept the smile on my face and the dread pushed to the back of my mind.

I THROW THE ball. My aim is off, missing the receiver, earning the opposing team an interception. He's immediately tackled to the ground, but my mistake will cost us. We're already falling behind because of my previous mistakes. With the remaining time on the clock, there is no way we are going to win this game. With two minutes left, we're still down my ten points. It's an automatic win for the other team now that they have the ball.

The coach is already waving me over to the sidelines, and by the look on his face, I have a lecture coming. "What the hell is wrong with you today, Garcia? That should have been a simple pass for you!" he bellows, the frustration emaciating off his face.

I keep silent. My only explanation is my pussy whipped ass cannot concentrate enough on the game because my mind is elsewhere, but I'm not going to tell him that; he would probably blow a gasket. I should be playing at my best, but somehow my mind is somewhere else. My silence irritates him as he orders me to take a seat on the bench. Trey jogs his way over to me, stopping right in front of me. "What the fuck was that, dude? I did my job, at least do yours," he growls after he removes his helmet.

"Back the fuck off, Trey."

He snorts as he shakes his head before walking away. We lose the game, my teammates feeling disappointed over the loss. As everyone gathers around to greet their family and friends who've come to see the game, I'm already walking away when I hear her voice. "Matt." I'm not surprised she's here.

I turn to face Laura, her tiny body making its way over in my direction through the crowd of people. Sighing to myself, I'm already thinking this may not end well. "Hey, Laura," I say, trying to keep it simple and nice as I give her a quick half hug with my arm.

She smiles up at me when I let her go. "I'm sorry you guys lost, but you played a good game," she sympathetically tells me.

Pushing her pity to the back of my mind, I give her a brief nod. "How are things going?" she asks, as if digging for something to start a conversation.

"It's going okay," I answer, already looking around at the crowd hoping to find a distraction. I know it may look rude, but at this point I'm already counting the seconds in which I can find my escape.

Her smile turns to a frown, her eyes turning glassy. "My

Nana Cuca passed away this week. I'm heading home tomorrow for the funeral," she says as a tear escapes her eye.

Feeling guilty, I drop my helmet to envelop her in my arms as my lips meet her head. "I'm so sorry, Laura. I know how much she meant to you," I whisper into her hair, giving her a kiss on the temple to try to comfort her as I rub her back.

Laura's grandmother moved in with her parents when she was young and her grandfather had passed away. Naturally, she was close to her. I knew exactly how she was feeling. I feel Laura beginning to sob against my chest as I rub my hand up and down her back trying to soothe her pain. I continue to kiss her head, reassuring her everything will be all right.

After a couple of minutes she calms and her lips are reaching up to mine. I pull her away so I'm whispering down to her. "Laura, I'm sorry, but I can't," I calmly tell her, trying not to cause her any more emotional pain.

"I'm so sorry. I don't know what happened," she apologizes. I know I should push her away, but her broken expression is keeping me from doing so. "I didn't mean to break down on you that way," she adds.

Feeling sorry for her, I give her another kiss on her forehead as she keeps her arms wrapped around me. "I understand," I sympathetically answer. "I wish I could go with you to the funeral, but I can't. I've already missed a whole week this semester. I can't risk missing anymore school."

She nods her head. "Where's your boss?" she asks around another sniffle, searching for Abigail. It's what it takes for me to put some distance between us. "She wanted to be here, but something came up and couldn't come," I say, already grateful she isn't here. Laura doesn't look convinced. "Will you tell everyone that I send my condolences? I'll make sure to send some flowers to the house."

It's my way of ending our visit, knowing I have to head to the locker room to shower. I make my final goodbyes to Laura, promising to call her during the week. I give her one last tight hug and a kiss on her cheek as I do. She still looks grief-stricken and deep down inside I'm feeling like an asshole for not staying longer, but I keep walking away.

After showering and arriving back at the hotel, the first thing I do is call Abigail, wanting to hear her voice. She doesn't answer, so I leave her a message, begging her to call me. I text her and tell her I miss her, hoping she will call back soon. Time passes with no call back, but I tell myself it must be because she's busy or on a run. It's my excuse as to why she hasn't responded. An hour later, I try calling her again as I'm getting in bed, needing to hear her voice before I fall asleep. When she doesn't answer her phone or the text message again, I grow worried. I check my earlier text message and notice she hasn't responded to it either. I text Kelly next, hoping she will have an answer.

Have you spoken to Abigail today? – Matt

No, she's been gone all day. Don't ask, I don't know. – Kelly

It's not the answer I wanted, but I continue on.

Did she at least pack her stuff? – Matt

Her overnight bag is gone. Where was she going? – Kelly

I have no clue. I'd thought maybe she would have told you. – Matt, I lie to her.

I don't want to go into a detailed explanation with Kelly about Abigail moving back in with me over a text message, but knowing her overnight bag is gone is telling me she's probably already back at the house. I try calling and texting her again thirty minutes later and I still don't receive a response. So I try the next person she would be with—Julio.

Is Abigail with you? – Matt

He immediately responds, but the answer he gives me worries me more.

Yeah, she's with me. – Julio

His answer alleviates some of my worry.

Why isn't she answering her phone? – Matt

I don't want to be in the middle of it, but she says to stop calling and texting her – Julio

I try calling her again, but it goes straight to her voicemail, telling me she's turned her phone off. She's pissed and I hate not knowing why. Is she still pissed about this morning? It's the only explanation I can come up with.

Julio *–Is she at the house? – Matt*

Not right now. - Julio

It's not the answer I wanted to read, but I know that if I push Abigail any further it's going to backfire on me. My hope of getting an explanation as to why she's ignoring me will have to wait until I return and I can talk to her in person. Until then, my mind will be in turmoil of possibilities as to why she's angry. My heart drops to the pit of my stomach with ideas. Desperate to talk to her, I try calling Julio instead, but he doesn't answer either. Now I'm pissed because he's pulling the same shit.

Just tell me what's wrong with her. I'm worried about her. Is she in trouble? Is she hurt? – Matt.

Nothing is physically wrong with her. – Julio

What the hell is that supposed to mean? Knowing I have to give up until tomorrow, I try one final attempt.

Can you just tell her I love her? – Matt

He doesn't answer, but from the confirmation I know he's read it and I pray he's done as requested. Tomorrow cannot come soon enough. I need to get home to find out what is wrong with her.

Abigail

I DIDN'T TELL Matt I was following him to San Francisco for one reason: to test him. I'd known deep down inside why he didn't want me there and I was proven right when I'd seen him with her. The first thing I did when I arrived back at Kelly's was book a flight for Julio and me and arranged for us to stay overnight. I hadn't told anyone of my plans, not even Julio. I'd told him to pack an overnight bag and be ready for me to pick him up. Kelly was at work when I left, so I wrote her a note stating not to worry and that I'd be back tomorrow. I had Julio with me so she had nothing to worry about. I wish I could have brought her, but she was scheduled to work the weekend and I don't think her boss would have appreciated her having to leave work then calling in sick the next day. So it was simply Julio and I.

I couldn't book a room in the hotel where they were staying. It was completely full when I had called. So I booked something nearby. The delay was with the rental car. I forgot that little detail, so it took Julio and I a while to find a company that had a car available. Julio wasn't too happy with the choice of car that they had given us, but I wasn't complaining. It was a car that was going to get us from point A to B. But the look on Julio's face when we had to climb into the little two door Focus was comical.

I made sure to stay hidden amongst the crowd. I didn't want any overdrawn attention, especially because I didn't want Matt to know I was there. It was upon watching Matt play that I knew something was bothering him. He didn't seem focused and I couldn't understand why. As I watched with the crowd when he threw the ball during the last play, I instantly knew something was wrong. Matt had never played so horribly. When the game ended, I stayed, waiting until most of the crowd had made its way down to the field before I got up from my seat. I was still waiting to see if my predication was going to come true and when I'd spotted her, my heart stopped. It shouldn't have surprised me she would be here at his game. I should have expected it. The college was near the city she resided in, but physically seeing her here waiting for him hurt. It kept me from making my way down to the field where he was. Instead I hid myself below the bleachers out of sight, watching them.

I knew Matt couldn't see me. I'd made sure to keep myself hidden from his view. I'd practically held my breath waiting to see what would happen between the two and at first I told myself I had nothing to worry about. It wasn't until I'd seen him kiss her that I'd known I'd been fooled. My heart was torn from my chest, shattered to be left behind on the ground of the field. I could do nothing more than to stand there and watch as he affectionately hugged her liked he had done with me that morning. Sharply watching them, I could make out his lips promising to call her during the week. Her nod told me she wasn't expecting anything less. I was watching the nightmare play all over again in my head.

Even after I watched him walk away from her, I could not move. It was because of Julio tugging my spiritless body away that my legs moved.

After checking into the hotel, I begin hearing the announcement of Matt trying to call me, but I ignore his phone call. I cannot bring myself to look at his text messages. I don't want to see his words. To me they are lies, as he did nothing less than deceive me.

How can I have believed him when he told me he had chosen me over her, when I had seen with my own eyes hours ago that it was all a lie? It had proven he was nothing more than a liar. I had learned my lesson with Bill and there was no fucking way I was going to let it happen to me again. With my heart now shattered, it was now my turn to break his heart in return and give him a taste of his own medicine.

I'M ANGRY. NO, I'm furious. It's bad enough he did it once, but to make a promise to never do it again, telling me that he had chosen me instead of her, then to turn around and lie. It was a slap in the face. I was teaching him a lesson this time. I was taking no prisoners.

I'm walking up to her, bat in my hand. She looks so innocent sitting there. She has no clue what I plan on doing to her. My blood is boiling from rage. I have no self-control at this point. The image of Laura in Matt's arms is still running in my head, like a video that is on constant repeat. It's the only thought taking over my mind at this point. He's broken my heart one too many times. It was time I broke his.

When I get close enough to her, I raise the bat up high, closing my eyes one last moment as I take a deep breath. Inside my head I know I shouldn't do this. If I still had a heart, I'm pretty sure it would be the one thing telling me to have mercy, but since I no longer have one because of him, I open my eyes and bring the bat down, swinging with all my might.

My body vibrates from the impact of the first hit, the bat cracking the window into a web as I shout to the car, *"This is for fucking Lisa on our dining room table. You couldn't keep your dick in your fucking pants long enough for me to come home!"*

I swing again, this time shattering it completely as I make contact with the window. *"This is for all the times you told me I was beautiful and I believed you!"*

I lift the bat back, swinging it forward, now aiming for the mirror. It breaks off with my first swing. *"This is for the first time you kissed me, making me feel like I was worth something to you!"*

The bat comes up above my head, I bring it down with all my might on the windshield, and the impact sends a vibration up my arms, as if she's punishing me for hurting her. I don't give up though as I keep yelling. *"This is for telling me you'd be willing to take a chance at a relationship again, only to fuck things up!"*

I walk to the front of the car, taking out each one of the headlights, still having no mercy. I hit the hood next several times, making sure I leave my imprint on the car. *"This is for telling me you chose me. You fucking liar!"* I shout at the top of my lungs.

I keep moving, taking out the other mirror next. It's when I take my first swing at the driver's side window that I see Trey's Jeep pull up into the driveway. Just like the first window, it doesn't break on the first impact, so I swing at it again. I hear Matt shouting behind me, "What the fuck are doing?" but I ignore him as I keep swinging at the car, the window shattering to pieces.

At this point Matt is now standing in front of the car, blocking it with his arms extended out, protecting her. "What the hell is wrong with you, Abigail?"

I glare at him with all the anger in my soul. I don't care if he's blocking her. In my mind I want to finish her off, so I bring the bat up again ready to strike. "Get the fuck out of the way, Matt," I growl at him, still holding the bat up in the air.

He doesn't move, instead shaking his head, his eyes pleading for me to stop. As I'm about to bring it down on him this time, I feel someone grab it, preventing me from doing so. "Abigail, I don't know what is wrong, but please, you need to stop," he begs, his eyes watering up as his pleading words hit me. I can tell he's holding back the tears, but I don't care.

That's the same tone he always uses to sweeten me up and the thought of them makes me angrier. How many fucking times has he used that tone of voice on her?

I let go of the bat, not bothering to see who has taken it. My eyes are still locked with Matt's as he hesitantly steps towards me with sorrowful eyes begging for me to reach out to him. Instead I shove him back, his body slamming against his car. "Is your heart broken, Matt?" I shout to him. He lets out a muffled sob. "Now you know how I feel... What you've done to me. But unlike me, that car can be fixed!" I continue shouting, now pointing at his car. "I can't say the same about my heart," I declare before turning to walk away from him.

"Abigail, wait!" he shouts back, but I ignore him, heading straight for my car. I can hear Julio's footsteps behind me, both of us soon climbing into my car. He hasn't yet shut the door before I'm peeling out of Matt's driveway, leaving him behind. I don't give a fuck about the future he's willing to offer me anymore, because it's no longer going to include me.

Chapter Twelve

Matt

I WATCH ABIGAIL drive away. I'm both confused and unable to comprehend what has happened. Why would she want to destroy my car? What have I done to upset her? It pained me to see her so angry and upset. When I'd left I was one step closer to her moving back in. I'd made her accept nothing less than us being a couple again. For the last couple of weeks I've done nothing but prove to her how much I love her and that she's the most important person in the world to me. What the hell has made her see otherwise?

Her taillights disappear into the darkness as I ponder the questions in my head. When they are no longer visible, I reluctantly turn to face Eleanor's damaged state. My heart plunges to the pit of my stomach as I fully take her in.

"What the fuck was that all about?" Trey's muddled voice breaks me from my shocked trance. I still cannot speak at this point. I'm still trying to comprehend what's happened.

"I have no fucking idea," I rasp out.

"It had to have been something serious in order for Abigail to go all ape shit on your car."

Blinking, to push the abiding tears away, I rake my hand through my hair as I stare at my broken car. With my mind demanding an answer for her actions, I turn to face Trey. "Let me use your Jeep," I say, already holding my hand out for his keys.

His eyes go wide in shock. "Are you sure that's a good idea? She looked ready to kill you before I stopped her," he says, reminding me he was the one to stop Abigail from swinging at me.

"Just give me your fucking keys," I demand.

"Fine dude, it's your head not mine. Just make sure she doesn't come after my car next, or else you'll be fixing two up instead."

Ignoring his sarcastic words, I'm already stalking my way to his Jeep. Driving as fast as I can over to Kelly's apartment, I make it there within fifteen minutes. I pull up just in time to see her making her way into the apartment. I rush to the door, turning the doorknob to find it locked. Enraged, I start pounding on the door. "Abigail, open this fucking door!" I shout at it.

Surprisingly, David is the one yanking the door open. "What the fuck?"

I shove past him, uncaring of what he thinks. She's protectively tucked behind Kelly, but rage is still fresh in her eyes. My steps are halted when David yanks me to a stop. "What the hell is going on?" he shouts, his head whipping back and forth between Abigail and me.

Abigail keeps silent, but still staring daggers at me. "That's what I want to know."

"Don't fucking stand there acting like you don't know!"

A bewildered looking Kelly is still standing between us looking torn and unknowing of what to do. "What the hell did you do this time?" she asks, already shooting daggers at me as well.

"If I knew, I wouldn't be here."

She whips her head around to now stare down Abigail. "What did you do to piss him off?"

"She beat the shit out of Eleanor with a bat!" I answer for her. I hear a shocked "Fuck" leave both Kelly and David's mouth.

"You deserved it," Abigail snarls at me.

Still looking at her, Kelly asks, "Where did you go this weekend?"

Her eyes have been locked onto mine this entire time, but with Kelly's question I can see the wrath of fire form in them as she says, "San Francisco."

Her response tells me she saw everything between Laura and I. "It's not what you think," I defensively reply.

"I'm tired of hearing your fucking excuses, Matt!"

I try to step forward, but I'm prevented from moving when David tightens his hold on my arm to keep me from reaching her. "Look man, right now is not the best time to try to talk to her," I hear David say behind me.

I ignore him. "I swear it's not what you think," I repeat.

"You fucking liar!" she shouts. "I saw you kiss her!"

My heart stops, my blood completely drains from my body as I stand there shocked and speechless. Her chest is angrily rising and falling as she continues to narrow her eyes at me. "She kissed me, but I never meant for it to happen," I swear to her. "Please, you have to believe me, beautiful," I beg. "She'd just told me her grandma died and I was feeling sorry for her," I explain.

She shakes her head at me. "You liar. You knew she would be there. That's why you didn't want me to go. It's so you could be alone with her."

"That's not true." She still looks angry. "Please, you have to believe me." I know if I admit that she's right, I'd be hanging myself further. She furiously looks back at me and I know I've lost.

"I think it's best you leave, Matt. Give her some time to calm down," David calmly suggests, already tugging me towards the door. I allow him to pull me, but I take one last remorseful glance at Abigail, hoping David is right.

He follows me out to Trey's Jeep. "Even I thought something was going on between you and Laura," he admits as we reach the Jeep. "What really happened?"

His words shock me, but viewing it from an outside perspective, it would look wrong. "I swear I was only comforting her," I explain, raking my hand through my hair. "I know I should've pushed her away, but I didn't, and I'm regretting it now." He still looks skeptical. "I couldn't just turn by back on her when she told me her news. I was with her for years and it came naturally to me to comfort her when she was hurting. It doesn't change the fact that I love Abigail. It never will," I insist.

He's silent for a minute before answering. "I believe you, but she doesn't, and she's the one who you need to be convincing," he conveys. "Just not tonight." The sympathetic look he's giving me is pissing me off. "Why didn't you just let Abigail go?"

"I didn't want her to go because I had a feeling Laura would show up. I could not risk her upsetting Abigail." David crosses his arms across his chest as he considers my words. "In my opinion, it would have been better to have her at your side," he states.

"If the tables were turned, would you do it with Kelly?" I challenge him.

He frowns. "Of course. There isn't anything I would keep from Kelly." The realization of his words strikes me like lightning. I've been keeping too much from Abigail. Since the day we've met I'd been guarding one thing or another, which has been the cause of our mistakes. "You're right," I admit. "But what should I do now?" I pitifully ask.

The answer I receive is not the one I was anticipating from David. "You have to give her time." Taking in his words, I nod my head in agreement before I turn to climb into the Jeep. On the drive home, I have nothing but time to go over my conversation with David. My biggest mistake has been that I've grown used to keeping things to myself. I've learned to shut out the world from my emotions that were dwelling inside of me after Emily died. It took Abigail for me to love again, but I still made the mistake of not being honest with her. It needed to stop, and it was going to stop as of now.

Abigail

MY BODY STARTS shivering from the anger boiling through my veins as I watch Matt leave. When I'd seen him walk through the door, I wanted to physically attack him, the anger taking over inside of me like a caged animal demanding to be let out. It worsened with his explanations, his deceiving lies. I didn't know what to believe anymore.

Kelly's arm wraps around my shoulder to guide me to the couch. Taking a seat, I can already see her waiting for an explanation. "I needed to see with my own eyes," I rasp out, not knowing what I had intended to mean with my own words. "I'm sorry," she sincerely replies as if comprehending what I'd seen.

We continue to sit there together in silence as she sympathetically comforts me. Matt's words are still fresh in my head. My disoriented mind keeps me from doing anything more than stare ahead in a dazed filled trance. It isn't until David returns that I'm forced to leave it. Dishearteningly looking over to him, he looks torn whether to speak or not.

"What did he say?" Kelly asks, digging for the information I'm desperate to know.

He looks hesitant to answer. "Do you honestly think he was telling the truth?" I ask through clenched teeth.

"I honestly think this is all a misunderstanding," he says before I give him a piecing glare. "I know you both have a lot to work out, but it's never going to happen if you don't talk to each other," he bravely answers.

I don't know what has possessed me, but I stand and grab my purse, heading straight out of the door. I jump into my car and drive off, my destination clear in my mind. When I arrive I go to my trunk and pull out the duffel bag with my spare running clothes, changing in my car. I do the only thing I can do to help me logically think; I run.

The sun is starting to set and with each mile I add my thoughts keep bringing me back to Matt. It isn't until I'm done that I allow myself to cry. The pain is still taking over my body, but the despair of knowing I have to make a decision to either believe him or walk away is tearing at my mind. My heart feels empty when I began running, but with every memory of Matt, it begins to fill again; this time with love.

Taking a deep breath, I text him.

Do you remember the first run we ever took? – Abigail

Yes. I took you to my favorite park. – Matt

If my heart wasn't already sunken to the pit of my stomach, it would have with his response. I have to close my eyes to take a deep breath. Opening them back up, I type my next message.

I'll be here for the next fifteen minutes before I leave. – Abigail

I grow worried when I see the notification telling me he's read the message, but hasn't responded. I sit alone in the park telling myself I've made a fool of myself and I should just leave. Looking down at my phone, I see it's already been fourteen minutes. What's another minute if he hasn't already shown up? Standing up, I walk my way over to my car. As I'm about to open my door, I see Trey's Jeep speeding its way into the parking lot. The screech of the breaks as he brings it to a halt makes me flinch. Matt climbs out of the driver's side and rushes to me. Without giving me a chance to speak, he grabs my face in his palms and kisses me. I try to push him away, but I'm weak from his kiss and my heart is protesting my request. Instead, I fiercely grip his waist to keep him from pulling away.

Breathless, we part and his dark eyes are staring back at me. "That is how I kiss the person I'm meant to be with," he rasps out. "I will never kiss anyone else like that ever again, I swear."

"I'm sorry," I whimper. "I shouldn't have reacted that way."

Matt is about to speak, but I stop him. "Please, I have to let it out." His silence allows me to continue. "I hate the person I've become. I've turned into this raving bitch and my only excuse is because I'm afraid of losing you."

"Beautiful, that will never happen."

"You kissed her, though. When I saw you with Laura, I snapped. I felt like your words were nothing but a broken promise. How am I supposed to believe your words when you do things that make me believe otherwise?" I whimper out as I lay my head on his shoulder.

Lifting my chin, I look up at him once again. "It was a mistake. I know that now," he confesses. "At the moment it seemed like I was in the past with her. I never meant for any of it to happen, beautiful," he apologizes with a whisper. "You can tell me to go to hell if you want, but even if you did, I'd still find my way back to you," he says against my temple. "I'm going to fix this, Abigail," he promises.

His words are my breaking point. My weakened heart has succumbed to them as I lean my head against his shoulder again. "Can we just put this all behind us, please? I don't ever want to talk about it again."

"I'd like nothing more," he whispers.

Minutes pass and the sky has now darkened as we stand wrapped in each other's arms in silence. "I'm not moving back in now," I indicate, feeling his body stiffen, but I add, "I need more time, Matt."

I feel him nod his head before answering. "Not too much time. I can't stand not having you near." I don't respond. I'm too exhausted from fighting with him to bother.

Chapter Thirteen

Matt

AS I DRIVE up to Lisa's apartment, I start to grow anxious. I'd been dreading the thought of taking her to the doctor, but now that the day has arrived and I'm waiting outside her apartment to pick her up, I'm excited.

Although I still have my doubts about the entire situation, I have to force myself to push them aside. As much as I fear being a father so soon, the thought is starting to grow on me. I see Lisa come out as she briskly walks her way over to Trey's Jeep. She climbs in with a radiant smile on her face.

"Where's your car?" she curiously asks, looking around inside Trey's Jeep.

I focus on the road ahead as I pull off. "It's in the shop," I curtly reply without any further explanation.

"You excited?" she enthusiastically asks and I'm thankful that she's changing the subject.

I force a smile as I answer, "Sure."

"How was school today?"

"It was good," I shortly reply, looking down at my phone to double-check my directions of the address she texted me earlier.

She continues on with her bubbly conversation, but I focus on my driving to shut her out. Out of the corner of my eye I can see her face turn to a frown, looking agitated.

"Well?" she annoyingly asks.

"Well what?"

"I was suggesting we go shopping for baby supplies together."

Her statement takes me by surprise. "Don't you think it's too soon to be doing that?" I say, looking down at her stomach. I haven't seen her much but on occasion around campus. It's usually brief, as I make sure not to linger so not to give her the wrong idea.

"It's never too soon," she states as she starts rubbing her stomach and my mind forms a vision of Abigail's hand doing the same. Directing my eyes back on the road, I give my head a shake to bring myself back to reality. "Do you have a preference?" I hear her ask.

Confused, I ask, "About what?"

"Do you want a boy or girl?" she clarifies. "I want a girl, but I know most guys want a boy so they can name it after themselves."

"Look, Lisa, I'm sorry I don't seem as excited as you, but to be honest, I'm still trying to take it all in."

"How can you not be happy?"

I look at her like she's lost her mind. "I'll just let you be excited for the both of us," I clip out, focusing on the road again. I hear her utter something under her breath, but I pay no attention.

Before long we're at the clinic and when inside they give Lisa her paperwork to fill out. Taking a seat in the waiting room with her, we're surrounded by several different pregnant women and a couple in front of us. I watch as the man caresses the belly of his significant other. My mind returns to my earlier thought, this time envisioning my hand on Abigail's swollen stomach. The thought makes me close my eyes and swallow the lump now lodged in my throat. When I open my eyes, I look over at Lisa who is giving me a smile before she returns to filling out her paperwork.

As I wait I use the time to send off my daily text to Abigail.

I miss you – Matt

Within a minute I receive a respond.

I miss you too – Abigail

I take in her response and my mind returns to the conversation we had after we left the park.

I'm miserably lying in bed thinking of Abigail. It's been an hour since I've left her, but her dispirited expression I left her with has been haunting my mind. I hear the ping of a text message. I look down at my phone expecting it to be Lisa again, but instead I brighten up when I see it's Abigail.

I miss you, too. - *Abigail.*

Her words can't keep me from calling her. As she answers she says:

"Are we ever going to stop making mistakes?" she whispers into the phone.

My heart sinks. "I hope so," I sincerely reply.

"I never meant to hurt you," I remind her. "Please, Matt, we agreed to not talk about it anymore," she reminds me.

"Okay, but just remember that I love you too much to lose you," I explain.

She sniffles. "I love you, too. I just wish it would have never happened," she whimpers into the phone.

"Me, too," I agree.

My thoughts are broken when they call for Lisa. As we're walking, Lisa curiously asks, "What are you smiling about?"

"Abigail," I happily answer.

Her expression turns sour, almost angered. "I thought you guys broke up?" she mutters, her question laced with a hint of bitterness.

"No, we didn't," I reveal to her.

We follow the nurse who is a couple of steps ahead of us. "How does she feel about you having a baby with somebody else? I doubt she likes being a fourth wheel," she claims. The nurse is peering over her shoulder, looking confused from Lisa's words.

Ignoring the both of them, I follow them into the exam room. The nurse immediately begins to give Lisa instructions to remove all her clothes and put on a papered gown for examination, pointing to something sitting on an exam table.

Realizing what Lisa needs to do, I speak up. "I'll wait outside," I tell her.

"Oh, you don't have to leave the room. It's not like she has anything you haven't seen before," the nurse jokes, but I don't bother responding, already exiting the room. The only naked body I want to see from this day forward is Abigail's.

The nurse follows me out of the room, asking before she leaves, "I take it you don't want to be there for the vaginal exam either?"

I don't need the details to what that exam entails. The words alone are enough to tell me I don't want to be there. Giving her a quick shake, she chuckles again and tells me I can take a seat in a chair placed across from the exam room. Before long, I see a doctor knocking on the door to enter. Ten minutes later the door opens again and I see the doctor.

"You can come in now. I've finished my exam," she informs me.

Following her back into the room, I take a seat in the chair against the wall. "Lisa wanted you to be here for the rest of the visit," she informs me.

Giving her a short nod, I see her pull a machine from the corner of the room over to the side of the bed. "Lisa tells me you're the father. Are you excited?" the doctor asks, not bothering to look at me when she asked. Instead she's making notes in a chart. I don't bother to answer, not wanting a repeat of what happened in the car.

The doctor looks up at me as Lisa's eyes bore into mine. "Of course he's happy," Lisa answers for me. I'm about to dispute her response when my phone starts to sing *Here Without You,* the ringtone I'd designated for Abigail after she left. It was fitting at the time. The chorus doesn't get too many words into it before I'm digging it out of my pocket to silence it.

"Sorry, that was my *girlfriend*," I slowly clip out, earning me the continuous narrowed eyes from Lisa.

For a moment the doctor looks confused, but professionally continues at her task. Within seconds my phone starts ringing again, but this time it doesn't make it past the first three words before I push ignore on the screen. The doctor dims the light and a minute later I hear the ding informing me Abigail has left a message. The regret of not being able to take her phone call is coursing through me. It's the first time I've ever had to ignore her call. Another minute later it's followed by the ping of a text message and curiosity gets the better of me.

I'm sorry for bothering you. – Abigail

Her message stabs at my heart knowing she's resenting me for not taking the call. I silently question whether she knows I'm at Lisa's appointment with her. I know I didn't tell her. The only way she would know is if she's spoken to Trey and that's why she's calling. I'm forced to push the thought away when I hear a loud, fast thumping coming from the machine the doctor is standing near. When I look up, I see a black and white blur on the screen. At first I'm confused, until I realize it's *my baby.* My heart speeds with the realization of knowing *this is a life I've created.* I stand up to take a closer look and I'm left breathless when I see it flutter on the screen. A hundred different images of my future with this child course through my mind in that spit second.

"Since you said you can't remember when your last period was, we'll just take some simple measurements to determine how far along you are, Lisa," the doctor mentions, concentrating on the screen while pushing at some buttons.

"That's the baby, right?" I ask the doctor, wanting confirmation.

She looks over at me, a smile on her face. "Of course."

My breath hitches as my heart is rapidly beating with the sound surrounding the room.

"According to the measurements, I'd say you're about twelve weeks along," the doctor informs Lisa, punching at buttons with her hand. The excitement is further rising through me, but when I take in her comment, my heart completely stops as the blood sinks to the depths of my toes. "What did you say?" I utter.

The doctor looks over at me. "She's twelve weeks along," she repeats.

Doing the math in my head, I know that cannot be right. "It's only been nine weeks since Chicago," I say, trying to contain the anger replacing my excitement as I look over to Lisa.

Her face pales, looking just as shocked. "Maybe she's wrong, Matt. Right, doctor? Those measurements can be wrong. I'm nine weeks like he says, right?" she asks, sounding desperate at this point.

The doctor is looking between both Lisa and I, confused and apprehensive to say anything. "I'm sorry, Lisa. The measurements can be off by maybe a week, but not by three. You're sitting at around twelve weeks, maybe thirteen since the baby is sitting on the larger side," she conveys, sounding confident in her assessment.

"You lied to me?"

Lisa doesn't respond, but instead begins crying. The doctor immediately stands up, reaching for some tissue to give her.

"Why did you lie?" I demand of her.

She continues to cry, but I'm no longer sympathetic because of her deceit. Lisa looks at me with desperation in her eyes. "I didn't know what to do," she cries out.

"What the hell is that supposed to mean?" I snarl out at her.

The doctor is standing there, looking uncomfortable over the entire situation. "Lisa, why would you lie and say this young man is the father of your child when he clearly isn't?"

"Because I don't know who the father is," she announces with a wail.

"What do you mean you don't know who the father is?" the

doctor asks, beating me to the same question I wanted to ask.

Lisa's crying is now making her convulse. The doctor tries her best to calm her, informing her it isn't good for the baby. "I went to a frat party and I got really drunk. All I remember is having sex more than once that night, but it wasn't with the same guy," she says between sobs. "I *think* Trey was one of them. That's why I went to your house that night. I wanted to tell him I was pregnant, but you were drunk and it was easy to have sex with you. I knew that if I told you I was pregnant you would help me raise the baby."

The doctor looks surprised, while the blood drains from inside of me all over again.

"How could you expect me to raise a baby that isn't mine?"

"Why not?" she whines out.

I watch as the doctor's eyes, along with mine, go wide. "Because I love someone else, Lisa. I can't believe you did this to me," I bellow before storming out of the exam room, not bothering to wait for Lisa. I know it's wrong to leave her there, but at this point I'd rather leave her than risk strangling her for her little stunt.

Making it back to the Jeep, I sit there, angry. I cannot believe I let myself fall for her shit. The moment I saw that baby on the screen I'd looked forward to holding that baby in my arms, only to find out it's not even mine. The rage inside of me is already taking over as I turn the ignition and speed out of the parking garage.

Abigail

"HOW MANY ARE we planning on running today?" Julio skeptically asks, looking up at the grey sky that is beginning to darken by the minute—a downside of living in Portland.

The weather is always unpredictable. It's always hit or miss on good weather, especially now that the winter is upon us. I look up to the sky with him, praying the weather holds up long enough for me to finish my run. "According to my schedule, I'm supposed to run sixteen today, but I doubt it will be that much."

Julio's lips go flat as he looks back to me. "Let's hope. The last thing I want is to get caught up in the rain storm," he states, not sounding happy about it. "Neither do I," I add.

We begin walking over to the entrance of the trail that we've chosen for today. Julio is already climbing onto his bike and I'm about to bring my playlist up on my phone. I hear the ping of a text message and when I open it up, my lips turn up wide.

I miss you- Matt

Without hesitating I respond.

I miss you too – Abigail

I look over at Julio who is already pedaling on his bike, making me chuckle as he gains distance on me. I still can't get over the fact that he cannot keep up with me sometimes, even with the bike. But then again, once I hit my zone with running, I forget he's even riding next to me half the time. I get so lost to the music blasting in my ears that my legs automatically move faster against my own will. When I reach into the pocket of my jacket for my earphones, I come up empty handed. I check the top pockets, but find them empty as well.

"Julio, did I drop my earphones?" I yell at him as I jog to catch up.

"I remember seeing them on the counter before we left. Did you forget to grab them?" he shouts behind his shoulder, his words taking me back to the thought of when I placed them there to fill my water bottle before we left.

Crap, I did forget to grab them.

Julio sees the disappointment registering on my face. "Did you want to go back and get them?"

I shake my head. "No. I can't risk wasting any more time. I guess I'll have to run without them," I inform him, already dreading the idea.

Julio is used to running and riding without them. He prefers not to be distracted so he can stay focused on our surroundings, for my safety. I continue my usual slow jog to warm up, but within minutes I pick up my speed. I glance down at my watch to take in my pace time when I grow bored and notice it's only been two minutes that have passed. That's it? I think to myself, two lousy minutes, but I keep running.

Taking in the view, it helps, but not as much as I would have hoped it would. How the hell do people claim it's more relaxing and beneficial to run without music? Looking down at my watch again, it now says eight minutes and I still haven't found this so called Zen runners claim to find within seconds. Running without music is not going to cut it. Lesson learned, buy an extra set of earphones to keep in the car for these circumstances.

I glance over at Julio who isn't affected from the lack of music. "How the hell do you do it?" I question him, earning me a confused look. "Do that without music? I think I'm going insane. How the hell am I going to make it an hour?"

He gives me a chuckle. "How about we talk? It can help distract you," he suggests.

"Fine," I say, sucking in a deep breath. It's more of a sigh, but being that I'm running, it's how it comes out. Feeling the need to begin with the conversation, I hesitantly ask, "So why don't you have a girlfriend?" I'm hoping he doesn't become offended with the question, but I'm nosey and I've always wanted to know.

I don't know much about Julio, but strangely I want to know. He's never mentioned anything about his personal life before, but I always thought it was because of the whole "*being a bodyguard*" thing.

"Watching the drama that occurs between you and Mateo is enough for me to not want to have one," he states with a chuckle. I whip my head in his direction to stare daggers at him. At this point I'm debating if I can shove him off his bike because of the comment. When he notices my reaction, he lets out a full-hearted laugh. "I'm kidding, Abigail. I can tell from watching the two of you that you're still in love. It's something worth fighting for. That wasn't the situation with my ex-wife," he adds, shocking me out of step.

I quickly try to recover to keep from stumbling, my jaw still hanging near the ground as I look at him. "What do you mean ex-wife?"

Giving me a simple nod, he explains. "I was married once. Biggest regret of my life," he states. If I weren't already shocked, I'd be now. "Why would you say that?" I ask, it comes out sounding just as shocked as my expression is most likely conveying.

He laughs at my expression before starting. "We met through mutual friends. She was great at first, friendly and up-beat. We started dating soon after we met. Not a year later I proposed. I should have known from the wedding alone how our marriage would play out. I wanted something simple, but she had me blow all my life savings to pay for the wedding. After the honeymoon, when I couldn't buy her a house, she threw a fit," he states. I'm still looking ahead, but the image of what he's portraying is making me feel sorry for him.

He continues on. "Her family and friends had a large influence on her decisions. To them I was a lowlife asshole because I couldn't provide for her the way she wanted, yet I had a good paying job and she chose to live the life of a housewife," he takes a pause in his story so he can maneuver around a tree stump, but I'm left pondering his words.

"So was that the reason why you got divorced? Because you couldn't buy her a house?"

"No, that came three years later when I had gotten a job offer I couldn't resist turning down. Growing up, my dream was to always work for the Secret Service, which is something I think I would have accomplished had I not given up on it. Before I moved up here I lived in San Antonio. I had made it my goal to follow my dream."

"You're from San Antonio?"

He shakes his head. "No, I was born and raised here in Portland. My ex-wife is from San Antonio. I ended up there because it's the first job I got offered after the police academy," he explains. "I met her, fell in love, and married her. It wasn't until after tying the knot that her true colors came out. She was selfish," he adds.

"I had secretly applied for a position without telling her. I did it because I didn't want to get my own hopes up. She knew my dreams, but I guess she wasn't as supportive as I thought she would be. When I got offered the position, she refused to move, stating that our life and family were in San Antonio. She demanded I turn the job down, but I didn't. I followed my heart and took the job. I'd hoped she would change her mind, but of course she didn't. To punish me she maxed out our credit cards, completely wiping out our savings, and even went as far as refusing to pay my car, which eventually got repossessed," he adds, with a heavy sigh. I feel so sorry for him at this point. "That was the finishing point for me. I filed for a divorce right away."

"Is that why you were working a dead end job when I found you?" I ask. He responds with a simple nod. "I had to eventually file bankruptcy. The government does periodic credit checks and they want you squeaky clean. I was going to be forced to resign after I filed bankruptcy. After I had filed for the divorce they were doing layoffs, it was almost a blessing in disguise. I made the decision to move back to Portland and my mom offered for me to move back in. I'm still trying to recover my credit, but at least she's no longer a burden to me," he adds, his voice dropping low as if he's saddened by the declaration when he finishes, almost sounding relieved from the declaration, and can't I blame him.

We both continue running, our silence growing heavy throughout the fog that we are moving through. "You probably think I'm an asshole like her mother and family label me." I look at him shocked. How can he think that? But then again, of course he would think that about himself if that were all he's been hearing since he married her. "Not at all, Julio," I reply. "You made the right decision in my eyes by divorcing her. She was only thinking of herself. As you stated, she wasn't working, so she could have easily moved to wherever your dream took you. If she couldn't see it that way, then she didn't deserve you. It's her loss," I admit before adding, "And no, you're not an asshole. You look scary, but you're definitely not an asshole," I tell him, earning me another laugh.

"In a way, I understand what you went through. You have to remember I had an embezzling fiancé. It's not the same, but it's similar. She took what was yours without your permission. So you have every right to be angry," I proclaim.

It earns me a curt nod of approval. "What's going on with the whole Bill thing if you don't mind me asking?" Julio's curiously asks. The question came out sounding restrained, as if he was fearful of asking the question, but still wanted to know.

I sigh before I answer. "I don't' know," I tell him around the lump in my throat.

It's terrifying not having an answer. I had hoped to put that chapter of life behind me, never having to open the book again and read the words, but I was wrong.

I'm so lost in my thoughts, my attention of the trail has lapsed and my foot sinks into a pothole. I feel the sharp pain stabbing at my ankle, shooting straight up my leg as I stumble to the ground. I try to stop my fall, but it's unsuccessful as my hands meet the ground, feeling as if they are being stabbed as well. I roll to my side, grabbing onto my right foot, which feels like it's on fire.

"Abigail, you alright?" Julio frantically asks, already at my side assessing my foot. I'm forcefully containing the scream that wants to be let out as I take deep, long breaths. "Where does it hurt the most?" he asks, already grabbing onto the foot that's within my hands.

"Abigail, I know this is going to hurt, but I have to get your shoe off to see how bad it is," his expression looking frightful to try. "It's the only way," he explains. The process shoots another joint of pain up my leg and I cannot hold it in anymore as I let out the bellowed scream I was holding in. It hurts to damn much.

He's already untying the shoelaces and he looks at me for permission to remove it. I give him a short nod as I suck in a deep breath for courage. When he pulls it off, the sharp pain travels up my legs again this time feeling as if somebody has pounded me with a hammer from the bottom of my foot, forcing the pain to travel up my leg. He removes my sock as well and I can already see it turning all shades of purple and it looks double the size of what it normally would, making me cry.

Julio looks around before he places my foot on the ground. "There is no way you can walk back to the car. I'm going to have to ride back and drive it up as close as I can to the path. I'll carry you the rest of the way," he instructs me.

"Okay," I whisper through the pain, hoping he's heard me.

Standing to take off his jacket, he wraps it around my shoulders. "Your body will go into shock any minute. The jacket will help keep you warm. I'll be back as soon as I can," he says looking around. "You're off the path, so you should be safe here. You have your phone with you, right?" he asks. He's looking at me as if he's waiting for me to show him that I do. I reach inside my own pocket of my jacket and show him. He nods his head. "Call Mateo," he instructs. "I want you to stay on the phone with someone while I go retrieve the car," he orders.

I proceed to call Matt, but he doesn't answer. I try again, but this time it goes straight to voicemail, making me sob into the phone from the disappointment of him not answering. I don't say anything. What is there to say when you're speaking to an automatic machine? I hang up and shoot him a quick text, so he doesn't worry about my silent message. When done, I call the next person I can think of—Trey.

He answers immediately, and when Julio confirms he's on

the phone, he speeds off on the bike, leaving me to have a conversation with Trey. It isn't the person I would have preferred to speak with, but he does the job well in calming me by making me laugh. Now if only Julio would hurry up because now that I'm growing cold I realize, I really have to pee.

Chapter Fourteen

Mattt

I KNOCK AGAIN, and wait, which is causing me to grow impatient. I should have called before showing up on Kelly's front door, but I wanted to surprise Abigail. The door opens and instead of it being Abigail as I'd hoped, it was Kelly.

"Whatcha want, lover boy?" she annoyingly asks. She has her eyes narrowing at me, as she stands guarding the door. I gently push past her, my eyes searching for Abigail. "She's not here," Kelly states behind me.

Turning to face her, she has her arms angrily crossed over her chest. "Where is she?"

She shrugs her shoulders. "I just got home a little bit ago. Maybe she's out with her Sancho. If you can have someone on the side, why can't she?" she sarcastically states as her lips curve up to one side.

Sancho, my ass. She is not having a Sancho over my dead body. More likely his, since I'd be killing any fucker that gets near her. "I *don't* have anyone on the side," I respond, marching my way back to Trey's Jeep.

Climbing in, I dig for my phone and notice the icon reminding me Abigail had left a message. I press on the screen making it play. Instead of hearing Abigail speaking, I hear whimpering on the other end before the call ends. Unbelieving of what I heard,

I replay the message, hearing the exact same thing. When I play it for the third time, I finally comprehend what the whimpering is. It's Abigail crying, and once again the blood drains to my toes. Without hesitating, I dial her number and it goes straight to voicemail. I try Julio, but the same happens with his number. I'm left sitting there numb, unable to move from the worry rising inside of me.

My mind goes to a hundred different scenarios of why she could have been crying. Was she kidnapped? Did Bill find her again? The thought of knowing she is somewhere out there and I ignored her call is gnawing at my gut. Why did I allow myself to ignore her phone call? I should have taken it instead of wasting my time with Lisa.

With the worry still inside of me, I try calling her again, and still I get no answer. My worry has now turned to panic. Climbing out of the Jeep, I head straight back to Kelly's door, pounding on it this time as I demand she open it. She swings the door open, looking angry. "Has she called you at all today?" I frantically bellow out, making her eyes go wide.

"No, why?"

"She called me when I was at Lisa doctor's appointment, but I had to ignore her call. She left a voicemail, but she was crying, and now she won't answer her phone," I reply, the panic taking over my voice. Kelly's eyes go wide in shock before she glances down at her phone, shaking her head in response as she pushes on the screen before bringing it up to her ear. "It goes straight to voicemail," she states, swallowing hard before pressing on the screen of her phone again.

"If you're trying to call Julio, I tried that too," I tell her, her body slumping, as she looks up at me, frantic. "What did he say?" she desperately asks.

"He didn't answer either. She *knows* not to go anywhere without him, right?"

She nods her head. "Yes," she replies biting her lip, her gaze wondering to the side, as if she's thinking. Then her eyes light up before she walks over to the kitchen, leaving me to follow her. "She printed out this schedule a couple of days ago," she says, her finger going to a chart that is being held up by a magnet on the fridge. Her index finder glides down it and when I take it in. I know exactly what it is; it's a running schedule. Kelly's finger stops on a specific day, today's date, and it states sixteen miles.

"What route was she taking?" I ask, as she turns to face me.

"I don't know," she squeals out. "I'm not into that running shit like you guys!" she panicky shouts.

Her answer doesn't leave me satisfied, but I know it's all she's got. I search my mind, thinking of all the places she could have gone, but being that it's Portland, she can be anywhere in the city. They have trails everywhere.

I rake my hand down my face, growing frustrated again. Kelly starts punching buttons on her phone again before speaking into it. "Hey douche, have you heard from Abigail?" her eyes locking onto mine when she asks.

I already know she's talking to Trey. He's the only one she calls by that name most of the time. Her eyes light up and I get a hint of hope that he might know, and she confirms it when she nods her head at me with a smile. I yank the phone from Kelly's hear, earning me a scowl, but I don't care. "Where is she? Is she in danger?" I bark into the phone.

"Dude, calm the fuck down, she's at the hospital," he casually replies as if it's no big deal. How the fuck can he think it's no big deal? "What's wrong with her? Is she okay? What hospital is she at?" I blurt out to him, knowing it's probably more questions than he can focus on at once, but I need to know.

"Hell if I know," he answers.

I swear to God, if he were standing in front of me I would shove him against a wall or pound his face in right now. "She was running and got hurt. Julio was taking her to the hospital. She was screaming and crying in the background that she didn't want to go. She said she'd call me when she left," he adds.

"How long ago was that?"

"I don't know, like maybe half an hour, maybe an hour."

Looking at the clock on the wall, it's the exact time she called me and I didn't answer, making me feel guilty. I was off dealing with a liar when my girl needed me the most and I couldn't be there for her. Handing the phone back to Kelly, I sternly look at her. "If she calls you, call me," I demand to her.

"Of course."

Walking out of the door again, I run to the Jeep, speeding off. My heart is racing and I cannot help but to feel like the biggest asshole in the world all over again. I promised to always be there when she needed me and yet again I'm breaking that promise because of my fucking dick. No more, it has to stop, and it will. For now I need to find Abigail before I go insane.

Abigail

"ARE YOU SURE you don't want me to return his phone calls?" Julio hesitantly asks for what seems like the hundredth time since we've arrived at the hospital.

"No," I quietly reply, watching as his lips go flat, his normal reaction to my answer. I can tell by the way he's deliberately looking between me and his phone, he wants to call him.

My body begins to shiver again. "You cold? You want me to request another blanket from them?"

Shaking my head, I try to bring the shivers under control. I'm not cold. I just hate hospitals. I haven't been able to get the nervousness of being here under control; the memories of the last two visits are making me petrified. In all reality, I'm wishing Matt were here with me, but when Trey told me he was with Lisa at her doctor's appointment, I knew I could not bother him anymore.

My body shivers again and the desire to have him at my

side wins. "Fine, call him," I bitterly reply before I throw my body back to lean against the hospital bed. Bringing the sheet up to my chin, I watch as Julio's lips turn up to one side as he starts dialing Matt's number, making me roll my eyes. Within seconds he's conversing with him, giving him details of which hospital we're at.

"He's on his way," he states, hanging up the phone.

Sighing, I wait.

It isn't long before Matt is pushing the door to my exam room open, his lean tall body staring back at me. His expression is both full of relief and despair. Rushing to my side, he immediately places a kiss upon my temple as he cradles my head within both his palms, his lips lingering upon my brow.

Closing my eyes, to savor his kiss, my mind is transported to another place. A playground. There are children running around us, but my main focus is the little boy in front of me. He's holding his wrist in his other hand, grimacing as he holds it. The pain is evident on his face. Leaning down to place a kiss across his temple as I shush to calm him, the tears are already running down my own eyes. Pulling back to better see him, my vision is blurry, my eyes rapidly blinking to push the tears away. But it doesn't help much with the anguish of my guilt taking over.

"Don't cry, Em. It doesn't hurt as bad as you think," he whispers back to me, already wiping away the tear that is falling from the corner of my eye. It never fails to amaze me, how strong this little boy can be during the most difficult of our situations. No matter how strong I try to be for him, he's capable of proving that he's has the tenacity to be the stronger of us two.

Sighing, I look down at his wrist. I already know it's broken by the way his bone is protruding within the skin. Just looking at it I know it must be painful, even if he says it isn't so. "Okay, mijo, let's get you to the hospital to get you fixed up," I say down to him, already trying to help him up.

As I grab for his elbow, forgetting it's his injured arm, I hear him suck in his breath, wincing at the same time. "I'm sor-

ry," I guiltily say.

"It's okay."

No, it's not okay. I should have been more careful with him. I should have been watching him better. Had I done so, this would have never happened. He wouldn't be hurt. I can only live with the regret now as I continue walking with him to the car. Helping him into the car, I carefully buckle him in, giving him one last kiss on his head to reassure him everything will be okay, but it's when he speaks again, that I'm left speechless.

"This isn't your fault, Em. Please don't blame yourself," he says, squeezing my hand. He's now the one reassuring me. "I shouldn't have tried jumping off the swing. I'm sorry for scaring you. Everything will be okay, Em, you'll see."

My heart drops into the pit of my stomach. I don't know how it's possible for this little boy to always know what I need to hear to make me feel better. With a smile, I give him one more kiss, knowing he's right; everything will be all right.

I already know this little boy is going to grow up to make me proud and the girl that claims his heart will be one lucky girl.

I'm brought back to the present when I hear Matt speak to me. "You scared the shit out of me, beautiful," he whispers down to me, bringing his temple down to mine, the panic evident in his words as he lets out a deep sigh against my neck. I don't pull away because he's now holding me, it's the comfort I was seeking to take my anxiety away.

With my body still wrapped in his arms, I remember how his sister felt when he was hurt, realizing how lucky I am to have Matt at my side right now. My fear is completely gone, replaced with a giddiness of wanting Matt all over again. When he does pull away, his eyes rake over my body, stopping at my injured ankle. "How bad is it?"

"I don't know, they haven't taken me to get x-rays yet," I respond, already impatient with the wait, but I don't have to wait any longer since a technician is already entering my exam room.

As he's about to wheel my bed away, he notices how Matt

and Julio are both ready to follow. "I'm sorry, You're both going to have to stay behind while I take her for x-rays."

"No," they both respond in unison, challenging his demand.

His head looks back and forth between the both of them.

"I'm her bodyguard. Where she goes, I go," Julio demands, standing tall with his arms crossed over his chest. "And, I'm not leaving her side," Matt adds.

The technician now looks frightened by both their glares. "Fine, but both of you have to stay outside the radiology room," he orders, earning him a nod from both Matt and Julio.

To be honest, I was not going to let Matt leave my side, either. I already hate hospitals, but knowing he's at my side somehow makes the anxiety disappear. Almost thirty minutes later, with the films now taken on my ankle, I'm being wheeled back into my exam area in the emergency room. When the technician leaves us, I look over to Matt. "How did the appointment go?" I reluctantly ask.

His body goes stiff as a board, obviously surprised by my question.

"I'll give you guys some privacy," Julio says off to my side, already walking towards the end of the exam room. Closing the door behind him, Matt reaches down to grip the edge of the bed. His shoulders slump forward as he drops his head, looking frustrated as he takes in a deep breath.

He gradually lifts his head to look at me. "Not as I had planned, but it's for the best," he replies, looking drained. "You won't ever have to worry about Lisa, she was lying the whole time."

His words confuse me. "What do you mean? She isn't pregnant?" I hesitantly ask him, holding my breath for his response.

He steps closer to me so he's standing right in front of me. "She's pregnant, but the baby isn't mine," he answers with a slow shake of his head. "She tried to pin the pregnancy on me to find herself a father for her baby. The doctor confirmed it couldn't be mine; she's too far along. She admitted how she showed up at the house attempting to seduce Trey, but I was an easier target because I was already drunk. I know I fucked up, beautiful, but I promised you I wouldn't fuck up again," he says cradling my head in his hands to bring our heads together. "And I'm going to make sure it never happens again. I won't let anything come between us *ever again."*

I close my eyes as he holds me. "I hate this," I say into his neck.

He pulls away to look at me. "They'll be here soon, don't worry." Obviously he didn't get my true meaning. "No, I mean I hate how all these lies are coming between us," I clarify. "If Lisa wouldn't have lied in the first place, I would have never left. We wouldn't be fighting all the time." From his expression I can tell he now understands. "All these lies are the cause of me not trusting you. Not trusting you is the reason why I thought you were cheating on me with Laura and why I took it out on your car."

Closing his eyes he bleakly replies, "Did you have to remind me?" With a smile he adds, "Like you said, a car can be fixed, but you are my heart, beautiful, and without you, I'm heartless," he insists before kissing me.

Savoring his kiss, I pull him tighter to me as I pull him down on top of me. With a quick knock on the door we break away, both our heads snapping in the direction of the door to see a doctor and a smiling Julio behind him.

"I'm sorry to interrupt you, but I have your films from your x-ray," he says, looking embarrassed.

Matt pulls away from me to stand at my side again. The doctor goes straight to a computer in the corner of the room, waking it up. "Due to the results to your x-ray, I'd like to refer you to an orthopedic specialist. You have quite a bit of tissue swelling in your ankle and I'm not getting a definite result as to whether it's fractured or not. I went ahead and called one of the best specialist in town and made you an appointment for the end of this week, but until then, you're going to have to stay off it completely to avoid any further injury," he explains.

It's not the answer I want to hear. "That's it? She waits until she sees the specialist?" Matt asks, still demanding further clarification.

"I'm sorry. I know you want an answer whether it's fractured or not, but it's best we wait until some of the swelling has subsided and it can be looked at by an orthopedic specialist."

Leaning my head against Matt's chest, I nod my head in defeat. "Just make sure to RICE. Rest, ice, compress, and elevate during this week. I'm going to prescribe an anti-inflammatory for you to take to help decrease the swelling, but other than that, stay off it," he says before turning to face the computer again to take notes. "We can put a temporary splint on it to keep you from moving it, but you can't get it wet for the next week either."

"How am I supposed to take a shower?" I screech.

"You can wrap your ankle in a large garbage bag, just make sure you tape it tightly around the edge so no water seeps in, but other than that, I'd recommend baths with your ankle hanging over."

Growing irritated by the answers he's giving me, as if my whole ordeal is not a big deal, I shoot him with a glare at his back as he types away on the computer. I hear Julio and Matt chuckle at my reaction before I feel Matt's warm breath against my neck. "Don't worry, beautiful, I'll be happy to bathe you," he says against my skin before nipping my neck.

Normally, it would turn me on that he's kissing me this way, but right now I'm ready to take anyone down who messes with me. The doctor turns to face me. "Don't worry, doc, I'll make sure she follows your orders this week," Matt says from my side.

"Great. You can pick up your prescription at the pharmacy on the first floor after you're discharged. A nurse should be in shortly to have you sign your discharge papers and you'll be ready to go," he announces with a smile before quickly exiting the room.

If it wasn't for the fact that I cannot physically walk because of missing the mobility of my right ankle, I would be getting up from this bed and strangling that man. Julio's reaction is to laugh, making me now convey my anger towards him. My glare doesn't affect him at all as he responds by shaking his head at me.

It's not long until I'm being wheeled out in a wheelchair and picking up my prescription. With my car already at the pick-up lane in the front of the hospital, Matt helps me into the car, shutting the door after I'm safely inside. Expecting for Julio to climb into the driver's seat, I'm stunned when I see Matt climbing in instead. "What are you doing?" I ask him as I watch him start the car.

Without a sideways glance, he puts the car into drive and is soon pulling away from the hospital. "What does it look like I'm doing? I'm driving you home," he replies. "Being that you've made sure to put my car out of commission, I figured you wouldn't mind me using *your* car. You can't drive anyway, so it's better this way," he adds, with a mocking grin.

Folding my arms over my chest, I turn to face the other direction to look out the window. He's right. Even if I don't like the idea of him driving my car, or anyone else for that fact, I cannot drive myself around since it's my right ankle that is injured. And I am the reason why he cannot drive his own car, the guilt of my mistake taking over again.

Having to admit you've fucked up is tormenting, but I can now understand how Matt feels.

Chapter Fifteen

Matt

I CAN TELL by the scowl on Abigail face as she stares out of the passenger side window that she isn't too happy about me driving her car. To be honest, I'd much rather be driving my car as well, but I can't. It isn't long before we're pulling up to the house and I'm killing the engine.

Climbing out of her car, I make my way over to her door to open it. She looks up at me with perplexed eyes. "Why didn't you take me to Kelly's?" she asks as I reach down to wrap my arms under her body to pull her out. Without hesitation, she wraps her arms around my neck as I start walking with her. "I'm taking you inside," I inform her. "We made a bet and you lost. I'm claiming my prize," I remind her.

"Where's Julio, isn't he supposed to be following behind us?" she states, craning her neck to peer over my shoulder.

"He isn't coming. I told him to take Trey's Jeep home with him and I'd go back for it later."

"You already had this planned, didn't you?" she teases with a hint of humor in her words.

"I told the doctor I'd make sure you would rest your ankle and I intend to keep my word. This is the only way I can make sure you don't disobey me."

Already shutting the door behind us, we enter the house.

She doesn't say anything as she lays her head on my shoulder and I walk with her down the hallway. Reaching the room, I place her down on the bed, fluffing the pillows behind her so she's able to sit upright.

"I'm going to go get you a glass of water so you can take your medication," I tell her, placing a kiss on her temple before I walk out of the room.

Heading to the kitchen, I see Trey lying on the couch. "So what's up with supermodel?"

Opening up the fridge to grab the water container, I grab a glass next as I say, "They couldn't really tell us what's wrong with her ankle. They scheduled an appointment with a specialist for the end of this week," I explain to him as I pour Abigail's water. I'm already walking back towards the room when Trey drops a bomb with the next question. "How did your appointment with Lisa go?" he asks, making me stop dead in my tracks.

I turn to face him. "You're one lucky fucker I was the one here that night, because had it been you, you'd be the one I'd be congratulating on her pinning you as her baby daddy," I convey.

His face grows confused as if not comprehending my words. "She came over that night, already knocked up, looking for you. She planned on pining the baby on you, but I was the stupid one to fuck her instead."

"No fucking way!" he barks out.

Nodding my head, I tell him, "She saw you as an easy target."

"Good fucking thing I wasn't here," he cheerfully says with a smile. "So how did you find out?"

I relay what happened at the doctor's appointment to him, his eyes wide in shock when I finish. "Man, that's some fucked up shit she pulled."

"Yeah, because of her the last month has been a living hell between Abigail and I. You fucking owe me one for taking your place that night," I state before turning to make my way back to Abigail, but not before I hear Trey shout, "Anytime man. Just let me know when it is I can have my turn with Abigail."

"Not a chance in hell!" I shout back at him before entering the room to find Abigail already asleep on the bed. She has the covers pulled up to her chin, her angelic face on the pillow as she peacefully sleeps. Shutting the door, I walk over to the bed and place the water along with medication on the bedside table. Taking off my shoes, I go over to the other side of the bed to climb in next to her. She must have felt me because she turns her body to face me, her arms wrapping around my body, and her face finding the crook of my neck. Careful with her ankle as I entwine my legs with hers, I pull her body tighter against mine. My thoughts return to the events of the last month and all the trials that our relationship was put through. Then my mind turns to thoughts of Emily. I'm pretty sure she has something to do with everything that has happened. I have Abigail back now and I wasn't letting her go this time.

Abigail

WE'RE SITTING IN the exam room. A combination of both relief and anxiety is building within me as I rub at my ankle.

"You look pretty happy to have the splint off." Matt's teasing words make me look up to him. "Yeah, more than happy. That stupid thing was starting to drive me nuts. I didn't realize how much I'd miss taking a shower until I could no longer take one," I reply.

With a light chuckle Matt gets up from the chair he was sitting in to stand next to me. "You didn't like the baths you took?"

"It wasn't fun trying to get in and out of them, even with your help."

The anxiety returns, making me tremble. "You cold, beautiful?" Matt asks, already wrapping his arms around me, rubbing my back to soothe me.

Resting my head against his chest, I listen to his heartbeat and it calms my nerves. "No, I'm just scared of what the doctor is going to say," I say into his chest.

"Everything is fine. We made sure to keep you off your ankle this last week, at least for the duration that I was home," he says with a mocking chuckle.

Pinching him in his side for his comment doesn't do anything but earn me a full-blown laugh instead. "You can't complain you didn't like it," he huskily whispers as he nuzzles my ear, making me shiver from the memory.

Instead of admitting anything, my mind goes back to the week of having to be on my ass, most of it being the entire time in bed. It really did suck having to hop around on one foot when I did have to get up from the bed, which is why I stayed in it, even when Matt was gone. I *was* able to catch up on all my favorite reality shows and brush up on my Spanish while he was at school or practice.

"If it wasn't for the TV you put in your room, I might have been tempted to get up sooner," I tell him.

He leans his body back to look down at me. "Our room, Abigail. It's our room, not *my* room," he reminds me. "When you learn to accept calling it *our* room again, I'll stop reminding you."

I'm about to agree with his words when the doctor walks in. "Hello, Ms. Adams. I've got the results of your most recent scan," he says, holding up an x-ray film before walking over to a box on the wall that lights up and sticking the film into it. The grey film of my x-rayed ankle glows with the illumination of the light behind it. "Looks like I've got an answer for you," he says with a smile.

A smile now spreads across my face; hopeful it's good news since he has a smile on his face. "You've got a High Ankle Sprain."

"That's good then, right? It's only a sprain, which means

it's not broken and I can start running again, soon."

The discouraging expression on his face makes my heart sink. "Unfortunately, this isn't a normal sprain. Although it isn't fractured, this type of sprain will most likely keep you off your foot for a minimum of eight weeks, sometimes requiring up to six months, depending on how long your foot *requires* to heal," he states.

I can feel my heart sink to my stomach. Matt pulls me tighter against his body, as if sensing my worry. "I don't understand. If it's only a sprain, why does she have to treat it as if it's broken?" he asks, the question traveling through my mind.

"This type of injury happens when the ankle bends in an unusual way. When Ms. Adams twisted it, her ankle might have rolled simultaneously with the twist, causing her to split a ligament that holds the two lower leg bones together. As I mentioned, she didn't fracture the bone, but she did tear a ligament. She's actually quiet lucky the tear is already healing and doesn't require surgery like most patients do. The good news is, she will most likely heal if she continues to not put too much pressure on it, and with the assistance of a walking boot, she may be able to walk around when needed," he explains.

I'm taking in his words, but as I absorb them, they're scrabbling around in my head as they all blend together. The only thing I understand is not being able to run. It's my worst fear, what I was praying would never happen. The anguish of knowing I cannot do the one thing I began to do to take the pain away is now gone.

I feel Matt trying to comfort me by holding me and whispering reassuring words into my ear, but it isn't helping as I take in the realization that the one thing that bonded us together is now gone for the next six months.

"It's okay, Abigail, it's not forever, it's only temporary," he continues to whisper into my ear as I sit in my shocked state.

"He's correct. You'll require physical therapy when your boot is removed, but you *will* be able to run again," the doctor adds to Matt's words.

Pulling my face away from Matt's body, I look over to the doctor to ask the one question that is most important to me at this moment. "Will I be able to run Boston?"

His face sinks, as if he's unwilling to answer my question. "We won't be able to know until we take an MRI of your ankle after you've recovered from you're injury. I would hate to give you false hopes in case you're unable to recover fast enough."

"Yes or no," I demand.

"Ms. Adams, let's take it one step at a time. First we need to focus on your recovering ankle, after that, you have therapy. Depending on the progress of your therapy, we'll have an answer then," he replies.

Pussy, as Trey would call him for not wanting to give me an answer.

"Why don't we get you fitted for a boot and schedule a recheck for eight weeks," he cheerfully says. "If all goes well and you follow instructions, you may just be completely healed and ready for physical therapy then," he adds.

I hate the solution he's providing me with, but I'm left with no choice at this point. Begrudgingly, I nod my head in agreement. I feel the brush of Matt's lips against my brow as he squeezes my body tighter in his embrace.

An hour later, I'm wobbling out of the exam room with the ugliest damn boot I will ever wear, I know for a fact, because I'm damn well not going to be wearing something like this ever again in the future. At least I hope I won't after this whole fiasco is over. I'm already exhausted from this morning and all I want to do is go *home*.

Chapter Sixteen

Matt

I'M LYING ON the couch with Abigail draped across my chest. The couch is wide enough for the both of us to lie side by side, but this is the way I prefer to be. I think she likes it just as much since she was the one who had climbed on top of me. At first another idea had come to mind, but when she made herself comfortable with her head facing the TV to watch what was on, I'd gotten the point she just wanted to lie here with me as she watched her show.

I could care less what was on TV, as long as it kept her with me. My hand slowly caresses up and down her back so I can feel more of her, even if it's through a layer of clothing. It's enough for me to keep this blissful feeling I have when she's near.

I know she's upset about not being able to run this morning. The weeks that have gone by and not being able to run are slowly catching up to her. The agitation was clear on her face when she woke up and the sun was shining through the window. Although the pancakes I'd made her brought a smile to her face, it was quickly diminished when the sun shined through the windows. It was the perfect day to run and she couldn't do it. I can't blame her. When she left, she took away the one thing that made me happy: her presence. It tore at my heart not to have the one person who made me smile, so I understand how Abigail feels.

A commercial comes on and she turns her face to look at me, her chin resting upon my chest. She gives me a simple smile and I cannot resist giving her a kiss on the nose. Her smile grows wider. "What do you want to do today, beautiful?"

I watch her smile turning into a frown as she sighs. "Since I can't do much, this is pretty much it," she resentfully says.

"I can think of something else we can do that wouldn't require you to move too much," I tease as I grab her ass, earning me a yelp.

I pull her head down with my other hand to give her a kiss, pushing my hips up between her legs. She moans into my mouth when she feels how ready I am for her. We deepen our kiss, and as I'm about to stand her up and carry her to our room, we're interrupted when Trey walks into the house.

"Alright," he exclaims, cheerfully pumping his fist in the air, "I made it just in time for the porno show." I break our kiss so I can scowl at him.

"What? Don't stop just because I'm here," he says, tossing himself onto the other couch.

"Why are you barely getting home?" Abigail asks him, already forgetting what we were doing. My hardened dick hasn't as it pushes itself against her hip. I lift myself again to tease her and she looks down at me, warning me to stop. I ignore her as I lift my head to kiss her on the neck, lightly sucking on her skin. I know this would normally make her weak, but instead Abigail pinches me on my side, making me wince.

I look back at Trey. "I didn't know I had to check in with you, too. I'm not the one who's strapped at the balls," Trey sarcastically answers. "I was out DP'ing a young new freshman that was looking to have a little fun," he says, his lips teasing up to one side.

"What does Dr. Pepper have to do with you being out all night?" Abigail asks, looking lost from his words. Trey's booming laughter fills the room and I cannot help but join him, causing Abigail to become irritated. "What are you both laughing about?"

I mask the remainder of my laughter with a cough. "Beautiful, he's not talking about Dr. Pepper," I explain as I watch her grow even more confused. I lift my head up to her ear to explain what Trey was doing and when I pull my head back, her eyes go wide in shock as her mouth drops down.

"Trey Johnson, how can you do something like that?" she says, still shocked and obviously confused.

"It's quiet simple," he smugly replies. "Matt and I can show you if you'd like. We've shared plenty of times," he answers with a smirk.

"Shut the fuck up, Trey," I growl, hoping she doesn't comprehend the meaning of his statement, but by the disgusted look on her face she clearly has. She lifts herself off my body, making me let out an exasperated breath. I sit up with her, trying to pull her back down onto me, but it doesn't work as she yanks her arm back and starts walking away. "I'm going to go take a shower," she firmly states without giving me a backwards glance as she wobbles her way to the room.

I look over at Trey, shooting daggers straight at him. "You couldn't keep your fucking mouth shut, could you?"

He shrugs his shoulders. "What does she expect? She knows you weren't a saint before she met you. Why should it surprise her what we did?"

I'm ready to kill him, but I have to tame my anger and remember this is Trey. It shouldn't *surprise* me. "She might know I wasn't a saint, but I'd rather she didn't have to be reminded of it."

"If you want to live your life strapped to one girl now, then that's fine with me. Just don't expect me to," he demands.

"I can't wait until you find someone. I'll be the one laughing then," I tell him, already making my way over to Abigail's room to start kissing some ass, which I don't mind doing since it's her ass.

I find Abigail standing against the counter of the bathroom

using it to balance herself while struggling to remove a pair of yoga pants she's wearing. "Here, let me help you with that," I tell her, already reaching for her waistline. Placing her hand on my shoulder to hold on as she bears all her weight on her good leg, I carefully pull down her pants, stopping at the knees. She's looking at me confused until I lift her up to sit on the counter, doing it so she's not tempted to put weight on her other foot. Continuing with my task, I take her pants and underwear off, leaving her naked from the waist down. Her shirt comes off next as I make sure to keep my eyes locked onto hers.

She shyly smiles back at me and I know my tactic is work-ing. Although she has the hint of a smile of her lips, her eyes are telling me otherwise. They looked saddened. "Tell me what's wrong, beautiful," I bravely say, not wanting to upset her any more than she already is.

She looks up towards the ceiling as she sighs. "I just hate how I will always be reminded of your past. Whether it's from my memories or your friends, they will always be there," she grimly states. "I keep telling myself I have to accept it because it's *your* past, but it's harder than expected sometimes," she fin-ishes with a whisper. She leans forward to rest her head against my chest, but I force her to look up at me.

"Abigail, I've already told you, you're my future. It's all I want you to remember," I tell her before I kiss her. I slowly kiss her and by the way I feel her nails digging into my hair I know I've managed to distract her. My hands begin to roam up and down against her naked skin, teasing her. I reach for the clasp of her bra to unclip it so I can remove it completely from her body. I want to feel her breast in my hands. My lips gradually kiss their way down her neck, then down to her breast to take her nipple in my mouth, sucking vigorously just how she likes. Her nails dig deeper into my hair and her legs wrap around my waist pulling me tighter in between her legs. Letting go of my head, she starts tugging at my clothing, demanding I take them off. Pulling myself away from her body to remove my shorts, I use the opportunity to sink to my knees and take the center of her heat into my mouth.

I'm rewarded with a satisfied moan as her nails are once again digging into my scalp. Gradually I lap my tongue up and down her core, nipping and tugging at her clit as I purposely tease her, wanting to prolong her pleasure. It's never taken me long to bring Abigail to the brink of ecstasy. It's as if her body was made especially for me as I've memorized every touch needed to satisfy her. Hearing her breathlessly yell out my name should bring me satisfaction, but it doesn't; being inside Abigail when she does it is what I need.

Standing up, I'm staring at a flushed and breathless Abigail. Positioning myself at her opening I hear a banging on our door. "Go away, we're busy!" I yell out, earning me a chuckle from Abigail's lips as she nips at my neck.

Abigail's walls of her core surround my dick as I hear the banging once more, making me pause. I already know it's Trey at the door. His knock is unmistakable.

"If you don't fucking leave, Trey, I'm going to beat your fucking ass!" I yell to the door.

"You're going to want to come out here, Matt!" he shouts back.

By the way he says the words, I already know something is wrong.

Abigail is already trying to shove me away as she attempts to wiggle her way off the counter. I stop her, holding her firmly against the counter with my hands so she doesn't try landing on her injured ankle.

"It's probably nothing," I say against her lips as I kiss her to calm her nerves. "You stay here. If you move I won't be finishing what I started," I amusedly add.

Quickly finding my clothes, I dress and head out of the bathroom, but stop briefly to take one last glance at Abigail sitting on the counter. "I mean it, I don't want you walking around on your ankle any more than you have to."

I watch her roll her eyes. "Yes, doctor," she sarcastically replies.

My eyebrow raise high. "Hmmm, now you're giving me ideas. I'll make sure to thoroughly examine you when I get back." With the thought engraved in my head, I turn to leave the room, already coming up with the possibilities of what I can do as her doctor. My thoughts involve a lot more than simply *touching*.

From the hallway, I can see Trey pulling a beer from the fridge and I make my way straight to him. "I thought you were done being a cock blocker?" I say, watching his lips go up into a smug grin.

Within seconds my eyes avert to the reason as it catapults itself into my arms, forcing me to catch her. "I was afraid you weren't here because I didn't see your car outside."

"What are you doing here, Laura?" I ask her, confused as I attempt to push her away, but she holds on to me preventing me from doing so.

"You didn't call me when you promised you would. I got worried. I tried going straight to your room to leave my luggage, but Trey wouldn't let me," she expresses with a pout.

"What the hell would make you come all the way over here? You could have just called me." This time I manage to escape her embrace, but it's was too late as I see Abigail already standing beside me with her arms crossed over her chest.

"I told you to wait for me in the room." The reprimand un-intentionally comes out. Her eyes go straight to Laura. "I see why," she delivers through clenched teeth.

"It's not what you think. I didn't even know she was here," I tell her, feeling the need to defend myself for some odd reason. "I just didn't want you walking around on your ankle."

"What is she doing here?" Laura screeches from my side.

Turning back to Laura, I say, "She lives here."

"Oh man this is getting good," Trey announces from the kitchen.

I ignore him, making a mental note to beat his ass later for the remark. Laura delivers a disgusted look as her head whips back and forth between Abigail and me. "How convenient."

"What is that supposed to mean?" Abigail throws back at her, the anger radiating from her eyes. I stand in between the two of them, hoping to prevent Abigail from ripping Laura's eyes out.

"Holy, shit, I should have made some popcorn for this," Trey whoops from behind us. Abigail whips her head at Trey, glaring at him, my eyes finding Laura's. "She's always lived here. Since I met her."

"You told me you were only her assistant."

"What does it matter to you?" Abigail snarls at Laura.

Laura's eyes are raking Abigail's body. "Is she another one of your convenient fucks?"

I can feel Abigail trembling at my side. I know it's not from fear, but from the anger I can feel emanating from her body. "Laura," I groan out as a warning before Abigail can say anything. "What are you *really* doing here?" I ask, knowing she wouldn't just show up to surprise me, she never has.

With her lips in a pout she whines, "I wanted to get away from all the drama at my house. I figured I'd come stay with you for a while. You promised I was always welcome."

I hear Abigail snicker. "By all means, Matt, let her stay. I'd hate for you to break your promise," she sarcastically remarks.

Facing Laura again, I tell her, "You can't stay here."

"Why not?"

"Because you're not welcome!" Abigail throws back.

"Abigail, calm down."

Laura is now glaring at me. "Are you serious?" I know I'm playing with fire trying to stop her. "Oh, please. If you honestly believe he'll be faithful to you, then you're obliviously as stupid as your blonde locks make you out to be."

"Fuck you!"

"Abigail, let me handle this?" I try pleading, but from the

daggers she's still staring at me, I know I'm going to regret asking. "I can't fucking believe this! Either she goes or I do and I'm not coming back this time, Matt!" I know the words are not a threat.

"By all means, leave," Laura, mutters.

The fury is clear in Abigail's next words. "Get the fuck out!"

"You need to leave. I was in his life first," Laura replies.

I'm about to speak, but Abigail beats me to it. "You either get the fuck out, or I'm going to drag your short ass out and you'll be lucky if you leave with your limbs attached," she says with a sneering growl.

"Oh fuck. Please. I'd love to see that happen." Trey's enthusiasm is making the situation worse.

"No," Laura throws back at Abigail. "You're probably nothing more than a quick fuck when he needs it." Laura doesn't even see it coming as Abigail reaches for Laura's hair, yanking her forward and trying her best to drag her closer. Laura is frantically screaming at the top of her lungs as she stays rooted to the spot while trying to disengage herself from Abigail's grip. I try to help, but Abigail doesn't let up, instead her extreme force tugs Laura's head back and forth.

Laura is still screaming with all her might for Abigail to let her go, while Abigail is cursing her to hell if she doesn't leave. The entire time I'm begging Abigail to release Laura. Abigail finally lets up and releases her, allowing Laura to safely retreat a few steps away. The fury in Abigail's eyes is telling me she's ready to try again if Laura doesn't leave.

"Are you crazy?" Laura bellows out to Abigail while grasping her disheveled hair. "Matt?" she says, looking at me as if pleading for help as I try to bring an angry Abigail under control.

"Let me go!" she demands.

"Not if you're going to kill her!"

Laura is still looking back at me with fear in her eyes. She's obviously learned her lesson. "Beautiful, please, calm down," I whisper into her ear. I feel her body relax against mine, telling me she's heard me. "I'm done," she lets out, allowing me to breathe again. I release her from my hold, praying she doesn't attack Laura. My prayer is granted when I watch her stomp her way towards our bedroom.

"I wonder why I even took your ass back, Matt. This is what I meant by your past!" she yells from the hallway as I watch her slam the door behind her. Looking back at Laura, I see she's still holding her head, her eyes wide in shock. "You have to leave, Laura," I repeat, sternly pushing her this time.

My words make Laura's eyes go wider as she looks over in the direction of my bedroom. "You're seriously choosing her over me?"

"Yes."

"We've been together longer than you'll ever be. How can you think you have a future with her?"

"She gives me a reason to want a future. Which is why I chose her!" I shout, not knowing why I even bothered telling her, but hearing myself say it gives me some sort of fulfillment.

"Don't come running to me when she breaks your heart," she throws back at me as she stomps past me.

"It won't happen."

I don't know whether she heard me or not, but I'm already happy to see her reach for her luggage. I look over to Trey. "Can you make sure she gets somewhere safe?" I ask him, still feeling guilt ridden over everything that just happened.

He looks torn. "I'll make sure she gets to the airport," he replies, before adding, "I better not get my assed kicked by Abigail, or I'm coming after you for it."

Rolling my eyes at Trey's remark, I walk my way to the bedroom, finding Abigail pacing back and forth.

"Get out!" she shouts, her earlier fury still evident. "You're going to strain your ankle if you keep pacing that way," I calmly reply as I ignore her request.

She pierces me with her glare. "Why did you stop me?"

"Orange isn't really your color, Abigail." I tease. My remark is not what she wanted to hear. "You think I like putting up with the sluts from your past?" she throws back at me.

"Abigail, you knew from the beginning what my past was like. You chose to accept it. I don't understand why you're always making this my fault."

Snorting, she answers, "So I'm just supposed to smile while putting up with it?" My silence accompanied by a sigh doesn't help. "Why should I even have to?" she asks, still pacing.

"Because you love me." She freezes as she turns to face me, her eyes furiously looking back at me. This may or may not end well with that look.

Gradually she steps her way to me, her arms wrapping around my waist as she lays her head on my chest. "You're right," I hear her say barely above a whisper. "I'm so sorry."

"Abigail, I can't promise this will be the last time you'll have to deal with my past, but it's part of me. I can't change that."

Abigail

KNOWING HIS WORDS are true, I can only accept them. I don't say anything because in all reality, I have nothing to argue against. He's right. He had a past when I met him. I knew there would be consequences to it, but I was willing to follow my heart and fall in love with Matt. His past was now something I would have to learn to live with and accept … because I love him. In time, I know it will be worth it.

Chapter Seventeen

Abigail

"JUST PICK A fucking tree already, my balls are freezing. I may not want kids right now, but I *do* want them eventually. I'm not going to get them if my balls freeze off," Trey shouts from the next aisle of trees over.

Rolling my eyes, I take another turn looking at the rows and rows of trees ahead of us. I'm still indecisive over which to choose. They're either bald or ugly. I just want the perfect tree. Is that too much to ask?

Matt walks up to my side, his labored breathing forming a cloud of mist around us. "Beautiful, I'm beginning to regret this idea," he huffs at me.

With a chuckle I start walking again, leaving him to follow.

"If you don't pick a fucking tree, Abigail, within the next five minutes, I'm cutting down the one next to you," Trey shouts as he makes his way to join us. Rolling my eyes again, I look at which tree he's referring to, and surprisingly it looks like a winner. "I like it," I voice to Matt.

"You serious?"

Looking at him I see him eying the tree from head to toe. His head tilting back as he makes his way to the tip again. It's a tall tree, very tall, but it looks perfect in my eyes.

"I don't know if it's going to fit in the living room," he doubtfully adds.

Sighing, I fully take it in, already growing disappointed from the doubt. He's right; it might not fit in the living room. Trey, now standing beside us, plants his hands on his hips looking confused.

"Give up and admit you should've just bought a fucking tree instead of hunting one down."

"This wasn't my idea. It was Matt's. You could have stayed home if you wanted to," I remind him, remembering my offer before we left.

"What, and not offer my muscled man power to cut this thing down?" he says, holding his muscled arms up, displaying them. At least I think there are muscles underneath the sleeves of his jacket. He looks like a giant black marshmallow from the puffiness of his coat. He realizes were standing directly in front of a tree, now fully taking it in as Matt had done moments ago. "You've got to be fucking kidding me, right?"

"What, you scared you don't have enough muscle to carry this one?" I mock.

"I was only messing around. This shit is huge, supermodel. There is no fucking way that thing is going to fit in our living room." He confirms Matt's earlier statement, making me grow disappointed.

"You're right," I sadly admit before starting to walk away.

"You sure this is the one, beautiful?"

Turning around, I nervously chew on my lip as I take in the tree one last time before I nod. "Well, then, we're cutting the fucker down!" Trey shouts, holding the saw up high in the hair, imitating a lumberjack. I cannot resist laughing along with Matt.

Matt was the enthusiastic one that wanted me to have the full Christmas experience this year. It was his idea we come to a Christmas tree farm to cut down a tree. Apparently, a lot wasn't good enough for him, but in all reality, I think he secretly wanted to cut down his own tree. Trey wasn't too excited about the idea.

It was in the low forties outside, but we didn't have any snow on the ground. So what was he complaining about? It was Matt's declaration of calling him a pussy that made him jump up from the couch and beat us to the truck Matt had borrowed from a friend.

Both Matt and Trey are already on the ground sawing away at the base of the tree. Watching the back and forth motion between them makes me think a dirty thought, which I so kindly share. "Come on boys. I'm pretty sure you both have jacked off faster than that before," I tease.

"I don't know about you, Matt, but I don't need to jack off. I have girls falling on my cock all the time," Trey jokes, earning a protested moan from Matt. "I'm pretty sure it's what he was doing when you weren't around, supermodel."

"Shut the fuck up and cut faster!" Matt demands of Trey. "Or I'm going to cut your balls off next!" he shouts at him as he pulls the saw faster, making me laugh at the visualization of both statements.

It takes another couple of minutes before the tree is tumbling to the ground. Trey stands up to pump both fists in the air in triumph. His arms still are extended high above his head as he starts humming the chorus to the Rocky song, hopping back and forth on both feet. I cannot resist laughing at the sight of his cockiness.

"Alright, Rocky, now you get to carry the thing back to the truck," Matt reminds him, quickly bringing Trey's dance to a stop so he can flip Matt off with a puffy gloved finger.

Still chuckling, I begin walking to get a head start on both of them. It's takes me longer because of my boot. The walk here was already difficult enough, I'm not looking forward to wobbling my way back. I barely make it a couple of feet before I'm lifted up into the air and held within Matt's arms. I securely wrap my arms around his neck and look behind his shoulder to see Trey dragging the tree behind us.

"Why don't we exchange packages, Garcia? You can show

supermodel how manly you can be by taking this tree back for her."

"Nah, I do that enough with her in bed, she already knows I'm her man," Matt shouts over his shoulder. I chuckle at his words as Trey continues dragging the tree by its stump, grunting most of the way, but still pulling it effortlessly. The sight is comical, but nevertheless, I'm grateful for the both of their efforts today.

With us soon piling back into the truck, I lean my head back onto the seat and it's then that my ankle begins to throb, announcing I over did it today. Matt must have noticed the reaction on my face. "Is your ankle hurting you?" he worriedly asks.

Nodding my head, I take a deep breath to ward off the pain. "I'm sorry, beautiful. I shouldn't have made you come today," he guiltily admits.

I snap my head towards him. "I wouldn't have missed this for the world. It was wonderful," I say, grabbing for his chin to pull him in for a kiss. With our lips lingering, I close my eyes savoring the taste of our kiss.

"You can at least turn the heat on while you both play all lovey dovey over there. Someone's balls still need to defrost over here," Trey announces, making Matt and I laugh against each other's lips.

With a shake of his head, Matt starts up the truck, turning the heat on full blast. It's cold at first, but within minutes the truck begins to warm up. Laying my head on Matt's shoulders, my hand still entwined with his, I think back to the events of the day. The pain in my ankle is worth the memories I'm making with Matt. I'll take the pain tenfold just to be able to remember this day.

AM I DREAMING? If feels as if I am, but my surroundings feel so real, yet it still feels strange. I feel like two people in one body; one observing and the other experiencing it. This *has* to be a dream. Right?

I'm in a hallway that looks to be in a hotel. Looking to my left, I see him. The half of me that's experiencing it gives him a forced smile, while the other half of me is panicking. My breath hitches. My heart feels as it's stopped and just as rapidly began beating again.

My finger impatiently pushes at the elevator button, willing for the elevator door to open. "No matter how many times you push it, Abigail, it's not going to make it move any faster," Bill says.

"Fuck this. I'm taking the stairs," I say, already walking around him. I hear him following me and when we enter the stairway he speaks again. "We're not staying all night," he informs me as his voice echoes in our surroundings.

"Why not?"

"And I don't want you getting plastered drunk again like you did last night. You looked like shit for your photo shoot this morning. I don't want a repeat for the show tomorrow night," he lectures.

I stop to turn and face him. "You need to stop acting like a prude. I delivered during the shoot, didn't I?" He stays silent knowing I've proven my point. "So back the fuck off, Bill," I add.

I'm about to start resuming my descent when I'm halted to a stop by a hand digging into my arm. I'm yanked to look at Bill again, there's fury in his eyes. "You need to remember you're nothing without me." His words should frighten me, but they don't. "I don't need you anymore, Bill," I throw back at him. "I'm Abigail Adams and it was me who made that name for myself. I'm pretty sure it's you who needs me now," I state as I attempt to yank my arm from his grip. Instead my body is shoved back, causing me to lose my balance. My body drifts back into the air before the darkness takes over me.

I awaken gasping for air, my body uncontrollably shivering from the shock, and my body drenched in sweat. Looking around the room, I'm relieved when I see I'm in my room. Now rocking myself, I force myself to keep breathing. It's all I can do to distract myself until Matt gets home.

Matt

"THAT'S AN EXCELLENt choice, sir. The recipient is going to love it," the sales associate says.

"You sure this is what you want to do?" Trey doubtfully asks at my side.

I'm staring down at the ring in my hands, and for a second I doubt myself because of Trey's words, but I just as quickly answer, "Yes," with an excited smile.

I look up to the sales associate, giving him a stern nod. "Well, with the size of that thing, I'd be surprised if she says no," Trey mocks. I can only pray Abigail will say yes, but I have to wait to find out. I know Abigail is going to love it. At least I hope she will.

"Would you like me to wrap it up for you?"

"Yes, please," I say, handing the ring back to him.

"With pleasure, sir. I'll be back shortly."

"I can't believe you actually plan on doing this," Trey reminds me of his doubt. "I can't believe it either, but I love her and I want to do this."

He stays silent, but continues to skeptically look at me. "You'll understand when you find the right girl," I tell him.

He looks doubtful, but surprises me when he says. "I hope so, but I doubt it'd be anytime soon."

Understanding his meaning, I simply nod. The sorrowful look in Trey's eyes make me want to ask him what's wrong, but I know it's best not to pressure him. He will end up closing up on me. Instead, I focus on trying to picture Abigail's expression when she unwraps the present on Christmas morning. The glowing smile I envision is enough to light me up inside. I hope she doesn't find it until then. She's been snooping around the house, anxious to see what I've bought her. My thoughts are broken when the salesman returns with my package. The box elegantly wrapped, with a white bow surrounding it, it's the perfect looking gift.

Perfect for Abigail, just like her. She deserves nothing less.

"Happy holidays," I tell him as I take the box from him, already making my way out the door with Trey.

"Anything else you need to pick up for your family?" I ask Trey before stepping out in the brisk cold air. "Nah, I'm getting everyone gift cards this year. Can't go wrong with gift cards."

"That's not personal enough," I tell him as we make our way to his Jeep.

He delivers a snort before replying, "They should be happy I'm even getting them something at all." I cannot help but think of Abigail. Only one week until Christmas morning and she will be opening this little box. It's our first Christmas together and I'm determined to make it memorable. One she will never forget.

I may be nervous as fuck to give it to her, but deep down in my heart it's what I truly want. I tuck the box into my pocket to keep it safe, hoping that it's to her satisfaction. Only one week left until I find out.

Chapter Eighteen

Abigail

I'M IN MY favorite spot. My body draped across Matt's shirt-less chest. I could stay like this forever. Sometimes I wish I could. The sound of Matt's heartbeat against my ear and the warmth of his body radiating into mine, sends me to an element of complete relaxation. My worries and fears cease to exist while the rhythmic thump is against my ear. Add the soothing feel of Matt's arm snug around my body and it's enough to send me into a meditative state.

It's been cold out, which has kept us indoors, but I'm not complaining when it allows me to be snuggled up next to Matt. Closing my eyes, the rumble of Matt's voice vibrates in his chest, helping me drift off into sleep. Both him and Trey are discussing the game on the TV and I'm already picturing images of a dream in my mind when Matt's phone starts to ring. He shifts his body to reach for the phone, awakening me.

Shaking the sleep from my mind, I watch as he answers the phone. "Hello."

With my chin on his chest, I watch his face grow anxious as he listens to the caller on the other end. "Really?" his lips go up into a wide smile. "Yes, of course. I'll be there in about thir-ty minutes," he replies into the phone before adding, "Thanks, man!" with excitement radiating from him.

He hangs up the phone as I continue to lay on him, patiently waiting for him to share his good news with me. My patience isn't immediately rewarded, though.

"Hey, man, will you give me a ride?" Matt asks Trey before his lips find mine to give me a quick kiss. The smile is still radiating from his lips when he pulls back and I'm left staring back at him.

My expression doesn't faze him as he sits up, taking my body with him, gently shoving me off of him to leave me on the couch.

"Where are you going?" I curiously ask.

"I'm going to pick up Eleanor from the shop," he replies.

The word, *shop*, is a reminder of what I've done and the reason why she's there. No wonder why he didn't want to tell me who called. "I'll see you when you get back," I state, but the words unwillingly come out, sounding wistful instead of the marked blissfulness I was trying for.

"Uh, oh." I hear Trey playfully tease from behind us, already waiting for Matt. Normally his teasing would cause me to pierce him with a glare, but I don't bother.

He kneels in front of me. "What's wrong?" Matt asks with a chuckle.

"I get it, you don't want me near her anymore because of what I did," I state, feeling pitiful with myself.

Staring right at me, he says, "You're right, I don't want you near my car anymore," his expression confirming the reason why I should feel guilty. "At least not with any weapons that will hurt her again," he teases.

"I feel like the worst person in the world because of what I did," I say around the lump still lodged in my throat. "You keep telling me you don't care, but somehow I don't believe you. She was really important to you," I blabber out. "Oh God, I'm pathetic, I'm feeling guilty over a stupid car," I say, sinking my face into my hands. I don't know what's worse? Hearing Matt chuckle over my confession or the fact that I've finally accepted how much he cares for his stupid car.

He pulls my hands from my face so I can look at him. "Your right. She's just a car, who *I love dearly*," he admits. "As much as she means to me, you own my heart. I can always physically fix her, but it doesn't guarantee I can fix us, which is more important to me."

His words temporarily push the shame of my actions from my mind.

"I shouldn't have kept you from going to San Francisco. I shouldn't have kept anything from you. We've both made mistakes with each other, beautiful, and I'm pretty sure we're going to continue making them. No relationship is perfect," he claims. "Just promise me that no matter what happens, we can always trust each other," he pleads.

"Promise," I tell him.

Leaning forward, he kisses me on my temple, his lips lingering longer than usual. "Okay, let's go to Joey's and pick Eleanor up," he states, looking at me again. "Who is Joey?" I ask, not recognizing the name from his group of friends.

"Joey is the guy fixing what you broke," he says with a playful smile.

"Now you're the one reminding me," I tease back at him.

He looks back at me with a mischievous smile on his lips. "As I should. What did she ever do to you?" he says, striving to look mortified.

"You kept a secret from me," I reply. His smile turns into a frown. "You're right. No more secrets between us."

I understand how he feels, which is why I can easily agree.

Finding his lips, I say "No more secrets," against them with a kiss.

With a smile he tugs me up. "Let's go."

Closing the distance between us, his hands find my waist and he gently squeezes my hips. "No complaining about the smell of the shop," he adds with amusement.

Fighting the urge to scrunch my nose at his comment. I imagine the smell and give him a curt nod. "Okay, let me tell Trey we're ready," he states, giving me a kiss on the corner of my mouth before he heads to Trey's bedroom.

Wobbling my way over to the counter to where my purse is sitting, I grab it, already knowing I will need it. Twenty minutes later we're pulling up in Trey's Jeep to an auto shop and we all climb out. I take in the smell Matt had warned me about. My stomach turns a little knowing I'm a girl when it comes to things like these. Knowing I'm here for one purpose only, I force myself to ignore the smell and walk with Matt inside the office. An older gentleman is behind the counter, his face lighting up with a smile when he spots Matt. With a lift of his chin, he greets us. "Hey, boy, good to see you again," he says, with a smile on his face.

From my side I can feel Matt growing excited. "It's never been better to see you," he responds, pulling me to his side. "This is Joey. I used to play on the team with his son," he explains. "Max graduated three years ago, though. His dad is the only one I trust with any repairs on Eleanor," he adds before looking over to Joey. "So how bad was it?"

With a whistle, Joey begins speaking. "She was pretty bad as you know when you brought her in, but it wasn't as bad as we both thought. She's gotten a well-deserved makeover. Poor girl, I don't know what happened for her to deserve it, but she's shining real pretty now," he conveys.

I cringe from his words, completely ashamed of my actions. Behind me Trey bellows out, "It was this girl who beat the shit out of her."

Snapping my head up to glare over Matt's shoulder, I shoot Trey with a look. It doesn't faze him but makes him chuckle. Joey's whistle brings my attention back to him. "It was all a misunderstanding," I apologize.

"So, how much do I owe you?" Matt asks, already pulling the wallet out of his pants. I stop him by placing my hand over his, earning me a confused look. "I've got it," I tell him, my eyes already looking over to Joey. "How much do *I* owe you?" I say, digging into my purse for my wallet, opening it up to reach for my card.

Joey looks perplexed. "No, Abigail, you're not paying for it," Matt demands.

"I made the damages," I clip out, placing the card on the counter. "Please, Matt. I'll feel better knowing I've paid for them."

With a deep sigh, he gives in. "Fine, as long as it never happens again."

"I promise."

Looking back at Joey, I encourage him to take my card and this time he willingly accepts it. Within minutes, Matt has the keys to his car in his hand and we're walking to Eleanor.

"You're not coming home with me?" Matt asks, noticing I've stopped at the side of Trey's Jeep.

"Are you sure you want me anywhere near her?" I ask, eyeing his car.

He retraces his steps until he's standing in front of me. "Only if you promise to play nice with her from now on. You have to remember, she never did anything to *you*," he teases once again.

"Ha ha," I throw back at him, lightly shoving him on the chest. Without any notice, he tugs me to follow him, opening the passenger door so I can climb in. Within seconds he's at my side in the driver's seat, the roar of Eleanor's engine is soon heard. Leaning over to Matt, I reach for his face to pull it towards me, planting a kiss on his lips. "I'm sorry," I repeat against his lips.

"Let's go for a ride," he answers back.

Sitting back against my seat, I buckle myself up and he speeds off.

Chapter Nineteen

Matt

"MERRY CHRISTMAS, BEAUTIFUL," I whisper against Abigail's ear. She gives me a sleep filled mumble, but her lips turn up in a smile as she snuggles her body into mine. I cannot resist pulling her tighter against me to feel her warmth.

"Merry Christmas, Matt," she whispers back to me, her lips finding mine.

With my hand roaming down her body, I huskily whisper, "You don't want to get up and see what Santa brought you?"

I feel her chuckle against my lips. "I'm a little too old to believe in Santa anymore. But if you insist, let's get up," she replies, but instead of getting up and out of bed, she shoves me onto my back, straddling my hips. "I take it you were Santa?" she curiously asks with a smile as she takes in my already dressed state.

I fail to hide the smile I was trying to contain. "Maybe," I whisper, already running my hands on her silky smooth skin. Lifting myself up, I leave an open mouth kiss against her neck. "Although, I should have put you on the naughty list this year," I say against her skin, now trailing my lips down her shoulder.

Her body shudders in my arms. "If that were the case, I'll make sure to make a mental note to give Santa extra special favors so that doesn't happen," she purrs back at me.

"In that case, you're permanently on the naughty list from here on out," I tell her before slamming my lips onto hers. She grinds her body against my hips and I'm already aroused from our conversation. It doesn't take much when it comes to Abigail, my need to be one with her is easily awakened as I willingly give in to her request.

An hour later, our bodies are spent and exhausted and I remember why I'd woken Abigail in the first place. "That was the best way to wake up on Christmas morning," I whisper against her sweaty skin, leaving another kiss.

"Yes, it is," she says, still slightly out of breath, wrapping her body into mine to fall back asleep.

"Oh no, it's time to get up and open your presents."

Giving me a smile, she says, "Okay."

I watch as she sits up at the edge of the bed to put her boot on and is soon wobbling her way over to the bathroom. Without having to see her face, I know she's grimacing the entire way there.

Climbing out of bed, I grab for my clothes that are scattered around on the floor and dress. Before long, Abigail and I are making our way to the living room where the Christmas tree is twinkling with the white lights and bright ornaments she had chosen. The sight of the tree brings back the memory of the day we cut it down, my lips curving up into a smile as I remember. My goal to make this Christmas special for Abigail is proving to be effortless as her face lights up from the sight off all the presents I placed around the tree—the reaction I was hoping for.

Making ourselves comfortable, we sit near the tree. I watch as Abigail reaches for the presents, sorting the ones we obviously won't be opening to the side. Even though they weren't here celebrating with us, she made sure to get one for everybody, if not two. Trey had gone home for the holidays, leaving a few days ago, and David and Kelly were spending it between both their parents' homes. Julio was with his mom visiting their family in Mexico, a gift from Abigail for both of them, leaving

Abigail and I alone, which I was all too happy about.

I smile as I accept a wrapped box from Abigail and open it. Inside is a leather bound photo book. Opening it, the first picture I see is one of Emily holding me as a newborn. It was taken on the day my parents brought me home. Flipping the page, I find another picture of Emily and I playing in our childhood back-yard as kids. She's already a teenager and the gleeful smile on her face as she chases me brings tears to my eyes.

"Where did you find these pictures?"

"I hope you don't mind, but I went through the garage to find them," she replies in a whisper. "I know it hurts to look at them sometimes, but I wanted you to have something you can eventually look back at from time to time that reminds you of Emily."

Flipping through more pages, they continue to remind me of her and I cannot help but keep a smile on my face. "Hopefully one day you'll be able to share it with your children," Abigail adds.

My head snaps up at that remark as hopeful thoughts of children with Abigail run through my mind. "Thank you, beau-tiful. It's perfect," I tell her, giving her a kiss. "I'll treasure it forever," I add against her lips. Almost an hour later, we're both surrounded by a mountain of wrapping paper, when I hear Ab-igail say, "I think that is all of them," with a giggle, already gathering the wrapping paper in her hands.

"Nope, I think you missed one," I say, nodding my head up at the tree.

With a look of confusion she says, "I don't think so. Those left aren't ours."

With a smile, I reach forward and push a couple of boxes aside to grab the one present I hid in the tree. I made sure to use the decorated ribbon to hide it. My nerves are on end as I'm reaching for it. The sooner she opens the box, the sooner I will see the smile on her face.

I bring the box out and hand it to her. I watch as her eyes

go wide and stay locked on the small turquoise box in my hands, her body now rigid as she stares down at it, worrying me. She doesn't reach for it, but instead she looks at me with haunted eyes that are turning glassy.

Swallowing, she asks, "Is this what I think it is?" the fear clear in her eyes.

"Why don't you open it and find out," I answer.

She shakes her head. "No, Matt," she whispers, making my heart plunge to the pit of my stomach. Looking back down at the box, I push it towards her. "Beautiful," I manage to muster before she holds up her hand to stop me from speaking.

"Don't, Matt," she says weakly.

"Why?" I fearfully ask.

I'm still holding the box, but the rejection is now creeping up inside of me. Her eyes are still frightfully locked onto the box as she slowly retreats from it. "I can't," she utters, before she stands and rushes to the bedroom as fast as she can.

Shocked, I sit there staring at the box in my hand trying to understand what just happened. I don't know how long I sit there alone, lost in a daze as I stare at the elegantly wrapped bow. When I come to my senses, I force myself to stand and make my way to the bedroom. I reach the opened door, already hearing her whimpered cries as I enter.

Abigail is lying on the bed, her face against the pillow trying to muffle her cries, but it fails. I place the box on our dresser, ignoring the fact that she still hasn't touched it. Walking my way over to the edge of the bed, I gaze down at her.

"Why?" I repeat.

She turns her face from the pillow. "I'm sorry, Matt, but I can't give you the answer you want. It wouldn't be fair," she whimpers out.

"Why not?"

"I don't think we're ready for this," she says before sniffling.

Her denial is tearing me apart. I never in my mind envisioned her rejection. Instead I'd pictured a cheerful, *"Yes."*

She's looking at me with pleading eyes as if begging for my sympathy, but I cannot grant her wish. Instead, I give her the answer she would prefer to hear. "Fine, I won't ask again," I say before turning to leave her to cry alone in the room, walking past the perfect Christmas I had worked so hard to create for her, storming straight out of the house, wishing I could take it all back.

Abigail

I SIT IN the silence in which Matt has left me, wondering *what have I done*? My body is trembling from the shock of watching him leave. I can no longer control the tears streaming down my face; they're too fast for me to stop. My heart feels as if it's shattered, yet again. Why do we keep doing this to each other? Will we ever stop causing each other pain? There is no one to blame this time but myself. My selfish heart broke on its own, but I couldn't lie to him. It wouldn't be fair to either of us. I refuse to deceive him by giving him a false answer.

Pushing myself up from the bed, my eyes find the box staring back at me like a beacon brightly shining in my direction. I'm afraid to approach it, unwilling to acknowledge its existence. It pains me to think of the intention behind the single object. It represents Matt's passionate love for me, a love in which he felt the need to propose. I think of the possibilities it would have brought: a lifetime of happiness with Matt, the prospect of children, the acknowledgement of growing old with him. But can I truly believe it will always be the fairytale I craved in my heart? It was the same fairytale I believed I would have with Matt when he declared his love to me, but just as quickly my fairytale came crashing down the next morning. It's the reason why I still have my doubts of a future with Matt. I *truly do* love him, but I don't believe we're ready yet. I'm not ready. Why couldn't he understand that?

Still ignoring the box, I walk past it and out to the living room, stopping in the middle of what's left of Christmas morning. The sea of wrapping paper surrounding my feet is a reminder of my once joyful experience. From the corner of my eye, I see snowflakes slowly descending to the ground, bringing a smile to my lips from the thought of a winter wonderland. With the excitement of a child, I rush back to my room for a coat and my shoes, hastily putting them on before I'm rushing out the patio door. The feeling of the snowflakes hitting my body evokes my inner child.

I'm startled when Matt's arms tighten around my waist, my lips immediately saying, "I'm sorry." Turning by body, I step out of his embrace.

His head tilts to the side a moment before saying, "You have nothing to be sorry about, beautiful. You're right, maybe it's too soon, but I don't know any other way to tell you how much I love you."

His words demand I look up to him. "I don't need for you to propose in order for you to prove how much you love me, Matt. You show me every day."

He leans his chin against my head as I continue. "I love you just as much and I hope you believe me as well," I declare.

I feel him sigh before he answers. "I do."

The snow continues to fall around us as we silently hold each other. It's when I feel Matt shiver in my arms that I realize he isn't wearing a coat. "Matt, why don't you have a jacket on?" I scold him, trying to push him back into the house, but he keeps his feet planted to the spot, holding me.

"I swear, you're the most beautiful thing I've ever seen," he softly whispers into my ear. The words leave me breathless and dizzy, a reminder of why I love him so much.

"It is beautiful," I reply, holding my hand up to catch a

snowflake, my bracelet reflecting in the sun as I stare down at it melting in my hand. "I don't remember ever being in the snow before."

Matt looks down at me confused. "You don't? I know it snows in Seattle."

"It probably does, but I don't have any memories of it," I state with a sigh. "Another fault of my memory loss," I mumble.

His lips go up into a smile. "Good, then consider this your first time in the snow. Another first I get to spend with you," he conveys, making me smile with him.

"Yes, another first," I whisper as his thumb brushes against the charms on my wrist. "Do you miss it?" he questions.

Not understanding the meaning behind his question, I ask, "Miss what?"

"Your memory?"

My eyes look down at my bracelet as well. "No," I say, above a whisper. "The only memories I want to have are the ones with you. I promise," I answer without a doubt in my heart.

His answer is a continued silence that is slightly worrying me. "Matt, my *no* isn't forever, but it's my answer for now," I explain. "Will you please just give me time?" I plead.

I worry as I wait for his answer. "Of course," he replies, pulling me tightly into his body and I feel as if I can finally breathe again. Matt being the air I need.

Chapter Twenty

Abigail

I'M LOOKING AT the reminder staring back at me from the screen of my phone. I'm already grimacing with the thought of having to tell Matt. I'd forgotten about the stupid appointment and fear mentioning it to him. I glance over at him lying next to me as he stares into his book that he's supposed to be studying.

"Matt, I don't remember. Do you have class on Wednesday mornings?" I casually ask.

"I have an early morning class at seven. Why?" he says, now looking at me with interest.

Contemplating whether to tell him or not, I bite my lip as I watch his eyebrow go up high on one side. "What are you keeping for me now?"

Cringing to myself, I reply, "I wasn't intentionally trying to keep it from you, I simply forgot to tell you."

Rolling his body so he's directly above me, he cradles himself in between my legs. "And what is it you simply forgot?" he asks with a hint of laughter in his eyes.

"I forgot about my neurologist appointment," I answer, my finger tracing the outlines of his tattoo while holding my breath for the lecture I'm expecting. "Is it on Wednesday?" he asks.

Nodding my head, I continue to wait for a reaction, my eyes

focused on his arm. He surprises me when he leans down to give me a kiss on the corner of my lips. "Okay, then I guess where going to your appointment next week."

"But if you have class, I can't let you miss it. I'll just ask Julio instead," I say, already feeling disappointed.

He shakes his head. "Regardless if I had class or not, I'm not missing your appointment, beautiful," he says, and I smile. "I guess it's a road trip to Seattle on Wednesday," I reply, earning me a chuckle.

My mind cannot help but return to the worry I've had for the past month.

"Why so serious? Tell me what's wrong," he says, his voice laced with concern. "I feel like a disappointment," I admit.

"Is it why you've been keeping the appointment a secret?"

Glowering at him, I say, "I already told you, I forgot. I've had other things on my mind since I made the appointment."

He wags his eyebrows before his mouth dives below my ear to place a kiss. "Oh, yeah. And what specifically has been distracting you?" he asks, his warm breath laces against my skin. An uncontrollable shiver glides down my body as he kisses his way across my lips, trying to district me; It's working. My earlier disappointment is now gone.

"I still think you were purposely keeping it a secret so you wouldn't have to go," he mocks, still kissing my neck. "Like you haven't kept any secrets from me?" I throw back at him, now tilting my head back to allow better access to my neck. He snaps his head back and I'm expecting him to look outraged, but instead he looks guilty, my heart coming to a halt when he replies. "You're right. I've only kept one secret from you," he states.

Panic rises within me. "Oh, and what was that?" I ask, dreading his response. I can feel my heart racing as I think of the many possibilities.

Leaning forward, he kisses my lips as if to distract me. Instead of pulling away, he leaves our lips mere inches apart. I can feel the warmth of his breath against my mouth. "I should have told you sooner how much I loved you," he whispers against them. Closing my eyes I feel as if I can breathe again. "I love you, beautiful," he adds, making my heart swell.

I'M STUFFING MY mouth with another forkful of pancakes when my phone pings. My body tenses from the sound. "It's almost time to leave," Matt says near my ear before nipping at my shoulder. The arms that are securely wrapped around my waist tighten, as if reassuring me everything is going to be okay. Next his fingers dig into my sides, making me giggle. "That's more like it," he says.

Turning in Matt's lap to better face him, his tongue darts out to lick at the corner of my lips, making me shiver. "You had some whipped cream on your lips," he utters. "We better leave if we don't want to be late."

His words leave me disappointed. "We don't have to go. We can stay and do something else," I tease, pushing myself back against the hips I'm currently sitting on. I feel him moan against my skin. "If I'm not mistaken, I'd think you're trying to get out of going, beautiful. I don't know what you're so scared of," his lips whisper against my temple.

"That's easy for you to say. You didn't wake up in the hospital with amnesia," I remind him.

"True, but I'm positive we share the same memory from six months ago," he says, making me wonder which one he's referring to. "It was the day you knocked on that door," he says with a tilt of his head towards the front door, making me smile.

It reminds me of my dream. I've purposely pushed it to the back of my mind. The day it happened I sat trembling until I heard Matt walk in the front door. I'd composed myself enough for him to engulf me in his arms, instantly making me feel better. Since then, I haven't thought of it again.

Still staring at the door, I reply, "I can't believe it's been six months since we've met," As I tighten our embrace. "It was the best day of my life," he responds. "The first of many to come," he adds, as if promising me many more. Regardless of the circumstances of how it came to be, it will *always* be one of the best days of my life.

My thoughts are easily detoured into another direction when his lips find mine for a kiss. His intention was to simply kiss me, but the sweetness of his words awaken a hunger for something more than food. Deepening the kiss, I start tugging up his shirt, my hands already creeping down his stomach to reach for what I want. I can hear the clatter of the dishes behind us before his hands tighten their grip on my waist and he lifts me up off his lap and onto the table.

"You win, but this is going to be quick," he growls against my lips before his mouth dives back down to the hollow of my neck to kiss and torture me. The warmth of his palms slowly skims my skin, leaving a current of electricity in their wake as his tongue licks its way across my skin. My legs hook around his waist to pull our bodies closer together. Lifting my shirt off, his fingers are soon unhooking my bra, pulling it off and away. His mouth starts trailing its way down my body, his lips finding my breast as I hold his head in my palms.

My body is suddenly pushed back onto the table, his head still trailing down my stomach as I suppress a giggle. I try bucking him off as a reaction, but I'm firmly held down by his hands kneading my breast. The feeling of his tongue gliding against my skin is all I need to relax as I close my eyes again and allow him to pursue teasing me.

I'm so lost in the darkness of his pleasure that I barely register lifting my hips to let him pull my pants off. His mouth has never left my body as his teeth nip at my skin. When I don't feel anything at all anymore, I grow alarmed, wondering why he's stopped. Thinking it's because he's stopped to strip, I lift my head up and open my eyes to find him gone. What the fuck? Where has he gone?

I hear the fridge opening and closing, my eyes looking in the direction to find Matt already walking back, shaking a can of whipped cream. His eyes are hooded and dark. "We're going to be late now," he states with a husky tone.

Standing in between my legs, he continues shaking the can. "Seeing you naked and sprawled out on the table like this, beautiful, you look like a dedicate dessert ready to eat," he says before bringing the can down and dispensing whip across my body, making me gasp from the coldness.

He's left a trail from the hollow of my breast down to my stomach. Matt chuckles from my reaction before his head dips down to lick my body, his tongue lapping away the whipped cream. Shaking the can again, he applies a dollop to each one of my nipples, a gasp coming from my mouth again, but this time I cannot help but laugh as well. When his lips take in each one of my nipples to lick away the cream, I moan in delight. His mouth next finds my lips, allowing me to savor the sweetness he was just tasting.

I whimper as his lips leave mine, making me crave for more. As much as I love kissing him, I love the wicked things his tongue can do to my body. Including now. I throw my head back and arch by body when his lips slowly tantalize their way down. I'm staring up, hoping the white ceiling will help distract my mind from my ticklishness. I feel the coldness of the whipped cream being dispensed between my legs and his mouth finds my heated center. My eyes close to allow the sense of his touch to take over. My hands grip at his hair, needing something to hold onto to as a heavy moan escapes my lips. I struggle to resist the urge to let go, but it's impossible as I start to explode from his torturous tongue.

My body is still convulsing from the intensity of my orgasm. My breathing is labored as I attempt to catch my breath and the prickles are still traveling through my body. I feel his mouth nip its way up my stomach again and I continue to hold onto his hair to keep him from tickling me.

"Beautiful, open up your pretty eyes," I hear him say above me. I want to open my eyes, but my body is still trying to come back from the heaven it was sent to. "Abigail," he demands.

Slowly, I blink open my eyes while his hand makes its way down my thigh to hook my leg around his waist. My eyes lock onto his dark brown eyes as he plunges into me, causing me to throw my head back and cry out with blissful pleasure.

"Look at me, Abigail," he demands again.

Bringing my gaze back down to his, he slowly starts to rock against my body. I want to close my eyes, but the demand in his eyes is keeping me from doing so.

His hands find my hips and I soon feel the pressure of him fiercely holding onto me. My hands come down to lock themselves around his wrist, wanting to feel some part of his body. His once passionate thrusts have now turned ruthless as he pounds into me. My body is forced to absorb each thrust as he stares down at me with his dark eyes. The particular look in his eyes is transporting me to my past.

I slam my eyes shut to push the vision from my mind, but it doesn't last long. "Abigail," I hear Matt demand again, but I cannot look.

Unwillingly, my mind takes me back to the memory I associate with those dark eyes— his regret as I walked in on him with Lisa. The shiver I once had is now making my body tremble with anger as I remember him pounding into Lisa, anguish and need apparent as he turned to look at me with those same eyes.

"Stop!" I frantically shout, already shoving him off me. I still can't open my eyes as I scramble out from under him. I'm forced to open my eyes to catch my balance as I stand and attempt to walk away. Matt is already grabbing at my arm to bring me to a stop, but my adrenaline and anger has taken over as I shove him back to land onto the table. "Beautiful, wait," Matt orders behind me, but I continue hurrying away.

I'm brought to a halt when I'm forced to face him. "What's wrong?" his confusion mixed with worry stares back at me.

"What were you trying to prove while you were fucking me on the table, Matt?" I bellow out.

He seems confused. "What are you talking about?"

"Was fucking me on the table you're way of forgetting what you did with Lisa?" I throw back at him, my anger completely taking over.

"Is that what you believe?"

"Yes."

Matt rakes his hand through his hair. "When are you ever going to put the past behind us? You keep letting it come between us!" he shouts back, making me flinch.

He releases my arm and stomps back towards the table, leaving me shocked from his reaction. I watch him furiously dress himself with his back facing me the entire time. When he's completely dressed he turns to face me. "When you're ready I'll be waiting in the car," he says as he grabs the keys from the counter and stalks his way to the front door, slamming it behind him, making me flinch once again.

Chapter Twenty-One

Matt

IT TOOK US Three motherfucking hours to get from Portland to Seattle, the entire drive spent in utter silence. It would have been the perfect opportunity to resolve our fight, but the animosity I have over our fight is still with me. Abigail made no attempts to approach the subject either, which I was happy about. Instead, there was a darkened remorsefulness between the two of us. She kept her gaze out of the passenger window, her lips tightly pinched in agitation. From the corner of my eye I catch her glancing at me every so often, but when I'd glance back she averts her eyes back out of the window.

My mind keeps returning to the words she threw at me that are now burned into my soul. The shame of knowing Abigail had exposed me for the true reason why I'd started making love to her on the table leaves me tormented. When I'd first begun, I'd wanted to see her beautiful eyes, to know it was Abigail's eyes I was peering down on. It soon became an obsession to erase the memory of my mistake with Lisa on the table. Instead of fixing my mistake, I only made it worse. I knew the minute she demanded I let her up I'd done wrong.

Reaching over, I grab onto her hand, expecting her to wrench it out of my hold, but she surprises me as she entwines our fingers. I bring her hand up to my lips to kiss the back of it. I want her to understand how much I love her. She turns her head from looking out of the window and smiles at me. At first the smile looks forced, until I tell her, "I love you." The words sound simple, but they're true. It's then that she gives me the smile I want, the one telling me she loves me in return. It's the answer I need to know that regardless of the struggles of our relationship, everything is going to be okay in the end.

Before long we're arriving at the medical center where Abigail's appointment is scheduled and I'm parking the car. I can already feel the tension radiating off her body. She's been dreading this appointment since the moment she told me about it, and no matter what I've done to ease her worry, it isn't working at this moment. I knew how important it was for her to be here, not because she hasn't recovered her memory, but for closure. I could care less if she doesn't remember her past. All I care about is her future.

Looking over at her, I see her eyes glazed as she stares at the building ahead of us. I give her a few minutes to sit there, lost in her thoughts. It's the least she deserves. Hearing her sigh, I know she's as ready as she will ever be. Getting out of the car and heading over to her door, I open it, waiting for her to step out, but she still looks petrified.

Pulling her out, I shut the door so I can lean her body up against it. I engulf her in my arms and her head immediately leans on my shoulder for comfort. I stroke her back for a couple minutes as we stand there in silence.

"I'm scared, Matt," she mummers into my neck. Placing a kiss on her brow, I hope to take her fear away. "Everything will be fine, beautiful," I tell her, knowing it could be a lie.

"What if it's not?"

Pulling our bodies apart so I can take her face in my palms, I kiss her, more for my selfishness of craving the feel of her lips against mine than anything else. When done, I look at her, making sure my eyes are locked onto hers. "No matter what happens, I love you, and nothing will ever change that," I promise before giving her a quick peck on the lips and walking with her towards the building.

Two hours later, after being put through an MRI machine as part of her recheck, we're back in the exam room where I'm now comforting Abigail. She's not fond of being put through that machine, so her silence is not surprising. As the minutes slowly trickle by Abigail's fidgeting increases and the wait starts to feel endless.

After a quick knock on the door, the doctor walks in with a hopeful smile upon her face. "Hello, Abigail, it's good to see you again," she greets, reaching out to shake her hand.

Abigail's face goes pale the moment she enters and I can feel her breath catch. With a forced smile upon her lips, Abigail shakes her hand. "Hi, I'm Dr. Kumar, Abigail's neurologist," she says, now holding her hand out for me to shake. "I'm Matt Garcia, Abigail's boyfriend," I happily reply.

"Nice to meet you."

Heading straight for the computer in the room, she asks, "Any new progress you'd like to share, Ms. Adams? Have you fully recovered your memory?"

She swallows nervously before she answers. "No."

Looking discouraged, the doctor says, "Well then, before I start asking questions, let me go over the results of today's scan with you." Within seconds a flat screen TV mounted on the wall ahead of us comes to life with images of the results of Abigail's MRI. Stepping towards the TV screen, I examine the images, trying to better understand what they mean. To me it looks like foreign language, until the doctor begins explaining the images.

Using her finger to point at an image, she begins to explain. "Abigail, this is the original scan we took after your accident. You had a severe amount of swelling in your brain, which is why I put you in your medically induced coma. It was to help bring the swelling down." The image changes on the screen. "This is the scan of your brain we did after you awoke from your coma six months ago." Moving her finger to the right, but it looks exactly like the previous one. "These are the results from your scan today. As you can see, there isn't any difference from six months ago to today," she finishes.

"Is that good or bad?" Abigail asks, still looking as confused as I feel.

"As far as I can tell there are no changes at all, which is a good thing. Now, besides not fully recovering your memory, is there anything unusual you can think of that I should know about?"

"There's only one thing I remember," she announces. "And what is that?" the doctor encourages.

"There was a conversation I remember while I was in the hospital. I think it was from when I was in my coma," she replies.

"Hmm," she says again while crossing her arms over her chest as she leans against the counter. "That doesn't surprise me. It's been known that patients in a coma will hear conversations surrounding them while they're in their deep sleep. But other than that, have you recovered any memories out of the norm that you didn't already know when you woke up?" she asks again, still hopeful for an answer.

Abigail quickly glances in my direction, as if she is apprehensive to say anything. "I don't know if it was a dream or an actual memory," she states.

I grow nervous and hold my breath, eager to see if Abigail will mention my sister's memories, but what she reveals is not what I was expecting. "I had a dream. At least I think it was a dream. It was the night of my accident," she murmurs.

The doctor's eyes go wide and my heart feels as if it's been slammed against my chest. "What specifically do you remember, Abigail?" I demand to know.

"Just falling down the stairs, but nothing more," she answers before ducking her head.

The doctor starts scribbling notes onto a clipboard she's holding in her hands. The doctor might be satisfied that is Abigail's complete answer, but I know her too well now. She hiding something and its pissing me off she isn't telling the truth.

"Do you have any further questions for me, Ms. Adams?"

Looking hesitant, she asks, "Will I ever recover my memory?"

The doctor now looks woeful. "You may or may not. Only time will tell," she relays and Abigail accepts her answer as if it's no big deal.

"Unless there is any significant changes, I can write you off as recovered. You're welcome to schedule another scan for a year from now, but from the results of today I really doubt there'll be any changes," she announces.

The doctor's words pierce at my ears. "That's it? We just hope she'll one day remember who she is?" I throw at the doctor. Both Abigail and the doctor snap their heads towards me. The doctor looks shocked by my words, but Abigail looks frightened.

"I'm sorry, sir, but there is nothing I can do about Abigail's memory. It's something she has to regain on her own."

"When?" I ask, earning me a confused expression from the doctor.

"There isn't some magic solution to how she can recover her memory, it's up to Abigail if and when she recovers it," she sternly states. It's not the answer I want, but it's the only explanation I believe she's willing to give us.

"Matt, please," I hear Abigail plead. When I look over at her, her eyes are glassy and I can tell she's fighting the tears. Feeling like the biggest asshole for my reaction, I step towards her to wrap my arms around her. "I'm sorry," I tell her. "I just want you to have answers, beautiful. I hate knowing you don't know who you are," I whisper to her.

"I don't care anymore," she states. "I'm happy the way I am," she says loud enough for me to hear. If Abigail is happy with her outcome, then I have to be as well.

Looking over at the doctor, she now looks apologetic. "I really am sorry."

"I just want to go home," Abigail states.

I soon hear the click of the door shutting, announcing the doctor has left us all alone. Deep down inside I'm still pissed over the visit, but only because of my own selfish reasons.

Abigail

THE ENTIRE CAR ride home I can feel the tension between Matt and me. I sat in turmoil as I consider what to say to Matt, but could not find the courage to speak. It was a darkened cloud that was hovering above us the entire three hours back to Portland. My thoughts keep returning to the feelings I have for Matt. Surrounded with the silence, I kept asking myself how it was possible that our relationship still existed. Was it the memories I held for him, or was it truly the bond of our love? Three hours is long enough for your mind to wonder to the unknown, and today was no different. Although we made small talk, I knew Matt was keeping his true feeling locked up within himself. It angered me more to know he couldn't trust me enough to speak to me about them, but I know that makes me a hypocrite. Here I was sitting next to him, refusing to broach the subject. The resentment I knew we felt for each other was building with every minute that went by.

Pulling into the driveway of the house, I feel both bittersweet and uneasy of what was yet to come. Would we discuss what happened in Seattle, or push it aside as we've done for the past three hours? My thoughts are broken when I'm startled back to reality as the door slams behind me and we enter the house.

I watch as he tosses the keys and they skid across the counter. It is the final indication I need to confirm he's still angry. He takes a seat on the couch with his elbows landing on his knees, allowing him to lean his head forward into his hands. Raking his hands through his hair before he grips it into his palms, the strain of his grip telling me he's trying to keep his anger under control.

My anxiousness to ask him what is wrong is building, but the fear of angering him any further is keeping me from forming the question. I can't move, but keep my feet rooted to the spot, watching from a distance.

He releases his grip to rake his hands down his face before enfolding them into each other as he stares out into the distance. Our silence takes over the room as it lingers longer than I want it too, but I still cannot find the words to ask him why he's mad. I don't have to wait long, though. "Why didn't you tell me about the dream?"

I've been expecting him to ask. "Because that's exactly what it was… A dream."

He lifts his head up and his dark eyes are staring back at me. "I know it was more than you just falling down the stairs, Abigail. *I want to know the details of the dream,*" he demands.

"I think Bill pushed me down the stairs," I rasp out.

"What!" he bellows as he stands. "And you didn't think that was important enough to tell me? We should be pressing charges against that asshole for trying to kill you!"

His words are the reason why I haven't told him. "Even if I tried to press charges, it's his word against mine. What proof do I have besides a stupid dream?" I yell back. Raking his hand through his hair again, his frustration radiates off him. "At least it's a start, Abigail. He needs to be behind bars in order for you to be completely safe. Until then all I can think about is what will happen if he gets to you again. I won't be able to live with myself if something happened to you."

His words are now making me feel guilty. "I don't understand why you choose to keep everything to yourself?"

"Just because I didn't tell you about a dream?"

"It's not just the dream. You didn't tell the doctor about my sister's memories."

"They're not my memories to tell, Matt. She asked if I've

gotten *my* memories back and I haven't," I truthfully tell him.

He whips his head in my direction and his eyes are dark and full of anger. "But you are getting *some* memories. You should have told her about those," he clarifies.

"I just want to understand why you're getting them," he explains. "Don't you?" His question throws me aback. "I thought it was the reason for seeing the neurologist today." He demands.

The realization of why he's been insisting I see the neurologist finally hits me. "That's the reason why you've been insisting I make that follow up appointment? So *you* can get answers as to why I've been getting these memories?" I ask him, demanding the truth as I watch him grow confused.

He turns sympathetic and all signs of his anger suddenly disappear. "It's not about me, this is for you."

"No it's not, Matt. If it was, you wouldn't be so angry at me right now," I throw back at him, before adding, "You heard the doctor, she doesn't understand, either."

"Then why are you having them?"

"I don't fucking know!" I shout at him, annoyed from being asked the repeated question as if I would know the answer myself. "You think I *chose* these memories, Matt? You think I woke up from my coma hoping that I didn't have my *own* memory? No, I didn't. But I wasn't given a choice, and you're making me wish I'd never got them in the first place!" I shout at him.

Rising, he stalks his way to stand in front of me. His hands fist at his side as he looks at me with regret. "I'm pissed because no matter how much you say you don't care about your past, I know you do. I know how much you hate getting my sister's memories."

I'm shocked. "When have I ever said that?"

"You don't have to say it, Abigail. I've seen the way you react after you get them. You look either angered or upset most of the time."

I'm now thinking back to all the times I've gotten Emily's memories and most of the time I'm with Matt, but I never knew

I looked upset over getting them. On the contrary, they always seem to help me better understand Matt. Cautiously I step forward to reach for Matt so I can lay my hands on his chest. I can feel his rapid heartbeat telling me he's either nervous or still angry, but by the somber look on his face, I have to believe it's the first.

I make sure our eyes are locked as I say, "Matt, I never hate getting your sister's memories. I might not understand why I get them, but I will never hate or regret I get them. Because of them I fell in love with you and with every new memory I gain, my love for you grows."

My fist is now gripping onto his shirt as I continue to tell him, "I may never get my memory back, Matt, but that first memory brought me to you and I cherish every... single... one since then. Those memories alone are worth never knowing who I was."

Chapter Twenty-Two

Matt

ABIGAIL WINCES AS she pulls her foot from my hold. I must have caused her some pain. "I'm sorry, beautiful," I quietly apologize. "Do you want me to stop?" I ask, taking her ankle back in my hands to rub her foot. With a smile on her lips, she shakes her head. I continue to watch her from my side of the couch for any other type of reaction just in case.

I love days like today when we simply lounge on the couch with nothing to do but spend time with each other. It's the perfect opportunity to massage her ankle. I know her foot grows stiff and sore from wearing the boot, which is why every so often I'll take her foot and begin to massage it for her. This time I believe I've hit a too sensitive sore spot.

She's still staring at me; her eyes urge me to continue. "Don't stop," she nicely demands, giving her foot a light shove.

Still doubtful she isn't in any pain, I don't move. She nudges her foot into my hand again, this time with a little more force, causing me to chuckle. Resuming the massage, my fingers push into the heel of her foot, earning me a satisfied moan. I watch as she keeps her eyes closed and she lays her head back, biting down on her lip.

"You need to stop making those sounds," I groan as my cock grows in my jeans. Her head snaps up and her eyes are wide in surprise. "What can you expect from a sex deprived man?" I playfully tease, knowing I'm far from being deprived when it comes to Abigail. "You only put out once last night, claiming you were *tired*," I remind her, using my fingers to quote the word.

"Is that *all* you ever think about, Matthew Garcia? Sex?" she squeals.

"Most of the time, yes," I answer, still teasing her.

She narrows her eyes at me, but from the hint of laughter in her eyes, I know she's far from angry. Her other foot slowly starts rubbing against my groin as if to tease me in return, but instead I'm the one who wins when I gradually glide my finger up the inside her leg. Her once narrowed eyes are growing wide and I can see her pupils dilating as they radiate with her desire. "I *was* tired," she purrs. "You kept me up most of the night before," her lips now pouting as she continues to move her foot around and her breathing quickens. "You're lucky I didn't pass out on you during sex *last night*," she playfully says before taking her lip in between her teeth.

"By the way you were snoring seconds after I rolled off you, I'm pretty sure you did," I reply as I grab her other foot.

A small gasp comes from her lips. "I do not snore!" she says, yanking away the foot I was holding to shove it into my stomach.

I throw my head back to laugh. "I know, beautiful, I just love teasing you," I joke before reaching in between her legs to pinch her. She yelps as she clamps her legs tightly shut, giving me the opportunity to further tantalize her. I start tickling her just so I can hear her laughter, which I love. What I wasn't expecting was for her to further grind her hips into my hand, allowing me to continue teasing her. My mind is lost in the images of what I could be doing with Abigail instead, but my carnal thoughts are broken when I hear the front door open and closing announcing Trey's arrival.

Abigail groans as her expression turns sour, making me

laugh again as I stare at her now pouty face. Trey reaches the couch looking down at us as he stands behind us. "You guys up for heading to the Brewhouse tonight?"

Looking over to Abigail whose nose is scrunched up from the stench radiating off of Trey, she quickly answers. "Sure, why not? But you better take a shower first," she adds, waving her hand in front of her face.

"What's wrong, supermodel? Don't love the smell of a real man?"

She rolls her eyes before looking over to me. "Yes, I do, and it isn't you."

The dejected look on Trey's face is comical. "Whatever. Give me a few to jump in the shower," I hear Trey shout as he walks away.

Bringing her ankle up to my lips, I place a gentle kiss on it, keeping my eyes locked with Abigail's. It's my way of seducing her. I know it's worked when I hear her slightly gasp. Reaching down, I pick up the boot brace, carefully strapping Abigail's foot back in it.

"You want some water?" I ask her as I sit up from the couch.

Instead of an answer, her eyes focus on my semi-erect cock bulging inside my jeans. It's the reason why I stood up; I needed to breathe to make it disappear before we leave.

"Later," I joke at her.

Leaving her on the couch, I start walking into the kitchen to retrieve our water, but I suddenly hear the tapping of her boot brace, indicating she's following me. Turning, I'm surprised to see her already in front of me, glaring at me like a furious little a pixie.

"What?"

"What do you mean, *what?*" she utters with her hands on her hips. "You know exactly what you're doing, Matt, and it's not fair," she barks out, stabbing me in the chest with her finger.

I step forward to wrap my arms around her waist. "I have no clue what you're talking about," I tease, nuzzling my nose below her ear to further torture the both of us. Inhaling her scent, I'm already regretting telling Trey we were going with him. With her hands holding onto my arms, she tilts her head to the side, allowing my lips to trail down her neck. "Do I need to take you to the bedroom to help you blow off your frustration?" I whisper into her ear with a chuckle. "I promise, beautiful, when we get back I'll make sure to satisfy your every need," I quietly growl into her ear as I gently bite down against her skin. She shivers in my arms as I continue to torment the both us.

Abigail suddenly pushes me against the counter and I'm left watching her sink down to her knees. My eyes go wide in surprise. I'm pretty sure I know what she plans on doing, but I don't want to grow too excited since she's never offered to do so before. I hear the shower turn on reminding me Trey takes the fastest showers known to man.

Silently cursing to myself, I say, "Abigail, we don't have time." I stare at the bathroom door mentally praying Trey will choose to jack off in the shower today.

I feel her hands unbutton my jeans, reaching in to spring my cock from my boxer briefs. "Hmmm, someone is already excited," I hear Abigail purr before she wraps her hand around the shaft. I can't resist looking down at her as her tongue darts out to lick the head of my dick. Holy... Fucking... Shit! The sight of her on her knees licking me practically makes me blow my load that very second.

"Abigail, Trey is going to get out of the shower any minute now," I warn through gritted teeth. With a playful smile while looking up at me, she responds, "I guess I better make this quick," she states right before she wraps her warm mouth around my cock. My hands dig into her hair as I let out a tortured hiss and close my eyes to savor the warmth of her mouth. I feel her slowly pull her mouth back, sucking harder as she retreats and pushes forward. Tightening my grip in her hair, I help guide her as she bobs her head back and forth. I cannot restrain myself as she continues to torture me. Her hand is moving to the rhythm of her mouth as I listen to her sensual moans from below. I cannot help but add to her sounds with my own. Forcing myself to open my eyes and look down at her, I see her eyes already looking up to me for the next few minutes. When I feel the head of my cock brush up against the back of her throat telling me my dick is completely imbedded in her mouth, I lose all self-control. "Oh, God, Abigail!" I shout up to the ceiling as I relinquish my control to hold back any longer and I release myself into the warmth of her mouth.

She looks up at me with a satisfied smile as she stands and envelopes herself in my arms. Behind her I hear Trey already opening the bathroom door. "Thank you," I breathlessly whisper into her ear. Her lips place an open mouth kiss onto my neck. "You're welcome," she responds as I continue to slump against her, attempting to get my rapidly beating heart under control. Another minute later, I'm hastily buttoning up my pants as Trey walks into the living room.

"You fuckers ready?" he impatiently shouts.

With a smile still on her lips, Abigail turns and walks away saying, "Why do you have to rush?" Leaving me to think: *I'm one lucky man.*

Abigail

AS USUAL, ON a night when the guys want to drink and watch the game, we end up at the Brewhouse. As we're walking in the song *Angel* is blasting through the speakers as the hostess spots us. Giving us a tilt of her head to follow her to our usual table in the back, Trey walks ahead of us leaving us to follow. The music is about to play the chorus and from the corner of my eye, I see Matt rush a couple of steps ahead of me before he turns to face me. Placing his left hand over his chest and right arm pointing his finger at me, he sings along to the chorus.

"Girl your my angel, you're my darling angel. Closer than my peeps you are to me, baby. Shorty you're my angel, you're my darling angel, girl you're my friend when I'm in need, lady."

His eyes are hooded as his lips are sensually curved up into a smile. He continues walking backwards as I glance behind him and see Trey with what looks like a disgusted look on his face as he watches. Matt is unconcerned with the crowd watching him. He's singing the words only loud enough for me to hear them, but he's putting on enough of a performance with his body movements.

"You're a Queen and so you should be treated. Though you never get the lovin' that you needed. Could have left, but I called and you heeded."

With the next line he drops down to his knees as he brings his hands up in a prayer pose and continues to sing, and by now a small crowd has surrounded us.

"Begged and I pleaded, mission completed, mama said that now that I dissed the program. Not the type to mess around with her emotion. But the feeling I have for you is so strong. Been together so, and this could never be wrong."

I'm blushing like a giddy schoolgirl at this point by the scene in front of me. Taking a quick glance at the crowd, our small little group is a mix of blissful girls who are ready to swoon over Matt, or glowering men who are glaring at him for out doing them. He gets up and grabs for my hands, but instead of singing, he's bobbing his head to the beat with his body as he hums along.

Everyone is waiting to see what he will do next and with the next couple of lines, he lets go of my hands and starts up again as he continues his performance. Holding his hands to his chest, as in the beginning, he starts singing again.

"Girl your my angel, you're my darling angel. Closer than my peeps you are to me, baby. Shorty you're my angel, you're my darling angel, girl you're my friend when I'm in need, lady.

Uh, Uh."

With his eyes closed, he bellows out the last line. If I thought I felt embarrassed earlier, I am mortified now. I would have never thought Matt would serenade me in the middle of a restaurant.

"Girl, in spite of my behavior, said I'm your savior. You must be sent from up above. And you appear to so me tender, say girl I surrender. Thanks for giving me your love."

He finishes and comes up to me to give me a kiss on the lips as the song comes to an end. I hear cheers and whistles from the crowd before Matt pulls himself away to take several bows in all directions of the restaurant. When done, he grabs my hand with his and leads us to the back.

"Seriously, fucker? I know you're a pussy, but do you have to go and act like one in public, too?" Trey's lets out, his words never seeming to fail to kill the mood.

"Pussy or not, at least I'm in love." Matt tugs me tighter to his side as he smiles down at me while we walk. "Whatever, dude," Trey throws back, looking unfazed by the remark.

Taking my seat, I can see David and Kelly across from us bickering with each other. "I just don't understand why you can't do things like that every now and then," I faintly hear from her lips as David sighs while rolling his eyes. I know Kelly's bickering is for nothing. David may not give Kelly performances because every day he does something to make Kelly love him more. I, on the other hand, am still trying to understand why Matt felt the need to do it. My thoughts are broken when I feel Matt's lips meet below my ear, his warm breath adding to the blush that is still fresh on my cheeks. I'm still feeling giddy as he wraps his arm around me, allowing me to lean into his body as I shyly ask, "Why did you do it?" still confused over the performance.

Looking at me, I watch as his brow furrows. "Why wouldn't I?" I'm still contemplating how to respond as he leans his head down, our foreheads now touching, as he answers. "In my eyes, you'll always be my angel," he conveys only loud enough for me to hear.

My hand goes straight to his bicep to where his tattoo sits, the outline of his angel wing staring back at me as I stare down at it. My thoughts wander off to the day in the park when he told me the meaning behind why he got it in the first place. "No, Matt, she'll always be your angel."

I feel my chin being forced up to look at him. The sincerity coming from his eyes tells me he understands what I mean. He brings his lips down to mine and all the sad thoughts behind the meaning of those words vanish to the back of my mind. When we end the kiss, his lips are still inches away from mine when he says, "Your right. Emily will always be my angel up above, but you're my angel here on earth, beautiful."

The snicker that escapes my lips makes him chuckle. He always knows how to turn me into a puddle of mush within seconds. Why do we have to be surrounded by a crowd of people at this moment? I'd much rather be at home right now, finishing what we attempted to start earlier.

As if reading my mind, Matt lips go up to one side. "If you keep looking at me that way, I might just have to give in to your request."

"Don't make any promises you don't intend to keep."

His eyebrows go up as his eyes begin to wander the restaurant. He stands up, pulling me with him to follow as he leads us away. "Matt, where are we going?"

Without answering, he leads us to the restrooms in the front of the restaurant and straight into the ladies room. "It's probably cleaner," he states before pulling us into the bathroom and locking the door behind us.

With his body he gently shoves me against the counter as his lips slam down on mine. "You should know," he murmurs against my lips, "by now that I keep every," he continues as his hands find their way into my shirt to skim against my skin, "single," the words coming out before his mouth finds my earlobe, "promise," he seductively whispers into my ear, making me lose it completely. I need him, and I need him *now*.

My hands are already pulling at the button of his pants and reaching inside for him, finding him already hard. Wrapping my hand around him, I feel him moan against my lips as he kisses me, telling me I'm not going to have to wait long. I can already feel his hand at the buttons of my own jeans, forcefully pulling them apart and shoving them down. Within seconds my legs are being lifted onto the counter and wrapped around his waist, stretching my core as he enters me. He muffles my moan with his mouth and his hands are already grabbing the cheeks of my ass, gripping them with full force as he possesses my body. I hold on for the ride that I know will bring me to ecstasy.

The once slow thrusting of his hips quickens as proves his promising words. Gripping his shoulders for dear life, my nails are now digging into his skin, and I'm trying to control the moaning escaping my lips, but I fail miserably each time he slams into me. My desire is built to its peak and the only thing I can do is allow Matt to take me over the edge. The longer he pumps into me, the harder he grows, stretching me fully.

His hands are pulling me tighter against his body and my legs are tightening against his waist as I start to reach my peak. "Please tell me your close, beautiful. Because I can't hold out much longer," he quietly growls against my ear.

I cannot answer him with words, but I do by tightening the walls of my core around him, causing him to pump faster as my body explodes. Thankfully his mouth catches my screams and he soon follows me over; the vibrations of our screams echoing against each other.

Bringing his body to a stop, he drops his head onto my shoulder, my panting matching his own as we desperately attempt to catch our breath. I have no words, but Matt does. "I swear, Abigail, I can never get enough of you," he whispers, his words vibrating against my skin.

"Good," I say, still trying to catch my breath.

With a chuckle, he kisses my neck and my body is awaking again, but my thoughts are soon brought to an end when we hear a knock on the door. Matt yells over his shoulder, "We'll be out in a minute," making me blush from head to toe.

I cannot believe I just had sex in a bathroom. It shouldn't surprise me with Matt, but it still does. He pulls away from me just enough to look directly in my eyes. "I meant every single word I said earlier. You are my *angel*, Abigail," he says, making me smile before he places a kiss against my lips.

I feel empty as he pulls his body away from mine. Before long, we're both dressed and Matt is opening the door to the bathroom to find Carol standing against the wall. My body recoils from the glare she is shooting us, but Matt pulls me to his side, wrapping his arm around my body as if to comfort me.

"Sorry about the wait," Matt says. He's already pulling us away, but I pull myself to a stop when I hear Carol say, "At least you didn't make me wait long, which means you didn't take as long as you did when you fucked me in there." I feel the blood completely drain from my body.

Whipping my head around, I see her staring at me with a smug smile on her lips. She's waiting for my reaction, but I can't give her one because I can't even breathe at this point. I'm still in shock over her words.

"True, but the difference between you and Abigail is that I merely fucked you, I just made love to her in there, so that's what you'll smell when you go in there."

Carols mocking eyes are now full of rage. With a squawk, she stomps from the bathroom, rushing past us back into the restaurant. Matt tries pulling me to follow, but I angrily stay rooted to the spot.

He takes one look at me and understands. "I'm sorry, beautiful," he shamefully voices before placing his hand on my cheek. "Remember, you're my future and that's all that matters," he reminds me.

"I hate always knowing in the back of my mind that I might

see some girl you once fucked around every corner," I throw at him.

Heavily sighing, he says, "Abigail, how many times are we going to fight about this?" The question makes me realize it *may never* end. "How would you feel if our roles were reversed?" I ask, instead of answering his question.

"I wouldn't fucking like it," he growls.

"Exactly."

Without hesitating, he pulls me into his arms and his lips find my temple. I know our relationship will always have a past attached to it, but deep down inside I know it's worth it. "I'm sorry, beautiful. I know I can't change my past, but I promise to make my future yours, no one else's." His words are a perfect example of my thought just seconds ago. I don't have any words to return, but I know I believe him. We continue standing there for a couple more minutes before returning to the restaurant.

On the way to our table, I'm forced to walk past Carol, but instead of acknowledging her, I ignore her, knowing she isn't worth my time. When we take our seats, I pull Matt's face in my direction to give him a kiss. "I love you," I say against his lips when I'm done kissing him, meaning it from the bottom of my heart.

Chapter Twenty-Three

Abigail

MATT'S LIPS ARE trailing down my body, bringing a shiver to my body as his warm breath glides against my skin and his tantalizing fingers slowly float on the edge of my ribs kindling sparks in my blood. I open my lips to beg him to quit torturing me, but I'm startled awake from the sound of music demanding my attention instead. Recognizing the words of my ringtone, *Glowing,* I groan as I reach for my phone sitting on the nightstand. Even in my frustrated state, I cannot help but smile as the words remind me of Matt.

Silently cursing to myself, I continue blinking to open my protesting eyes, already acknowledging I won't be able to return to my luxurious dream. I'll have to wait until Matt gets home now to make it a reality. I'm rubbing the sleep from my eyes when the ping announcing a new voicemail. Taking in the time, I curse again. It's only 9:46 A.M.; it's too damn early to be up. In my opinion the day should begin at noon, but not many seem to agree with me, including the person who just called. Entering my code to unlock my phone, I go straight to the call log, not recognizing the number. Next, I listen to the voicemail.

"Hello, Ms. Adams, this is the Fallen Model Agency. We got your number from Samantha Clark over at Running World

Magazine. *We were unaware you were modeling again, but are interested in having you do a photo shoot for our agency. If you would please give us a call at 206-555-2764, I'd greatly appreciate it."*

The call goes silent after the last words and I'm left confused from the message. My mind goes back to the interview, remembering how persistent Samantha was about me giving her my number, stating she needed it for the magazine's chief editor in case there were discrepancies with the interview. Had I known she was going to be freely giving my number out to people, I would have never given it to her.

Pushing my infuriation aside, I push on the number, nervously waiting as I listen to the ringing in my ear.

"Hello, this is Karen," a girl cheerfully answers.

"This is Abigail Adams, I just missed your call," I cautiously reply.

You can practically hear the excitement in her voice as she continues introducing herself. "Thank you so much for calling me back. I'm a recruiter for the Fallen Model Agency." Her excitement radiates through the phone. "I was wondering if you were working again?"

I carefully choose my next words. "At this time I'm focusing on doing small jobs for now. I needed some time off."

"Yes, I understand. You'd probably want to take a break after your accident."

"Yeah," I reply, hoping it sounds believable.

"I have a job with a local designer who is interested in having you for her photo shoot. It'd be for tomorrow morning, if you were interested. I know it is short notice, but the girl who was scheduled to do the shoot had a family emergency and had to fly back to Brazil, so I'm in a bit of a bind to find someone. When the magazine hit the stands and I read the interview, I thought of you right away."

"The interview? What does the interview have to do with my modeling career?"

"You mentioned in the interview how you were anxious to get back into the modeling world," she states, as if I should have known myself.

Quickly scanning my mind, I don't recall *ever* mentioning anything of the sort, but I wasn't going to pass up the opportunity. "I don't have anything planned for tomorrow, so yes, I'd be available."

"Excellent. Where can I send the information?"

My mind is scrambled as I try to figure out where she should send it. "You can send the information to my email," I rush to tell her.

Minutes later after giving her the information, we're ending the phone call and I am both excited and nervous as I think of the day ahead. I don't have to wait long until the ping on my phone informs me I have a new email and my fingers are trembling as I open up the app. Scanning through the details, a groan rumbles from my throat when I take in the location and time I'm expected on set. With my nervousness it hadn't occurred to me to ask those details of the job. I'd been too excited with the offer. They expected me to be on set by seven for hair and make-up. Why can't people understand that not everyone is a morning person, especially models? I'm shocked at myself as I finish thinking the words. I would have never associated the complaint with my current life. Shaking off the thought, the first thing I do is text Julio.

It's time to get back to work. We're going to Seattle today and we won't be coming back until tomorrow. – Abigail

I don't have to wait long to receive a response.

No problem. What time do you want to leave and who's driving, Mateo or me? – Julio.

Remembering Matt has class all day tomorrow, I reply.

Matt isn't going. It's just you and me. - Abigail

I respond, looking down at my booted foot.

You're driving.

I'm reminded that I have another matter on my hands. I'd

forgotten I was still injured and managed to keep the detail from the recruiter. Shrugging off the concern, I make a mental note of stressing to the agency that I can't put too much weight on it. I am not going to risk being stuck with this thing any longer than I need to be by further injuring myself.

Julio's simple, "*Okay,*" comes through and I get out of bed to pack my overnight bag. The entire time my apprehensive mind is contemplating whether to text Matt or not. I know if I were to tell him the details before I leave he will come rushing home, expecting to go with me. As much as I want him at the photo shoot with me, I couldn't allow him to miss any more school at my expense. He's missed enough with all my appointments. It leaves me with my next decision, which is still a dreadful one, but I already know how to handle telling him. It's the only choice I have.

Packed and ready to go, I then book Julio and I a room near the location the agency gave me. Next, I send Julio another text to confirm he's on his way. Before long, Julio's arrived and loading up the car.

Nearly three hours later as Julio is nearing the city of Seattle, I look down at my phone to check the time. Matt should be home already. With a deep breath, I press on Matt's number and listen for the ring on the other end.

"Hello, beautiful," his loving tone making the dread of giving the news increase. "Where are you? And please tell me you have Julio with you," he says, the concern in his words adding to the guilt.

"Yes, I have Julio with me," I say glancing at Julio from the corner of my eye. "Matt, I won't be coming home tonight," I bravely tell him.

"Why not? Where are you going?" his voice pitched high with both concern and fury, most likely from not knowing of my plans.

"I have a photo shoot in Seattle tomorrow morning."

"Why didn't you tell me you had a photo shoot in Seattle?"

he asks with a restrained tone. I cringe as I picture his expression. "I got the offer this morning, Matt. I didn't tell you because I can't let you miss anymore school. If you do, you'll end up failing and won't graduate," I explain. "Weren't you the one telling me I needed to get back into modeling? I was given an offer and I took it. I even booked my own hotel suite," I proudly state.

"How did you get the job? I didn't get a phone call or email asking me. Everything has to go through me first, Abigail. I need to make sure it's what's best for your career."

His words piss me off, a reminder of my previous life. "You're not the one who makes the decisions in my life, Matt. I do! If you think for one moment you're going to control what I do with my career, then you have it wrong. I've already had enough of that shit when I was with Bill, and thankfully I don't remember most of it, but right now you're reminding me of him," I growl into the phone.

The other end goes silent for a few seconds, causing me to pull the phone away to see if he's hung up. In the corner of my eyes I can see an uncomfortable looking Julio. "Matt, are you still there?" I hesitantly ask when I've pulled the phone back to my ear.

I hear a heavy sigh on the other end. "You're right. I have no right to make you're decisions and I never meant for you to feel like that, beautiful. I just hate knowing that asshole is still out there and he can hurt you. I would just prefer to be at your side so nothing will happen to you."

I'm feeling relieved he hasn't hung up. "I know, Matt, but I'm tired of living my life in fear of him. If I do, I'd be proving he's still controlling my life," I somberly reply. Taking a quick glance at Julio staring at the road ahead of me, I feel a little better that I'm not alone on this trip. "I have Julio with me. I doubt Bill or anyone will be able to get near me with him around," I say with a chuckle, earning me a smile from Julio and a stern nod as well.

"You're right, that's what he's there for. But promise me

you won't let him leave your side," he demands before correcting his words. "His ass better have his own room in the suite. Other than that, he needs to be at an arms distance."

Now I'm the one smiling, imagining Matt's face as he makes his demands. I know the furiousness is still radiating off him, but it's when he's demanding that I'm most turned on. I already have an ache between my legs from the image in my mind. If he was standing in front of me right now, I would have him naked and in me in seconds.

I'm so lost in my fantasy that I barely make out Matt's continuing lecture on the precautions I need to take when out in public. Sometimes it's easier to have him at my side than to listen to him give me advice like a worried father.

I cut him off by saying, "Matt, I have Julio with me. Remember?"

He grows silent, but I can hear the defeat in his words. "I know. I just hate knowing I can't be there," he says, making me smile. "Needy much?" I throw back at him as I try to make him laugh.

"We'll see who's needy tonight when she can't sleep," he says, reminding me of how badly I've depended him to help me sleep. "But really, Abigail," his voice sounding serious again, "I don't want you leaving Julio's side."

"I won't."

Seeing Julio already pulling up to the hotel, I end the call, promising to call Matt back as I'm getting ready for bed. The hours trickle by and as I'm staring into the screen of my phone reading an article online, Matt's smile starts flashing back at me. Puzzled, I press on the screen to answer and the picture is transformed into a realistic smiling Matt looking back at me.

"Hey, beautiful," he huskily voices.

"Hello, handsome. I forgot that we can Face Time on our phones," I answer, a wide smile taking over my face.

From the background and the position he's in, I know he's in our bed and I'm already regretting not being at his side. Within that second I grow lonely without him.

"Thank God for technology. Do you miss me?" he taunts with his smile up to one side.

"Of course I miss you," I truthfully respond. "I wish you were here." I add, my heart miserably sinking with disappointment.

"Me, too," he whispers. "Are you excited about tomorrow?"

"A little, but I'm nervous too."

He looks surprised. "Why would you be nervous? You're Abigail Adams, remember?" Matt teases. "And you never got nervous before a game?" I jeer back at him as I laugh.

He laughs at my response, allowing me to take in his carefree expression although the dread of not sleeping at his side is growing with every second. It must show in my expression as his smile fades into a frown. "I wish I could kiss that frown from your lips," he conveys barely above a whisper and I can already feel the regret of leaving him behind building inside of me. "Wanna have sex?" he suggest, shocking me.

He's laughing again, but I'm grimacing from his amusement. "And how do you expect to do that? Unless you have some super magical powers you haven't disclosed to me, I truly doubt you can be here in a couple seconds to fulfill that promise."

"Phone sex," he replies with a wag of his eyebrows.

My once grimaced expression is followed with irritation. "Why do I have a feeling this isn't the first time you've done it?" I irritably say back to him. His smile is now matching my own. "Past," he reminds me through clenched teeth, now looking aggravated from my words.

The single word leaves me feeling guilty for approaching the subject. Heavily sighing, he rakes his hand down his face before I see his eyes again. This time they look resentful.

"Can we just talk instead? It may help calm my nerves so I can fall asleep," I suggest.

With a simple nod, he begins explaining his day and I lay

listening to every word. It isn't long before my body is relaxed enough and it helps soothe my nervous mind, allowing me to drift off into a dreamless sleep.

"WHAT IS THAT on your foot?" a skinny looking man walking in my direction demands to know. Reaching me faster than I can him, he gawks down at my boot without bothering to conceal his disgusted expression.

"A boot brace," I curtly reply.

"And how do you expect me to photograph you with that hideous contraption on your foot?" he asks, his nose disgustedly scrunched up. "The designer is not going to be happy with this," he huffs out while rubbing at his temple.

I sigh as my eyes roll at his words. "It's not permanently attached to my foot. *It does come off,*" I snarl back. His head snaps up, clearly irritated with my response. "As long as I don't put any pressure on my foot for too long, I should be fine," I finish explaining to him.

His eyes narrow at me as he studies me from head to toe. "You're lucky most of the time you'll be laying down," he mutters as he turns to walk away, leaving me to wonder what he means.

I'm about to give him a piece of my mind when a girl in her early twenties comes straight up to me. "I'm your production assistant for today, Ms. Adams. You can follow me this way," she announces as she tilts her head for me to follow her. I was already irritated from the lack of sleep I had from tossing and turning and the both of them are unraveling my temper as they act like asshats. Isn't it usually the other way around in this industry?

Leading Julio and I to a dressing room, I enter to find another girl already inside. The moment she hears me walk in she turns to greet me, already instructing me to take a seat in a director's chair. For the next hour, I'm primped and prepped to her satisfaction while I attempt to catch up on my sleep.

"Okay, Ms. Adams, here are your choices for today's wardrobe," the same girl from earlier announces as she enters the room. Since the make-up girl is still applying my eye shadow, I reply, "Thank you," without opening my eyes. When I feel the brush leave my eyelids, I open them and look straight behind me, my freshly make-up covered eyes going wide in shock from the lack of clothing.

She didn't bring in clothes. She brought in scraps! To be more accurate, she brought in lingerie. "There's more, right?" I hesitantly ask, already afraid she will tell me no.

Looking at me confused, she says, "What do you mean?"

"Where's the rest of it?" I ask, still shocked.

"Ms. Adams, you *were* aware you were doing a lingerie shoot today, weren't you?"

Shit! I really should have asked for more details before I had agreed to this. Shaking my head to answer, I continue staring at the scraps on the hangers with wide eyes. Both the girls laugh, but when I don't join them they realize their mistake and bring themselves under control. "I'm sorry. I thought you were informed by the agency," the wardrobe assistant apologizes.

Although she's apologized, she doesn't look regretful as she stares at me as if I've lost my mind. Gradually making my way over to the rack, I start to push the hangers aside, one by one. The garments are pretty, but don't look like they would cover much of anything on my body.

"We didn't think you'd have a problem with it since you're known for your lingerie shoots," the wardrobe assistant's words reminding me of a past I'm unfamiliar with.

Shooting her with a vicious glare to shut her up, I make her cringe. Taking a deep breath and one last glance at the wardrobe, I find the courage to answer. "Okay, let's do this," I say, hoping I look much more confident than I feel.

With a satisfied smile she helps me strip down to put on the first outfit, soon wrapping me in a silk robe so we can exit the dressing room. With Julio following me, I walk over to the set already beaming with bright white lights and umbrellas.

Stopping to stand next to the photographer to await instructions, he doesn't bother looking at me as he says, "The first round will be with you standing, so I need you to remove that hideous thing." Using his nose to point at my boot.

If he keeps up with his horrendous attitude, I'm going to end up using the boot to knock him out. I take my time removing the boot to irritate him before I hand it over to the production assistant. As I'm about to take my first step, Julio is already at my injured side helping me walk over to the center of the set. "Remember, if it begins to hurt say something. The last thing I need is Mateo chewing my ass out because of your foot," he says, making me quietly laugh picturing his words. He leaves me, not waiting for a response.

With a few quick instructions, I'm soon entering the zone I've come to love. Thirty minutes later as we're taking a quick break so the photographer can switch lenses, I'm flinching and can no longer bear putting any more weight on my foot. "How much longer?" I ask as another jolt travels up my foot as I place it down.

"We'll be done when I say we're done," he says, looking down at his lens.

Hating the tone he's just used, I signal Julio over with my fingers while demanding for my robe. Within seconds I receive both, along with a high pitched screech of words. "What is he doing?" I hear the photographer say as I'm covering myself up and asking Julio to carry me back to the dressing room. "I'm taking a break. If you don't like it, fire me," I snarl back at him.

I don't bother looking back for his reaction. "I'll bring you some ice for the ankle," Julio tells me as he places me in the chair I was in earlier. Minutes later he's back with a bag full of ice and I'm silently cursing to myself through the pain. Grabbing my phone, I cannot resist texting Matt.

I hate it when you're right. – Abigail. Remembering how Matt would always lecture me that I should never stand on my foot without the boot for too long or else it would cause me pain. Within seconds I receive a response.

As much as I love the message, why do I have a feeling I won't be happy for you admitting it? – Matt

Because you won't. I reply before adding in the next message.

They required me to take it off for the shoot. I'm taking a break and icing it now. – Abigail.

With the guilt slowly building inside of me, I wait for his response.

I'll make sure to massage it when you get home. I love you. – Matt

The words make me smile and leave me relieved he didn't lecture me through a text message. I expect him to call me for said lecture, but when I look down at my phone to check the time, I realize he's in the middle of class, leaving me relieved yet again. Twenty minutes later, I'm putting the boot back on and changing once more into another skimpy outfit. Hobbling my way back out for round two, I'm surprised to see a bed has now been added to the set. With every step closer I get to it, I grow nervous, even more so when I see a guy also in a robe conversing with the photographer. I can already sense the type of photo shoot that will take place in this session.

Spotting me, a smile spreads across his face as he walks over to greet me. "Hi, I'm Kaden. I'll be your partner for today," he states with a little too much enthusiasm. "Hi, nice to meet you," I shyly reply, unable to resist fully taking him in.

The photographer is already barking orders on what he expects, and from his instructions, I'm already dreading what is to come. The uncertainly in the pit of my stomach is increasing as he adds the positions he needs. My mind is telling me this is not going to go well, but I force myself to push it aside and nod at his instructions, telling myself *this is a job, nothing more.*

Done barking his instructions, the photographer walks back to his camera equipment as I hear Julio express, "I don't like him," he clips out. "Me either," I add.

Both of us laughing, I leave him there as I walk my way over to the bed where the photographer and Kaden are already waiting for me. Still repeating my earlier mantra as I sit and remove my boot, I'm soon removing the robe again and lying back onto the bed to make myself comfortable. It's when Kaden climbs above me that my breath hitches. It's what the photographer wanted and I should be prepared for him, but somehow it feels wrong.

It's not Matt, I know it isn't him, and it feels wrong. Ignoring the guilt ridden voice in my head, I focus on the clicking of the photographer's camera as I lose myself to my zone again.

"Now kiss her!" I hear from my side as Kaden's lips come down to me. I turn my face to avoid his mouth. "No!" I shout, earning me two sets of groans. "I never agreed to that," I let out, now glaring at a disappointed photographer staring back at me. Ignoring him, I shove Kaden up to put some distance between us.

"Fine. But I need sexy. So figure out how you're going to make it happen," the photographer snarls at me. With my blood already boiling, I angrily look up at Kaden who is now looking as if he's won. "No kissing on the mouth," I tell him.

With his lips curving up into a smile he answers, "Sure." His lips begin to place kisses along my neck. My traitorous body is already reacting by arching my back and lifting my head back to give him more access as Kaden's hands roam down my body. The feel of his hand gliding down my bare leg is unfamiliar, but rouses the same desire. I know it's not Matt, but sinfully I'm just as aroused as if it were.

I close my eyes attempting to push aside the desire building inside of me, but it's impossible as a vision of Matt surfaces. With the image of him in my mind and the feeling of Kaden's hands freely moving up and down my skin, my body is soon stirring to life and I'm unwillingly reacting to him. I open my eyes hoping it will help deter the two, but even with the brightened lights, I'm unable to disguise the longing to have sex that is rapidly building inside of me. Soon enough, salvation is brought to me when I'm required to do a wardrobe change, but when I return it soon starts all over again as the photographer continues demanding the same similar scenario. Four hours later, I catch myself feeling the familiar ache in between my legs as I react to Kaden's touch. My lip is chewed raw from the many times I bit down on it to stifle my moans. The yelling of the photographer calling it a wrap snaps me back to reality, shame now replacing my pent up desire.

Without lifting himself off me he whispers into my ear. "What do you say we finish this somewhere else?" he asks before placing a kiss below my ear as Matt usually does. It's the bucket of cold water I need to remind me of who's really whispering in my ear.

Shoving him off of me, I'm already yelling for them to bring me my robe and boot. "In your dreams!" I shout as I walk away, not bothering to look back. Reaching my dressing room, the smell of Kaden's cologne is overpowering my body and the feel of his lips are still on me. I'm shivering from shamelessly knowing how I reacted to him. I just want to get home to Matt and forever push Kaden from my mind.

Chapter Twenty-Four

Matt

MY PHONE VIBRATES on my desk, making me pick it up to look at the screen. It's another text message from Abigail.

I'm almost home <3 – Abigail

With my lips going up into a smile, I reply.

I can't wait. Love you, beautiful. – Matt

I love you more - Abigail

I read the message and my smile grows wider. She's been texting me all day. They began in the morning when she awoke and have been randomly coming throughout the day, but today I have gotten more "*I love you*" out of her than normal, worrying me something was wrong. The text I was looking forward to all day announcing she was on her way home pushed all the worry aside. Normally she wouldn't text me this much during class, but I don't care this time. I've missed her and she's more import-ant than having to hear an old instructor lecture away to a class that is barely half awake.

My excitement builds knowing she's almost home. She hasn't been gone a full twenty-four hours, yet it feels as if I haven't seen her in days. Even our conversation on the phone didn't feel the same. I'd much rather have her at my side. Thirty minutes later I'm rushing out of class, practically jogging to my car and pulling up into the driveway another twenty torturous minutes later.

Without hesitation, I rush into the house, already searching for her. "Hey," I tell her as I spot her entering the living room with an excited smile on both our faces as I rush to her. Picking her up so I can hold her close, she wraps her legs around my waist and I can already smell the scent of her lavender body wash. "You took a shower without me," I playfully scold to her before I kiss her lips.

She responds by moaning into my mouth as she tightens her arms and legs around my body. I ignore the pain of the boot kneading into my back because it's worth it to have Abigail in my arms. She continues to kiss me while I start walking us towards the bedroom to make up for our time apart.

"Wow. Miss me much," I tease her when we end our kiss, panting for air. She nods her head before diving in for another kiss and grinding herself into my hips. I don't need any further invitation to know what she wants and I'm happy to abide to her request. Gently tossing her onto the bed, I hear her giggle before she reaches up to pull me down above her, urgently pulling my shirt off. Within minutes we're both naked and I'm inside her. The sound of her satisfied moan as I enter her is happiness to my ears. The sex is fast, but just as satisfying as I bring us both to our peak.

Panting, I pull myself from her body to lie at her side, tucking her into my side. We lay there in silence, but from the way Abigail is tightly holding onto me, I grow worried something is wrong. "Tell me what's wrong?" I ask her.

"Why would you think something is wrong," she whispers. "I just really missed you," she whimpers out, a tear already falling from the corner of her eye.

I can tell from the way she said the words she's disguising her true answer. "Beautiful, tell me the truth. What happened in Seattle?"

"Nothing," she whispers, reaching up to give me another kiss. "Tell me the truth," I softly demand.

As I wait for an answer, a thought comes to mine. "Did you run into Bill? Because if he came near you, I'll kill him!" I say, already leaning up on my elbow to look down at her.

"No," she squeals. "I just missed you, I swear," she says, trying to calm me with her hand stroking my face.

My heart had dropped to the pit of my stomach with fear that she would encountered Bill. Although she's reassuring me she just missed me, the saddened expression is telling me there's more. She looks heart broken and my worry has returned. "Are you sure that's all?" I request again as I tuck her hair behind her ear.

Instead of speaking, she nods her head. "Okay, beautiful," I reply, kissing her nose. "Why don't you tell me about the shoot," I say with a smile, but her reaction is far from my happy one. I watch as her breath hitches and her eyes go wide. "Abigail," I demand.

Her lips are now pinched. "It was a lingerie shoot."

I'll admit at first I'm irritated from her answer, but I have to remember what her career entails and I push the resentment aside. "Did you get to bring any of it home?"

She looks surprised from my response. "No, I wouldn't have wanted to bring them home even if they offered," she answers before adding, "I'd much rather wear something you chose instead." Her answer makes me smile.

Kissing her, I roll onto my back, pulling her with me as I run my hand up and down her back to soothe her to sleep. Her breathing slows, telling me I've accomplished my goal. Instead of joining her, I lay there remembering our short conversation, realizing that although I know the details of Abigail's career, I'm still not mentally prepared to accept certain aspects of it. Knowing my girlfriend is once again going to be half-naked for the world to see isn't what I had in mind when I encouraged her to start working again, but I know deep down in my heart it's what I'll have to accept to keep her at my side.

Chapter Twenty-Five

Abigail

"HOW MUCH LONGER is he going to take?" I impatiently whine. Standing at my side, I hear Matt laugh. "Patience, beautiful."

"I wouldn't require patience if he'd be on time," I mention. "We've been waiting in this room for over an hour," I continue, knowing I sound like an impatient child, but I'm frustrated at this point.

The *only* reason I'm still waiting is because I need to know whether or not I have to endure wearing this hideous boot any longer, if not I would have left long ago. As if sensing I need comforting, Matt places a kiss on my lips, but I pull him closer to tease him. "There is something else I would've rather been doing for the past hour," I speak against his lips, causing him to moan into my mouth.

In return he trails his finger inside my thigh, tantalizing its way up to my center. I'm now moaning as I push myself up against his hand. "Be good, or else you won't find out your results because you won't be here to get them," he seductively growls into my lips. His hand is now rubbing against the center of my jeans, causing me to grow wet from both his touch and the thoughts of what he can be doing with his hand if it wasn't for the barrier of the material.

"And where exactly would I be?" I curiously ask before biting into his bottom lip. We're both heavily breathing as he tightens the grip of his hand. I sense him about to answer when the door opens, causing him to pull away.

I know I'm blushing as the doctor begins to speak. "Ms. Adams. Glad to see you again," he announces with a friendly nod as he walks straight to the computer against the wall and starts typing away at it. With an embarrassed smile now on my face, I'm about to answer when Matt whispers into my ear, "You'll have to wait now until we get home."

The reminder of his words agitates me as my body shivers from his warm breath against my ear. The doctor turns to face me with a smile on his face. "Looks like the boot gets to come off today. You did a really good job of following instructions and keeping off your ankle," he says with a proud smile. "Not many patients follow my advice."

"I believe I had a lot to do with making sure she stayed off it," Matt cheerfully admits as he coyly smiles back at me with a twinkle in his eyes.

I'm blushing once again. "That's good. I appreciate your help," the doctor says with a smile over to Matt, oblivious to the true meaning behind his words. "This doesn't mean you're completely healed, though. You still have quite a bit to go before you're back to normal. You'll need to continue being on light duty and require physical therapy as I had mentioned," he sternly lectures.

My heart stops from his words and the dread is already building inside of me. "When will I be able to run again?"

His expression is somber "I'm sorry. It won't be for a while," he regretfully says.

"But now that the boot is off why can't I start running again? What about Boston?" I fearfully ask, dreading his answer.

As if expecting me to argue, he's already explaining, "Although we're removing the boot today, your ankle still needs time to properly heal or else you're going to cause permanent damage to it. I know you'd planned on running Boston this year, but I don't think it's going to be possible."

I blink away the tears that are threatening to fall as I take in his words, refusing to allow my weakness to emerge. The time I spent forced to follow orders feels as if it was for nothing, the entire time I obediently followed Matt's orders to rest and not be as mobile on my ankle feeling wasted. I believed I would be able to start training again once I'd been given the clearance to retire the boot. Aggravated, I feel as if I've failed myself. I simply sit there staring off into the distance, wishing my outcome were different.

It isn't long before both Matt and I are walking out of the exam room. The excitement I'd expected to be feeling from no longer having the weight of the boot to slow me down is absent. Instead it's replaced with disappointment of imagining the length of time I have to continue to wait until I can fully run again. It's as if my heart has shattered all over again.

When we're back in Matt's car he reaches over for my hand, entwining our fingers. "It's not as bad as you think, beautiful. This is just a minor setback," he reassures me.

I look over at him, wishing I were convinced by his words as I miserably sit next to him. After starting the car, Matt takes my hand to entwine our fingers to place a kiss on the back of my hand before driving off. I continue sitting in silence the entire car ride home, pondering my thoughts. I may not be able to run Boston this year, but I do make a promise to myself which I intend to keep. Boston may not be mine this year, but *I am going to run it someday.*

IT'S BEEN ALMOST a month since I've had the boot removed, and in that month I've discovered something new about myself—I have no patience. At least not the patience I need to take things slow. An entire hour of hearing someone tell me to take my time and to slow down grows irritating after a while. Having physical therapy two times a week was testing my sanity. I've come to the conclusion it's the reason why I quickly fell in love with running. If I wanted to get to the finish line faster I simply had to increase my speed, *not slow down*. I was in control of the speed that got me there.

At least I managed to make it through one more appointment, which means I am one day closer to my own finish line. With a smile on my face, I recall the physical therapist's compliment on my progress and allowing me the clearance to do runway shows again, giving me hope that'd I'd be running soon.

It could not have come at a better time since I've already accepted a job offer from the agency to do a runway show for an upcoming designer in Los Angeles. When the recruiter had called me with the offer, I took it without hesitation. I was confident I would be able to do it. My dilemma now was breaking the news to Matt. He's been persistent about not putting too much weight on my ankle until the physical therapist gave me the clearance. He made me feel like a child who was still wearing the boot. His only explanation for his persistence was that he wanted me to recover without any further injuries. At least he was on my side about me getting back to running soon, but he was beginning to make me feel resentful towards him.

With Julio at my side, I walk out of the medical building and climb into my car to head home with a huge smile on my face. Even with the silence between us in the car, it gives me time to go over the words I plan on telling Matt about the trip. With the smile on my face and Julio in tow, I walk into the house to find a scowling Matt. He's staring down at the papers in his hand, just before he tosses them across the floor and they land in a scattered mess.

"What's wrong?" I ask, looking down at them confused out of my mind.

The anger is radiating off of him as he looks over to Julio.

"She doesn't go anywhere without you. At all! Do you understand?" he demands. Julio looks confused as he nods, answering, "Of course."

"Matt, you already know I don't go anywhere without him," I remind him. "Tell me what's going on?" Now I'm worried from his words.

"The temporary restraining order against Bill expired last week. You never went to court to get the permanent one placed."

Closing my eyes, I curse myself. "I'm sorry, I forgot I was supposed to go to court."

"How can you forget about something that important, Abigail?" he declares, pointing to the scattered papers spread across the floor.

Looking down at them, the guilt is already rising inside of me. "So much has been going on lately that it totally slipped my mind. How can you blame me? It's not like my life has been sugar coated the last couple of months," I throw at him.

Ignoring my words, he starts rubbing at his temple. "It doesn't matter anyway. You don't have anything going on besides your appointments, so you should be fine until we can file another claim."

My earlier excitement has vanished. "Actually, I'm going to L.A. this weekend," I inform him in a way I hadn't planned on telling him.

Whipping his head up to look at me, he looks angry again. "What for?" he demands.

"For a runway show."

"Why don't I know about this?" he asks, looking confused.

"I'm telling you now."

Crap. With the enraged expression he's giving me, I'm pretty sure he's figured out I've been keeping it from him. "I didn't want to get my hopes up in case I couldn't get the clearance from my physical therapist," I further explain, still not sharing the full details of when I took the job.

Expressionless, he stares at me as he continues to remain

silent. "Matt, I'm tired of sitting around and doing nothing. I like modeling and I'm going to continue doing it. You can't blame me for taking the opportunity," I state, unwilling to cave on my decision.

Closing the distance between us, he now looks regretful. "You're right. You should do it, but can you blame me for wanting to protect you from Bill?" he quietly asks.

Tormented by his words, I push the doubt of my decision aside. "I can't keep living my life in fear of him, Matt," I declare. "I'm doing the show."

He considers my answer for a moment. "I didn't say you couldn't do it, I just don't like the idea of Bill being out there without you having a restraining order against him," he explains. "When is the show?"

"This weekend."

"And you felt the need to keep it from me?" he asks, his eyebrow curiously raised high.

He's testing me. "I don't want to argue about this, Matt," I reply without any further explanation.

"I guess where going to L.A. this weekend," he informs Julio before adding, "I want to talk to you outside," as he looks back to me. "I really do hope you're not lying to me Abigail," his words stabbing at my conscience.

With my heart now lodged in the pit of my stomach, I watch both Julio and Matt walk out the front door. I can sense from Matt's last words that he knows I've lied to him, which makes me feel guiltier for not telling him the entire truth.

When I see the door close behind Julio, I start to gather the scattered papers from the floor to try to better understand them, but fail miserably.

I'm left standing in the living room alone with a set of papers that mean nothing to me, but enough for me to understand Bill still has enough power to control my life, regardless of how much I tell myself otherwise. I may have escaped him more than once, but he's still managing to make me live in fear of him.

Matt

REACHING JULIO'S CAR, I take a quick glance back at the front door, making sure Abigail hasn't followed us. "How good are you with a gun?" I get straight to the point and ask Julio.

He snorts before answering. "Now you're asking me stupid questions," he curtly replies. "Why are you asking?"

"You and I both know even if Abigail were to reapply for a restraining order, a fucking paper is not going to keep Bill away from her. I need to know she's safe," I state, looking back at the house.

"I don't like the idea of her being around a gun, but if it's what it takes to know she'll be safe, then so be it. I know you probably kept up to date with your gun license," I tell him, earning me a nod. "Which means you're going to start carrying a gun again for her protection. I'll pay for whatever you need," I inform him.

"I agree."

"Good. Let me know how much you'll need and I'll get it to you." He opens his car door as I add, "And I need you to have it on you when we go to L.A. this weekend."

"Of course," he answers as he gets into his car.

Turning to make my way back into the house, I don't find Abigail in the living room. I head straight to the bedroom to find her lying on the bed with her face buried into the pillow. Her body stiffens upon hearing me enter the room, warning me I may have a battle ahead of me. Removing my shoes, I climb into bed behind her, wrapping my arm around her waist to pull her up against my chest.

"I'm sorry, Matt. I swear I was going to tell you," she murmurs, her words full of regret. I place a kiss on her shoulder. "I believe you," I reply, not knowing if I truly mean the words.

"Are you still mad at me?" she somberly asks.

I'm silently thinking as she turns her head to kiss my lips. "No, but I just don't understand what is going on between us anymore, Abigail."

She sighs deeply before turning her head to stare out the window. "I'm scared," she states in a whisper.

Her words worry me. I tug her body so she's facing me, pulling her once again against my body. "What are you scared of?"

"Of everything," she rasps out. "I'm scared I'll never know who I am. I'm scared I'll never be able to run Boston. I'm scared I'll never get my career back," she declares, but she continues on, "I'm scared that Bill is still out there and I may have just messed up my only chance to keep him away. But most of all, I'm scared of losing you, Matt," she says with a sniffle as I feel her wet tears against my neck.

"Abigail, you're *going* to run Boston one day. You're a strong beautiful girl who I love *very much*, which is why I would never leave you," I promise, trying to comfort her. "Bill, should be the least of your worries because I would never let him get anywhere near you.

"As far as your career, you've got that under control," I tell her, thinking back to what helped start this all. "We're going to L.A. this weekend and you're going to show them who Abigail Adams is and it's going to open many more opportunities. You'll see," I reassure her.

"That's if I don't fall flat on my face," she teases.

Envisioning her words, I throw my head back and laugh. "I love you. No matter what happens, I always will," I tell her when I'm done laughing.

Her expression turns somber, but I kiss her hoping it will distract her. I don't know what the future holds between Abigail and I, but I'm praying it's a future of forever.

Chapter Twenty-Six

Abigail

I'VE LIED TO Matt, again and he knows it. His angered expression staring back at me tells me I've pushed my limit with him. The rain is pouring down. Our bodies are drenched, our clothes completely soaked through as they mold to the shape of our bodies that are beginning to tremble from the cold. Every droplet that hits me feels like a piercing shard of glass, but it's nothing compared to the pain inside my heart as Matt's narrowed eyes stare down into mine, straight into my soul.

As the rain picks up, the droplets become larger and pound harder against my skin. I'll take the pounding over and over again, anything to not have to feel this way anymore. I don't want to feel this pain. It's as if he's punishing me for every second of anguish and heartache I've caused him for the last six months.

Yes, that's exactly what this is. This is my punishment.

"Please, Matt, don't do this," I beg him, desperately pleading as I yank on his arm to keep him in place. He stays silent, the anguish spreading across his face. I never thought I'd see this day. I expected him to always be there, regardless of what I did. However, it's entirely my fault and the look in his eyes tells me he has finally given up.

He slowly shakes his head. I can barely see his expression now because my vision is obstructed from both my tears and the rain. I want to wipe my eyes, but I don't want to chance letting him go, because I know the minute I do he will walk away forever. It will finally come to an end.

I yank again, trying to pull him closer to me, but he's stronger than I am and instead he steps back as my body is pulled forward as well. I stumble to stay upright, still trying to hold on for dear life. "You wanted this, Abigail. You chose this, not me," he growls. "How many times did I come crawling back to you, but you only pushed me away? I can't do this anymore. I'm tired of begging."

"Please don't leave me," I shout back to him. "You promised never to give up on us," I say as the tears continue to rapidly fall, my breathing now labored, and my desperation weakening me by the minute.

Excitement builds within me when I see him step towards me. He brings his hand up to cup my face and I lean in, needing his warmth. When he leans down to place a kiss against my lips, my heart feels like it's going to burst from my chest with happiness. His kiss is simple. Gentle. I can feel every ounce of love he has for me in just this one kiss, but when my eyes find his again, even through the rain, all I see is pain.

He brings his forehead down to mine. "I will always love you, beautiful, don't you ever forget that," he whispers loudly enough for me to hear before he places one last kiss against my temple and turns to walk away. My efforts to pull him back have failed completely. Somehow I've managed to let him go as I watch him walk away from me without a backwards glance.

I try to run to him, but my body is rooted in place, frozen and unable to move. I'm desperately shouting at him to come back, but my words are muted, silently coming out. My heart is shattering inside of me, the pain slowly ripping me apart inch by inch. I no longer have strength as my knees give out and my body comes crashing to the floor. When I lift my head up to look for him again, he's gone, as if he was never there.

I feel like my soul has been taken completely from me. My heart is no longer there because he took it with him when he walked way. My purpose to live is no longer within me.

The convulsions of my crying have taken over my body and I feel like I can't breathe, the rain taking over my lungs and now drowning me. I'm frantically gasping for air, but the pain has taken over. I accept that I no longer have a reason to live.

Matt

ABIGAIL AWAKENS ME as she twitches in my arms. I should have expected it since it's been occurring more often these last two nights, leaving me with a restless night. It's as if she's having a nightmare, but when I try waking her, she grows angry from me doing so. I've tried asking her about her dreams, but she seems to not remember anything in the morning.

Tonight, though, she's stirred four times already. I know she's still asleep, but it's still worries me. Tightening my hold on her body, I rub my hand up and down her back to try to soothe her. Her contented sigh into my neck tells me it's working, but soon I'm proven wrong.

"Don't leave me!" she shouts as she sits up, damn near scaring the shit out of me, making me sit up with her. "It's okay beautiful, I'm right here," I say as I pull her into my arms to whisper the words.

The room is dark, but with a faint glow coming in through the window I can see her eyes are wide open. She's clearly frightened. "Shhh, it's okay, beautiful. I'm right here," I continue whispering in her ear, once again soothing her with my hand.

Her face is buried into my neck now and I can feel the tears trickling down my skin. "Do you want to talk about it?" I cautiously ask her. I'm disappointed when I feel her respond with a shake of her head.

"Please," I plead. "I think it will make you feel better."

I'm expecting silence from her, but she surprises me. "I dreamt you were leaving," she faintly whispers against my ear. "I would *never* leave you, beautiful. I promise," I reassure her, although bewildered by her words.

"You can't say that, Matt."

I'm disheartened she doesn't believe me. "Yes, I can, because I love you," I insist. She doesn't argue this time, but I don't push any further. Eventually I feel her body become lax against my own and by the calm sound of her breathing, I know she's fallen back to sleep. Her hold on me has tightened as if doubting my words. Readjusting our bodies so we can lie back down, I lay her across my chest before I feel her shutter from her silent crying.

It's almost dawn and instead of falling asleep with her, I lay awake reflecting over her words. The alarm soon goes off and it isn't until then that Abigail stirs again. I continue trying to rouse her awake by kissing my way down her shoulder and up to her ear. "It's time to wake up, beautiful."

She mumbles. "Sex or pancakes, you're pick," I say to her, knowing she will get up for either choice. Sleepy eyed, she looks at me. "That's not fair. It's like asking if I want to breathe," she protests before closing her eyes once more.

Throwing my head back to laugh, I soon feel her hand creeping its way down my stomach before wrapping itself around my shaft. I allow her to stroke me and it isn't long before I'm hard and ready for her.

Pushing her on her back, I position myself between her legs as she uses her hand to guide me inside of her. "Screw pancakes," I moan, completely filling her.

At first I take my time rocking my hips into her body, but she demands more. Her hips lift against my body as I continue to glide in and out of her, urging me deeper into her. Her desperate moans grow loader and desperate, telling me she's close to her release. I plunge harder and faster against her body, wanting to pleasure her. I can already feel her walls tightening and within seconds I hear her screaming my name as she comes; pumping a couple more times I'm soon following her over the edge. Exhausted and spent, I rest above her with my elbows at her side to keep me extended above her body, refusing to pull myself from her body just yet. Her legs are still tightly wound around my waist and her arms are still holding me, telling me she isn't ready to let me go either.

"Now that you're done, Julio is waiting for you," Trey shouts from the other end of the door, making us both laugh. I sit both Abigail and I up, keeping her legs wrapped around my waist. "Now I'm hungry," I hear her breathlessly say into my ear as her body slumps against mine.

"Sorry, beautiful, no time for pancakes now," I inform her with a chuckle, my lips tasting her salty skin. "Next time I say you mix while you thrust. I get both pancakes and sex," she mumbles in return.

I cannot help but laugh at her words imagining the image of her request. "Maybe next time, beautiful," I say already climbing out of bed with her still in my arms, walking us both to the bathroom.

Taking the quickest shower we can both take, we're soon entering the living room to find Julio and Trey watching TV as we walk in. "Do you have everything you need?" I ask Julio, earning me a curt nod. Grabbing our luggage already sitting near the doorway, I rush Abigail out of the door, hearing complaints that she's still hungry.

"They don't taste the same," Abigail complains after eating her first bite of the McDonald's pancakes I've ordered from the drive-thru. Looking over to her, she has her nose scrunched up as she continues to chew. I smile, feeling reassured she will never like anyone else's pancakes but my own. "Next time you'll think twice about your choice of breakfast," I badger her over her decision.

Soon we're at the airport with Julio checking in ahead of us. It's when he pulls his coat jacket back to remove his gun from its holster that I hear a shocked Abigail. "Why does Julio have a gun?" she shrieks.

Her eyes stay locked onto Julio as I urge her to the next available attendant. "I'll explain in a minute."

Shooting me with glare, she says, "You knew about it?"

"Abigail, right now is not the time to be discussing this."

Ignoring my words, she continues her protest. "How long has he been carrying a gun?"

"He's only been carrying for a couple of days," I answer, handing the attendant my ID and ticket information.

"I can't believe you didn't tell me," she utters, already crossing her arms over her chest like a stubborn child. "Now you know how I feel when you keep shit from me," I mumble.

From the corner of my eye I can see Abigail now staring daggers off into the distance. She's purposely ignoring me, which is allowing me a break before the storm in which I know will come. It's when we're seated in the lounge of our terminal that I choose to approach the subject.

"Abigail, I don't know why you're so upset. It's for your protection."

Still staring off into the distance, she continues ignoring me for a couple of minutes before she speaks. "I'm scared of guns," she quietly states barely above a whisper. Shocked, I look over to her. Her eyes are glassy, but I can see she's forcing herself to stay composed.

Wrapping my arm around her, I pull her closer to me so I can kiss her on her temple. "I didn't know. I'm sorry," I apologize. "But with everything that's going on with Bill, I'd rather Julio be carrying it," I explain.

Surprising me, she nods her head in understanding. "It doesn't mean I have to like it," she replies.

I cannot argue with her words. Instead I hold her as we sit in silence until it's time to board the plane. Even if she had continued arguing the subject, she wasn't going to win this fight. Her life was more important to me than her fear.

Chapter Twenty-Seven

Abigail

I BARELY HAVE time to check into the hotel before I'm whisked away in a town car hired to take me to the runway show. I'm both excited and anxious the entire ride there, but it's when I'm sitting in the make-up chair and surrounded by the chaos of everyone around me I realize, I feel at home.

The production manager announces the ten minute warning call and I'm whisked off to the dressing area to change. Next I'm standing in a line with my eyes closed helping myself find the zone I've become so familiar with. On cue, they point to me and I take my first step onto the catwalk to an abundance of flashing lights. I feel in control with every step I take, a small voice guiding me every step of the way.

Shoulders back, look straight ahead. Keep walking until you reach the end of the platform, stop, freeze into a pose, now turn.

Continuing the same routine as I walk my way back, I head straight into the direction of backstage where I'm ushered to an area with a rack of clothing and production assistants holding up makeshift dressing rooms on the spot. Within a minute I'm stripped and dressed into my next outfit. I have enough time to breathe before I'm pushed back into line, but strangely the entire routine feels familiar and without hesitating, I'm doing it all over again; the catwalk being my center stage high.

The entire show goes by in a repeated blur until the final walk thru and the crowd is proudly applauding us. With the show over, I'm gathering my personal effects backstage when Matt finds me.

Throwing myself into his arms, he catches me in a swirling hug. "You were amazing out there, beautiful," he proudly states.

"Really?" I ask, now feeling doubtful of myself.

"Really," he answers before giving me a kiss. "You were so hot I think we need to leave already so I can congratulate you back at the hotel," his seductive words creating an image in my mind.

"Promise?" I breathlessly ask. I'm about to kiss him when I hear someone call my name. Turning to see who it is, the blood drains from my body and my heart plummets into the depths of my stomach as I take the person in.

"Kaden," my heart stops beating and I'm rendered speechless trying to figure out what he's doing here.

Ignoring the fact that Matt is standing next to me, he comes straight towards me to give me a kiss, but I quickly pull my face away to avoid his kiss. He looks confused before saying, "It's good to see you again," as his eyes rake down my body. "You look different with clothes on," he finishes with a crooked grin before I see Matt's fist make contact with his jaw.

Kaden attacks back by shoving against Matt's body with his shoulder. I'm frantically trying to break them up, but Julio is already at my side beating me to it as he pulls Kaden away from Matt. From the fury in Matt's eyes, I know he's ready to attack Kaden once more, forcing me to step in. "Matt, calm down!" I shout in an attempt to get his attention, but it takes me holding his body back with my hands against his chest to stop him. Instead of looking at me his eyes are following Julio as he leads Kaden out of the area.

"Who the fuck is he, and what does he mean *with your*

clothes on?" he furiously shouts.

"We did a photo shoot together last month," I explain trying to calm his enraged temper, still stunned over what happened. "You failed to mention the shoot was with a guy," Matt sneers. "What the fuck was he doing in it?" he asks, pointing at the direction Julio left to.

"It's not what you think," I defensively say, still trying to defuse his anger, but it isn't working. "And I didn't mention it because I knew you wouldn't be happy with it," I throw back at him.

"Is he the reason why you didn't want me there?"

"No! I swear I didn't know he'd be there. I didn't even know what type of shoot it was until that morning," I defensively proclaim. "I don't know why you're so angry. I wasn't fucking him, unlike when you're half naked with the opposite sex," I throw back at him.

Pushing away from me as if I've slapped him, he looks back at me stunned. "I'm sorry," I let out, regretting my words. "It was nothing more than a job," I quietly whisper, remembering the shame I felt leaving the photo shoot.

"How do you expect me to trust you when you keep things from me?" he bellows out. "You kept the fact that you were half naked with a guy, *on the job,* from me."

"You expect me to believe you would've been cool with all the details?"

"I just want to know why you couldn't tell me?" he asks.

"I knew you would react this way. I knew you would get pissed over my doing a lingerie shoot with a half-naked model!" I shout back at him, trying to prove my point. "This is what I do, Matt. This is my career. You knew it when I met you. You're either going to have to learn to deal with it…" I say, still pondering what to say next.

"Or what, Abigail?" he growls out, looking furious at this point.

"Or nothing, Matt, because I'm not giving you a choice,"

I snarl back at him, already turning to walk away. My blood is boiling as I walk my way to the car. My once ecstatic frame of mind has now been replaced with fury.

The entire car ride back to the hotel is made in utter silence. By the time we arrive my fury has, for some odd reason, been replaced with disappointment. Matt's reaction proves he will never truly accept what my job entails, which is the reason why I need to do what's best for me, which may just pull us apart.

Matt

I'M SITTING ON the balcony of the hotel with a beer in my hand, my eyes locked onto the skyline in the distance as Abigail's words repeat themselves in my head. The moment she threw them at me, I was hit with the realization of the truth. It was *her* career and I knew she wouldn't allow anything or anyone to choose different for her. She had enough of that in her past.

As I'd watched her on the runway today, I had never felt more proud of anyone in my life. I now understood how Emily felt from every accomplishment I had made for her. But now that the tables are turned, I have to learn to face the demons I kept pushing away. Abigail is a model and would always be. There was no denying she was born to be.

Finishing off my beer, I stand up and head back inside to try talk to her. I know I need to apologize for being a stubborn asshole, but my pride had kept me from doing it since we argued. Instead we've both been stubbornly ignoring each other since we stepped into the car. I'd intended to talk to her as soon as we arrived at the hotel, but she rushed to the bedroom and quickly shut the door behind her, leaving me the chance to drink my misery away alone on the balcony.

It wasn't until I was on my last beer that I realized I'd reverted back to doing what I had done before I met Abigail. I was shutting out the world and attempting to drink the misery away. Placing the empty bottle on the coffee table, I stumble my way over to the room to Abigail, hoping she isn't still too upset. When I enter, I see her ending a phone call with a smile spread across her face as she stares down at her phone. Her smile alone is lighting up the room as it removes the darkened cloud I had dragged back in with me.

I can tell she hasn't heard me enter, which allows me to stare at her beautiful face as she smiles. When she looks up, her body jolts as if frightened from seeing me. Cautiously, so not to stumble from my drunken haze, I walk my way over to her and join her in the bed. "Can I see your phone?" I ask her, already holding my hand out.

Clutching the phone to her chest, she asks, "Why?"

"I want to change the ring tone," I answer, demanding for the phone once more. This time she willingly hands it over and I go straight to looking for the song I kept thinking about for the last hour. Handing the phone back to her, I dig mine out of my pocket and call her. The lyrics of *Hanging By A Moment* are announcing themselves in the silence of the room.

She awards me with a genuine smile as she leans in to kiss me. Without hesitating, I deepen the kiss. "You're lucky I love the taste of beer in your mouth," I hear her mumble against my lips.

I pull her down on top of me so I can lay her across my chest, needing to hold her in my arms. Without any hesitation, she makes herself comfortable on my body and my hand is already rubbing her back. "I'm sorry," I whisper into her ear.

"It was just a photo shoot, Matt," she responds into my neck.

"No more secrets," I ask of her and she nods her head to answer. "We just have to trust each other and no longer keep secrets from one another. It's how this all started."

"I know, but I love you too much to lose you over something stupid like this," she states.

Her words are a reminder of the asshole I became when my jealousy took over me earlier. "I'm sorry," I repeat, hugging her tighter. "Can we just put this all behind us, please?" she pleads.

Pulling my head away so I can kiss her, my lips find hers, needing to show her just how much I love her. Her kiss is like ambrosia or a drug I will never get enough of, as is her body. Stripping her out of her clothes, I do the same with mine, wanting to be one with her. I have an urgency to be inside of her.

Making sure she's looking into my eyes, I enter her. With my eyes never leaving hers, I slowly make love to her. It isn't rushed, as it was this morning. I want her to understand just how much she means to me, how much I truly do love her, and I do it by reminding her every couple of minutes as I whisper it into her ear as I take us to our world of ecstasy.

Chapter Twenty-Eight

Abigail

MATT IS LAYING in my arms with his head on my chest as he quietly breathes in his sleep. He had fallen asleep almost immediately after we made love. Ironically, it's usually me who immediately attempts to fall asleep afterwards, but the alcohol in his system may be the reason why. Instead, I hold Matt in my arms as my mind wanders back to right before he entered the room.

"Hello Ms. Adams. I want to congratulate you on such an amazing show. The designer, Rebecca Russell, had nothing but praise for your performance today," the production director announces.

"Thank you," I shyly respond.

"I'm calling to ask if you're currently in a contract with an agency at this time?"

"No, I'm not," I answer. As I'm about to ask why, she enthusiastically continues. *"Oh great! We wouldn't normally be doing this, but the designer was so impressed with your performance today she is insisting I add you to the show as her primary model."* If I weren't already stunned from her words, the next set would have thrown me into shock. *"She has insisted we offer you a contract for the remainder of the tour. I hope your*

passport is up to date, because you're going to need it," she playfully teases.

Confused, I ask, "What do you mean?"

"There are ten shows left and our next stop is New York for the next two weeks to prepare for fashion week, and the remainder of it in Parii," she replies, accenting Paris *in a French accent.*

I can't help but grow excited from the offer, but my heart plunges into the pit of my stomach when I think of Matt.

"Can I give you an answer in a couple of days?" I hesitantly ask.

She goes silent for a couple of seconds, but quickly responds. "Unfortunately I need an answer now. This is a very good opportunity for your career, Ms. Adams," she suggests.

I'm frightful I'd be turning away an important opportunity. "I accept," I announce, feeling my heart sink lower in the pit of my stomach.

"Good," she happily replies. "Let me know where I need to send you the details," she says, before we're soon exchanging information and end the call.

With a smile on my face I stare down at my phone, confident I've made the right decision and my earlier excitement has once again returned.

The offer still feels surreal, but I knew I couldn't pass it up. Dreadfully, it means I have to be separated from Matt the entire time. It was only temporary, but the fear of distance is worrying me. I had to keep telling myself that our love is strong enough to endure these minor obstacles. I have to believe deep down in my heart it would make our love stronger.

Closing my eyes, I pray the decision I made will not tear Matt and I apart. I do love him, with all of my heart, but I need to do this for myself. I know deep down inside it's for the best. I just hope Matt will understand.

THE NEXT MORNING we awaken to the ringing of Matt's phone. I listen, still half asleep, to the rumbling of his voice below my ear against his chest. Most of his words are full of excitement, but it isn't until we're eating breakfast in bed that it occurs to me to ask who was on the other end of the line.

"It's a surprise," he states with a smile. I climb onto his lap so I can straddle him. "Is there anything I can bribe you with so you can tell me anyways?" I say, teasing him as I rub myself against his body.

I can feel him harden a bit between my legs. "As much as I'm tempted to take you up your offer, we really need to leave or else their will no longer be a surprise."

Now I really want to know and I'm sure from the glowering expression on my face Matt can tell as he chuckles back at me. "Okay, you win. That was an NFL scout who came to one of my games. He's interested in talking to me about the upcoming NFL combine. I didn't want to say anything because I didn't want to get my hopes up until I spoke to him," he announces.

I'm left in utter shock from his words as I remember Matt telling me once how important the NFL combine was to a college athlete. It was every college player's dreams to be considered. Screaming, I say, "Oh. My. God. Matt!"

"Let's not get our hopes up, yet. I still have to talk to the guy to see what he's even offering."

"Then we need to hurry up and get back to Portland," I say excitedly as I climb off of him and drag him to the bathroom so we can shower.

I should have pushed myself to tell Matt about my plans before arriving in Portland, but I didn't want to return with the same blackened cloud we had left with. Instead, I keep a forced smile on my face, giving him the impression everything was back to normal. I'd approach the subject after his meeting with the recruiter. Until then, I wanted to savor the moments of happiness with Matt.

The entire plane ride back to Portland I was mentally preparing my speech in my head, carefully choosing which words I would use when I told him. Another dilemma on my hands was whether or not Julio would be joining me on my trip. I was going to need him at my side. But was he willing to pack up everything and go with me?

My thoughts are brought back as Matt squeezes my hand; my eyes find his as I give him a smile. Deep down inside I'm apprehensive of how Matt is going to react, but I'll soon find out as I plan on telling him before the weekend is over. The closer we get to the house, the more I prepare myself for what is yet to come.

Pulling up to the driveway, we see a Chevy Malibu with a plastic frame surrounding the license plate—indicating it's a rental car. My heart is excitingly beating for Matt as he parks next to it. Climbing out of the car, he waits for me to reach his side before I hear him say, "Here goes nothing."

Pulling him to a stop so I can look at him to say, "He wouldn't be in there unless you were worth it. You have nothing to worry about," I say before pulling him in for a reassuring kiss.

"I'm hope so," he replies, making me shove him towards the house for ignoring my words.

I look back to Julio, remembering I wanted to speak to him as well. "Can you come in for a moment? There's something I wanted to talk to you about," I relay.

Matt looks back at me confused, but I ignore him as I continue ushering him to keep walking. As we step inside, Trey is sitting on the couch with another gentleman, but upon seeing us walk in, he stands to shout, "It's about time you got home!" looking straight at Matt.

The gentleman stands, already heading over to us, his hand extended to greet Matt. "Hello, Matthew. My name is Eddie. It's nice to finally meet you."

"Nice to meet you as well," Matt says as he shakes Eddie's hand.

Everyone, except for Julio who stands near the kitchen

area, heads over to the living room to take a seat. The recruiter goes straight into a conversation with Matt. "I've been watching you for the last two years and you've shown some great improvement."

"Thank you," Matt shyly replies.

Behind Eddie is an excited Trey pumping his fist into the air. "Unfortunately, I have to make this meeting quick since I have to catch a plane soon. I arrived yesterday and barely missed you after you left."

"Sorry about that. My girlfriend had a fashion show in L.A. I didn't want to miss," Matt replies, proudly looking at me.

The recruiter's eyes find mine. "Yes, you're a lucky man to be dating this beautiful lady," he says with a smile. "As I mentioned, I'm here to invite you to this year's scouting combine to see what you've got. It'd be there that we determine if you have potential to be drafted this year or not," he explains.

I expect for Matt's jaw to drop, but instead he looks skeptical. "Are you sure they really want me?" he reluctantly asks. "I mean, let's be honest. I *know* I've been sucking this year. There has to be much better players out there you'd like to focus on."

My eyes go wide from his response before I hear the recruiter snicker. "I like you already, Matt. You're right, you haven't been playing so well these last couple of games. To be honest I shouldn't be here by the way you played your last game in San Francisco," the words a reminder of his poor performance. "But I've been watching you since last year and I know there must have been a cause for your distraction during that game. It happens to every player, but I know deep down inside you have potential, which is why I'm giving you a chance. It's up to you to prove whether you're willing to step up and show us what you've got," he states before standing up. "So what do you say? Will I be seeing you there?" he asks with a curiously raised brow.

"Of course," Matt answers.

"Good," Eddie says before looking down at his watch. "I

look forward to seeing you on the field. Good luck," he says before shaking Matt's hand again.

"Thank you," Matt replies.

Pulling out a set of half folded papers from his coat jacket, he hands them to Matt. "This is all the information you'll need and my contact information. Shoot me an email so I can set everything up to get you there. Once again, good luck," he finishes saying before rushing to the door.

It's obvious he was in a hurry by how fast he was rushing out the door, but at the same time I'm thankful he waited. Excited, I look over to Matt who seems shocked as he looks over the paperwork in his hands. I watch as his eyes quickly scan the words before looking back up to me with a beaming smile. "I can't believe this," he voices.

"I'm not surprised," I express to him. Behind him Trey is already pounding him on his shoulder to congratulate him. Commencing a round of congratulations from both Julio and I, he's soon calling David to tell him the news. With the excitement still in the room, a dreadful frown spreads across his face.

"It still doesn't mean anything. I may not be good enough for them," he claims. Giving him a shove, Trey shouts, "Shut the fuck up. You know you're good!"

As if doubtful, he goes back to reading the paperwork again. His head snaps up, his eyes bright. "It starts the week after next," he states, my heart dropping to the pit of my stomach and the blood draining from my face. His frown deepens as he asks. "You're coming with me, right?"

His question has rendered me speechless. "What's wrong, Abigail?"

Forcing myself to find my voice, I tell him, "I can't." I practically whisper as the words break from my mouth.

"What do you mean, you can't?"

I can feel the agony of my admission building as I say the words. "I'll be in New York, Matt," I dreadfully tell him. "I got offered a contract by the designer for the show I just did. She wants me to be her star model for the rest of the tour," I explain, my breath hitching with the words. I stand there frozen, watching him grow confused.

"When did this happen? How long have you known?

Swallowing the lump in my throat, I answer, "Since yesterday."

"And you didn't tell me?"

I nod my head as it falls forward to stare at the floor.

"What else are you keeping from me, Abigail? Because for some reason that's all you've been doing lately, is keeping secrets from me," he growls out.

"It wasn't a secret, Matt, I just didn't want to tell you until the time was right," I throw at him.

His eyes are narrowed down at me. "And when would that have been? When you were getting on the plane like you tried to do this last time?" he delivers, his words hitting me like a ton of bricks. His eyes grow dark in anger as he continues. "I don't even know who you are anymore, Abigail," he snarls before stepping around me and heading straight out the door, slamming it behind him, making my entire body flinch. I'm standing there shocked as I try to comprehend everything that just happened.

I look over to Julio who is standing there looking sympathetic. "It's for two months. Are you willing to come with me?" I sternly ask him, as I try to mask the pain coursing inside of me.

He expression turns serious again as he answers, "Of course."

"Good, we leave for New York on Thursday night," I clip out as I make my way to the room so I can cry my misery away in my own solitary world.

Chapter Twenty-Nine

Matt

AS I'M DRIVING around Portland, I cannot help but remember one of the most important memories Emily left with me...

I'm looking around my empty room recalling my most favorite memories: the first time I slept alone in the room, no longer fearful of being alone after my parents died, the first time I slept with Laura in my bed, and most recently, getting ready for my high school graduation. It was the day I realized I'd grown up. I was no longer a kid who would have his sister at his side to guide him every step of the way.

The creak of my bedroom door startles me back to the reality of the moment and I turn to see Emily slowly walking in. "Sam has everything you asked us to take in the car. You ready to go?" she cautiously asks, as if feeling my dread to leave. I have no choice but to nod my head. Stepping up to my side, she wraps her arms around my waist and lays her head against my chest, allowing me to rest my chin upon her head. "I can't believe you're leaving for college."

"Anxious to get rid of me?" I tease.

She doesn't immediately respond, but instead sighs, which tells me she's containing her emotions. It's typical of Emily as she always tries to demonstrate how confident she is. "I'll miss you," I sadly tell her, feeling the tears building in my throat.

Pulling herself away to look up at me, she has a smile on her face.

"*I hate knowing I have to leave you,*" *I declare.*

"*Just because we say goodbye today, it doesn't mean forever. It won't be long before we see each other again,*" *she states. "The days apart may seem like forever, but with every day that goes by, it's one day closer to seeing each other again. Distance makes the heart grow fonder, which means when we do come back to each other, our love will be stronger because we'll have learned to appreciate one another,*" *she finishes saying.*

I take in her words, but I don't want to fully grasp them. Instead I pull her to me and hold her tightly. "If you say so," I reply.

I feel her laugh against my chest. "I know so," she announces.

My mind is brought back to reality when I hear the honk of a horn behind me, notifying me the light has turned green. With a heavy sigh, I drive off remembering Emily and realizing how wise her words were that day I left for college. I might have dreaded leaving that day, but she was right. With time our love grew stronger, as will the love between Abigail and me. At least I have to believe it will.

IT'S BEEN THREE days now since Abigail and I came home from Los Angeles. We've been casually dancing around each other since then. We haven't acted this way towards one another since before we started dating and I hate it. It's a tragic reminder of the first obstacle in our relationship; although back then we weren't technically dating, but even then, my heart had already belonged to her.

As much as I hated her keeping her news from me, deep down inside I was still proud of the fact that she landed it. I was just too pissed at the time to admit it. Instead of congratulating her as she had done with me minutes before, I was throwing a most recent mistake in her face, and now the consequences of both our actions has been following us around like a darkened cloud.

It took the drive around Portland taking in all the sites and places I'd taken Abigail for me to realize she was right. I've been acting like the controlling asshole she so proudly left and I was regretfully trying to do it with her career. My only excuse for my actions is the need to protect her, but I was also afraid of losing her again. I knew I was wrong the moment I realized it and since then I've been doing whatever possible to portray my happiness for her, but deep down inside I was fighting the urge to tell her she couldn't leave, and I think she knows it. We're both miserable and it shows as we barely made small talk when we were together. To make matters worse, I had a shit load of studying to do for semi-finals this week, which limited the time we had for actual conversations. Instead she would lie at my side as I studied and helped me by quizzing me, but she never complained, and neither did I.

As I arrive home from class, I see her in the kitchen near the stove concentrating on the task in front of her. Taking in all the items spread across the counter, my lips go into the widest smile they have worn for days. She's cooking me my favorite meal. I can tell by how focused she still is that she hasn't heard me walk in and by the bobbing of her head I know she's listening to music. It allows me to walk over to her so I can step up behind her to wrap my arms around her waist. At first she's startled when she turns to see me, but soon she's greeting me with a smile and a kiss on the lips.

She pulls her earphones out of her ears, allowing me to say, "Thank you," I whisper into to her ear, feeling her shudder. Turning her body to better face me, she chuckles. "I wouldn't be thanking me yet. I don't know if I'm going to give us food poisoning," she mocks me with words I usually tease her with.

I throw my head back to laugh before I kiss her again.

"Even if you did, I wouldn't care," I tell her. "Do you want some help?" I ask, looking at the half assembled enchilada casserole in front of her.

"Please."

Quickly washing my hands, I help her finish. The entire time I make sure to stay as close as possible to her and it isn't long before we're eating. I keep her near me by having her sit on my lap. It's another reminder of a most recent event, but this time I push the memory aside and focus on keeping her close.

"What do you want to do tonight? Is there anywhere special you want to go?" I eagerly ask once we're done eating, wishing to make tonight memorable. Wrapping her arms around my neck, she hesitantly looks at me. "I want to go for a run with you," she declares.

Looking outside, I can see the sun already setting. "It's getting dark, beautiful, and I think it's too soon for you to be running," I remind her, but even I can catch the controlling tone I put into the words.

"It's a full moon tonight and we don't have to run at our normal pace. We can jog," she argues. "Please, Matt? I just want to go on a run with you before I leave," she pleads.

Wanting to make her happy plus the thought of running with her persuades my decision as I nod in agreement before I place a kiss on her neck. She's practically jumping from my lap as she drags me along with her to the room to change. Thirty minutes later, we're at the only flat trail I know of that will allow the full moon to illuminate our path.

"Remember to keep your pace slow and if at any time your ankle is bothering you, tell me. I don't want you injuring it again," I order, earning me a short nod.

Without waiting another second, she's already taking off, leaving me to follow. Both lost in our thoughts, we run in silence the entire time. My mind returns to the first time I ever ran with Abigail, the first race we ran together, but most of all, the first time she told me she loved me. Before I know it, we're back to our original destination and I'm saddened we're walking back to her car. Somehow, I can feel deep down inside it will be a while before we'll be running together again, so I better make this one memorable.

Abigail

MY BODY IS beaming from the inside out. I was doubtful I would be able to keep a good pace because of my ankle, but besides a little discomfort now that we've finished, I feel great. Still trying to catch my breath, we reach my car and I turn to face Matt. He surprises me by urging my body against my car, my ass meeting the metal of the hood as he leans my body to lie upon it. Pushing his body between my legs, our bodies meet as his lips descend down onto mine. My senses are awakened and I'm already hungry for him. Matt's kisses will be one of the most cherished acts I will miss of him when we're apart. I always feel as if I can never get enough of them, yet I'm going to have to live without them.

As he bears his weight on me, I can feel the muscles of his body and my hands automatically grab at his waist, pulling him closer as I grind myself against his hips. He leaves me breathless when he ends the kiss to trail his lips down my chin. "Hmmm, you taste salty," he mumbles against my throat. His warm breath sends a chill down my body, making me shiver from excitement. "I'm stinky and sweaty," I correct him as I remember how hard I pushed myself during our run tonight.

He moans against my skin. "You're tasty and I'm hungry," he clarifies as he nips on my neck, causing me to moan. Leaning my head back to allow him to further torment me, the grip of my hands tightens to keep me under control. In return, his hands grip at my thighs as he grinds into me, his hardened erection telling me he wants me as well.

My eyes find the twinkling stars above my head and Matt's hands start tugging at my shorts. My head snaps up in shock to look at him. "Wait. We're not going to have sex out here, are we?" I frantically ask, looking around at our surroundings.

Although we're alone in the public park, the last thing I want is some stranger pulling up as Matt is making me scream his name.

Ignoring me, he continues disrobing me of my shorts, leaving me naked from the waist down. It's the answer I need to know that we *are* going to have sex out here. My only protest for him as he enters me is, "Why on my car? You've never offered to fuck me on *your* car," I breathlessly declare as he rocks his hips in and out of me.

Stopping, he looks at me. "First of all, beautiful, I've never fucked you," he replies before resuming the rocking of his hips. "Second of all, I've never considered fucking *anyone* in or out of my car but you," he softly growls into my ear, his voice sounding strained as he continues to thrust in me. "But, I'd much rather get your juices all over your car, than mine," he huskily adds before biting down on my earlobe. It's what throws me over the edge to scream his name, making those said juices he just mentioned to drip from between my legs.

His speed increases, our moaning getting louder with time from the multiple orgasms he gives me under the moonlight, until he finds his own, leaving me breathless and sated in his arms. Wrapping me in his arms, I slump against his body. I can feel the panting of his breaths against my chest as his lips continue to kiss their way along my skin. Eventually when we do pull apart, he places his forehead against mine. "I love you, beautiful," he whispers, his words conveying every ounce of love I feel for him. "I love you, too," I whisper back.

Closing my eyes to savor the moment, I know I'll need it to hold me over for the next two months.

Chapter Thirty

Abigail

I WAKE UP dreading to open my eyes. Instead I tighten my hold on my pillow, inhaling Matt's unique scent, knowing the next time I wake up it won't be in his arms. I'm exhausted from barely getting any rest, but my night with Matt's constant love-making is worth it. Time will only tell when will be the next time I will be able to wake up in Matt's arms.

I finally climb out of bed to begin packing. I'd purpose-ly left it until last minute, dreading the thought of having my packed bags sitting around to remind me that I had to leave. As I'm closing the last of my luggage, I take one last glance around the room to make sure I have everything. It's when I run my hand down my arm I realize I'm not wearing my bracelet and I step towards my nightstand where I usually leave it to find it missing. I panic as I turn in every direction I can search, still not finding it. My heart has dropped to the pit of my stomach, fearful I won't find it in time. Dropping to my knees, I begin looking under the bed, still disappointed when I find an empty floor.

"I'm really going to miss this view," I hear Matt's husky voice say from the doorway. My tears have fully obstructed my vision at this point and I can barely make him out when I turn to face him. Sitting back on my knees, I wipe my nose with the back of my hand as a sniffle escapes my lips. "What's wrong, beautiful?" Matt asks, looking just as worried as he kneels at my side.

"I can't find my bracelet," I whimper out, attempting to contain my tears.

Pulling my head to his chest, he kisses me on the temple as I feel him chuckle. "I'm sorry, I tried to get it back to you without noticing it was gone. I guess I failed."

Confused, I feel him move and within seconds my bracelet is sparkling in my view. "I took it to the jeweler's to have something added," he says in a whisper.

Relieved, I breathe again. Looking down at it as he wraps it around my wrist, he maneuvers it so I see two new charms facing up in my direction. It's a key, along with a sparkling diamond encrusted heart. Brushing my finger against it, I hear him say, "This heart represents my own, and the key is you."

"The key to your heart," I whisper back to him.

"Yes."

The tears I was desperately trying to contain are now falling from my eyes as I kiss him. "Thank you," I say against his lips as I grip his head in my hands, not wanting to let him go.

I soon hear Julio's unique knock on the bedroom door, notifying us it's time for me to leave. Since Matt had classes today, he had briefly come home in between them to see me off. It's why I scheduled the hired car to arrive at a specific time. We had a small window of time to say goodbye to one another, leaving us with a window of fifteen minutes together before I had to leave. I hated that we had such a small amount of time to say goodbye, but I was grateful we had the opportunity.

I made sure to say my goodbyes to Kelly and David last night, and Trey this morning. I could not handle the thought of all of them hovering around as my car drove off. The guilt of seeing their faces as my car drove off was unbearable.

Gradually standing with Matt, I feel better as I take the final glance around my room, my eyes locking onto my drawer in the dresser making my heart sink as I remember what it contains. I haven't taken the box out since the day Matt gave it to me and I had safely tucked it into my drawer Christmas morning.

Today was still not that day.

Walking at Matt's side to the living room, I watch as the hired driver takes the last of my luggage out of the house and we slowly follow him out to the side of the car.

"It won't be too long before I see you again," Matt says into my hair as we're wrapped in each other's arms. Nodding my head in agreement, I tuck my head into his neck, taking in his scent, trying to engrave it into my mind.

My heart is still lodged in the pit of my stomach knowing I have to climb into the car. With his arms still wrapped around me, I feel him look over to Julio. "You've got all the paperwork you need for your gun?" he asks.

As much as I hate the idea of Julio carrying a gun near me, I've finally come to accept the idea that he needs it for my protection. My one rule was he never takes it out in front of me unless he had to. The less I was reminded of him having it, the better I was about allowing him to carry it. I kiss Matt one more time, holding back the tears threatening to escape. I told myself I wouldn't cry. I didn't want to remember crying in front of Matt as I left.

"Take care of Lola for me?" I ask.

With a hint of laughter in his eyes, his lips curve up to one side. "I'll make sure to keep the bats away from her," he teases. Shoving at his shoulder, I lightly laugh with him. "She's safe with me. I promise."

"I love you," I say with trembling lips.

"I love you more," he says against my own. "We're not saying goodbye forever, Abigail," he assures me. "The time apart will make our love stronger," he quietly says against my hair, squeezing me tighter. "You show them who Abigail Adams is," he says, making me laugh as I remember the last time he told me those words. "You're going to do great," he adds.

"Can I have your phone for a moment?" he request, holding out his hand. Handing it over to him, I see him tap at the screen, already knowing he's changing the ring tone. He hands it back to me, saying, "I'm going to call you when you drive away. Don't answer it. Just listen," he says down to me as I contain the tears still threatening to fall.

"Abigail, we have to go if you want to make your flight on time," Julio says at our side, reminding me why I'm saying goodbye. Kissing me one last time, Matt helps me into the car before taking one last glance at Julio as he climbs in after me. "You take care of her," he demands. With a stern nod, I watch him climb into the car and we drive away. Matt stands on the curb watching us drive away, even through the darkened tint of the window and the distance growing between us, our eyes are still locked onto each other's. My heart is completely shattered knowing I'm leaving. The farther we drive away from the house, the heavier it feels. I can no longer see Matt's silhouette and somehow I feel as I've left him behind, *forever*. My heart feels as if it was left behind with him and all I have is a blackened hollow inside my chest.

My phone starts to sing the lyrics of *All of Me*. I'm not strong enough anymore. The tears are freely falling now as I do as Matt has instructed and listen to the words.

With every teardrop that falls, I have to force myself to breathe, but it's harder when all I want to do it succumb to the pain. Leaning my head back on the seat, I close my eyes and picture his face, holding onto the memory of his smile. It's the only thing I have left of him now. A memory I'll hold onto to forever.

Chapter Thirty-One

Bill

"FUCKING BITCH!" I scream in a fit of rage, hand slamming down on my desk as I take another glance at the article, the fury inside of me uncontrollable. I never expected Abigail to land one of the most prestigious deals of the year without *me*—the kind of deal I would have locked down had she been under my control.

Would have... A fact I was still infuriated with myself about. Because of her I was now cowardly hiding and running low on funds, the latter caused mostly by Susan's extravagant spending throughout our affair, which was finally over. I couldn't take it anymore. I'm not used to living this way and I would not have to had Abigail not been clever enough to transfer her funds to God knows where.

I underestimated her.

I never once thought Abigail would be smart enough to consider it, but I'm not stupid, either. I knew that little boy toy of hers had something to do with it, but there is nothing I can do about it without getting caught by the authorities. No, I had to continue laying low until the time was right... Which was soon.

Picking up the phone, I dial the only other person who could manage to get a deal this important for Abigail, but if I find out he is helping her without my knowledge, I may just have to hurt him as well.

"Evan Warren," he answers.

"Evan, Bill speaking," I curtly deliver. "I want to know if you've been in contact with Abigail Adams," I say, getting directly to the point.

I hear a chuckle on the other end. "Why am I not surprised that you're calling me?"

"Answer the fucking question," I demand.

"Yes, I have," Evan, answers.

"When?" The fury inside has risen to a murderous level. "And why didn't you tell me!"

"It was a couple of days ago and she flatly refused. I wanted to test the theory of amnesia rumor floating around. She isn't fucking around. She truly had no clue who I was."

Interest piqued, I ask, "She didn't jump on your offer?"

"No. Rumor has it she's still a free agent and refusing to sign with anyone. She's pulling in her own jobs."

I'm surprised. The Abigail I knew was always looking for the fastest way to climb the career ladder. There is no possible way Abigail would be working alone. There *has* to be someone behind her, I think as my mind drifts to the boy she's been living with. I already know from a little digging around that he was the reason why she got her initial job.

"Are you sure?" I ask again, still feeling doubtful of his answer.

Sounding serious, he says, "I know what you're thinking man, but I'm surprised myself." My hand on the phone tightens and I can no longer control my anger as I pound the desk with my fist again.

"Look, man, a little word of advice. I'd stay away. You're in enough trouble as it is with the shit you pulled with her."

"Fuck you," I growl into the phone.

Evan chuckles at my response. "Let me see what I can find out and I'll get back to you. Just keep laying low or else you can say goodbye to your career."

Feeling my temper beginning to calm, I reply, "Thanks, Evan."

"No problem. What are brothers for?"

Ending the phone call, I stare off into the distance as my anger slowly subsides, the reminder of what I have succumbed to because of Abigail Adams keeps a small part of it banked.

Why couldn't she just fucking die that night? I should have fucking pulled the plug on her in the hospital and finished her off completely.

"You're going to regret the day you fucking messed with me, Abigail," I snarl to myself. "This time I'm going to make sure you die."

To be continued in Matt and Abigail's story... UNSPOKEN *Endings*.

Acknowledgments

To my husband and children. Thank you for putting up with my grouchy attitude through this journey, it was a tough one, but I wouldn't change it for the world. You stood by me during the frustration of and I love you so much for that. To my mom, Rosa, who I love more than words can ever express. You helped me discover my passion for reading, which led to writing and has never let me give up. I love you dearly, mommy.

To my crazy girls in my blue box, although you distracted me enough through this journey, I still love you at the end of the night and at the beginning of the day. Yamara and Cezanne, you should have looked in the front first.

To my editor, Edee M. Fallon aka my "Heroine." She always has the best advice, day or night. Wendie Lynn Williams from Sweet Book Swag for always sending me presents to cheer up my day. You make the best swag. To Matt's Beautiful girls: Thank you for all your support and helping me believe this story is worth writing. To my beta group who helped guide me in the right direction; Yamara Martinez, Cezanne Dilbert, Juliana Cabrera, Colette Noak, Tara Bersano, Janett Gomez, Lynsey Sabin, Jennifer Weeks and Keri Greear.

Sarah Hansen, from Okay Creations, without a doubt you've made my stories come to life with your awesome covers. You always know how to amaze me.

To EMI Music Publishing industry for allowing to me to use the lyrics to 'Angel', without it, my story would have not been so musical.

Last, but not least, to all the readers, and bloggers who took the time to read Unspoken Promises. Without you I wouldn't have a reason to write. Thank you from the bottom of my heart.

About the Author

Gabbie is a Southern California native, who lives with her wonderful husband, two amazing kids and a senior citizen kitty. When she's not writing you can find her reading or sneaking off for a run. Some might say it's a crazy life, but she wouldn't change anything about it.

Author page: http://gabbiesduran.com/
Facebook: www.facebook.com/authorgabbiesduran
Twitter: @gabbiesduran
Goodreads: https://www.goodreads.com/author/show/7093957.
Gabbie_S_Duran